OUT OF BREATH

OF

BREATH

SECRETS OF BROOKHAVEN

BOOK TWO

ISBN: 978-1-951447-39-7

ABOUT THE BOOK

A carefree day on the lake turns deadly when a boater dislodges the skeletal remains of a woman from her watery grave. Nearly thirty years ago Misty Collins vanished from her home in the middle of the day, leaving nothing behind but a note. Everyone assumed she'd run away, but the truth is far more sinister...

The deeper he delves into her mysterious disappearance, the more Lieutenant Campbell McCoy uncovers a tangled web of deceit and betrayal that stretches back decades, ensnaring both past and present. As secrets come to light, each revelation brings him closer to a dangerous adversary who will stop at nothing to protect their hidden past.

When a young local woman is abducted, Cam must unravel the truth before the lake claims another victim. Because her next breath may be her last...

CHAPTER
ONE

The sun glistened off the calm surface of the lake, casting a shimmering path that stretched out before the sleek speedboat. Jared revved the engine, causing the boat to leap forward. Gabby clutched the side, her knuckles white as they sped across the water, much too close to the shore for her comfort.

"Jared, slow down!" Gabby shouted, her voice nearly drowned out by the roar of the motor.

Jared just laughed, the wind whipping through his hair. "Relax, Gabs! We're fine!"

But Gabby wasn't convinced. "Seriously, Jared, stop it!"

Jared grinned and whipped the wheel hard. Gabby screamed as waves slapped against the side of the boat, making it lurch frantically from side to side. Gabby grabbed the edge of the seat, clinging to the fabric with all her might. "Jared! You better stop before you get caught!"

They were already deep into the no-wake zone, and the waves crashed against the shore with violent force, frothy and white.

Jared rolled his eyes. "We're not going to get caught. There's no one out here."

"The people who live here will be pissed," she said, gesturing toward the homes tucked within the canopy of trees along the shoreline. "They're going to call the cops on you."

"Fine." He turned the wheel again and pushed the throttle, sending them back out toward the middle of the lake.

The boat shot forward, and a scream caught in her throat as Gabby was jolted off the seat. A sickening screech filled the air as the bottom scraped against something below the surface.

"Shit!" Jared eased off the throttle, and the boat slowed to a stop.

"I told you," Gabby shot back. "There's all kinds of stuff this close to shore. You better hope you didn't ruin your dad's boat. He'll be pissed."

Gabby peered over the side of the boat, straining to see into the depths. A dozen feet away, a patch of blue bobbed in the water.

She pointed at the object. "What's that?"

Jared squinted, then shrugged. "Probably just some trash. Grab it before it gets caught in the propeller."

Gabby dug out an oar then leaned over the side, using the paddle to slap at the water, dragging the object closer. It drifted toward her, trapped air lifting it to the surface. From here she could make out what appeared to be fabric, once bright blue but now faded with age and stained from the lake.

Gabby angled the oar downward, trying to pin the fabric and drag it toward her. It was heavier than she expected, and she struggled to pull it in. "It's stuck on something," she muttered, giving it a harder tug. "You probably hit a log or something down there."

She tossed a look over her shoulder at Jared, who shrugged sheepishly. "My bad."

Rolling her eyes, Gabby turned her attention back to the task at hand. *Nice of him to help*, she thought to herself as she dragged the fabric closer, aided by the gentle rolling of the water.

"Almost got it..."

She bit her lip and strained her muscles, reaching just a bit farther. She dragged the oar over the rippling water, the fabric trailing in its wake. The surge of satisfaction that shot through her quickly turned to dread as the fabric rolled under the pressure of the oar and something began to take shape.

"What the...?" Her brows drew together as the object dipped below the surface, then reappeared.

The fabric slipped free of the oar and as it did, something dark began to rise from the depths. Terror slid through her as Gabby found herself staring into the empty sockets of a human skull, its mouth agape in a silent scream.

empty sockets of a human skull, its mouth agape in a silent scream.

CHAPTER
TWO

The old, decrepit farmhouse loomed in the distance, its silhouette dark and foreboding against the cloudy gray sky. Lieutenant Campbell McCoy's knuckles were white with tension as he gripped the steering wheel and turned down the long gravel driveway.

He pulled to a stop in front of the house and scanned the exterior. The lawn was overgrown, machinery and discarded trash littering the tall grass. The paint on the house was peeling, and several broken windows had been covered with newspaper and duct tape.

"Nice place," Sawyer said, his tone wry.

"The Cottrells lived here as long as I can remember," Cam said as he put the transmission in park. "Wade was the last of them, at least locally."

Sawyer turned his way. "Think it's empty?"

"I sure as hell hope so." But one never knew what

Wade was into at any given time. It was far better to be alert, especially given the events of the past twenty-four hours.

Yesterday morning, Lindsey Gill had been abducted from her home on the west side of Brookhaven. Shortly afterward, Ainsley Layne and her sister, Kinley, had been attacked in Kinley's home.

The oldest Layne sister, Ainsley, had recently moved back to Brookhaven to be close to her family after leaving her abusive boyfriend. Suspecting that something wasn't quite right, Sheriff Dare Jensen had rented her the live-in suite at his home where she would be safe under his watch. Naturally, Ainsley's ex, Dr. Joel Parsons, didn't take kindly to her leaving. For weeks he'd hunted her, even going so far as to kill her friend to draw Ainsley out into the open.

The sheriff's office had been called to the scene when Lindsey was abducted, and Ainsley had gone to Kinley's house to pass the time. The police could only speculate that Parsons had followed Ainsley to Kinley's house, where he'd knocked her unconscious before attacking Ainsley. Things hadn't worked out as planned.

Unbeknownst to anyone, Wade Cottrell had his eye on Ainsley as well. Several years ago, Dare had shot and killed Wade's older brother, Beau, when the man had fired on him after a traffic stop. Wade had apparently held a grudge and saw an opportunity for revenge when Ainsley and Dare began to date.

Wade had broken in through the back door, then

killed Parsons before going after Ainsley himself. By a stroke of sheer luck, Cam and Dare had shown up just minutes later. It was a tangled web of deceit, with several innocent women caught in the crossfire. Ainsley and Kinley had been admitted to the hospital with their injuries, and Lindsey Gill was still missing. Coupled with the recent murder, it was almost enough to push Cam over the edge.

Just a few weeks ago, Jayla Simms had been found dead in the center of Brookhaven, her body posed on a park bench. Initially, they'd speculated that the perp who'd killed Jayla Simms had abducted Lindsey. But now Cam wondered if it had all been a diversion. Wade and Joel both intended to draw Ainsley away from Dare. Had one of them abducted Lindsey to distract the police?

They slid from the car and approached the house cautiously, eyes and ears alert. Cam wouldn't put anything past Wade, and he refused to let down his guard despite the fact that the man was dead.

Dodging splintered, rotting boards, Cam climbed the steps to the porch, one eye tuned to the windows, watching for movement. Standing off to the side the front door, he gave a hard knock. "Sheriff's Department. Open up."

A heavy silence followed, and Cam knocked again, calling out louder this time. "This is Lt. Campbell McCoy with the Brookhaven Sheriff's Department."

When no one responded, he leaned forward to peer

through the single pane of glass in the door. It was dingy, covered in dust and grime, making it almost impossible to see inside.

He signaled for Sawyer to take the back while he entered through the front. Cam grasped the doorknob, surprised when it twisted easily beneath his fingers. He gave a push, but the swollen wood refused to budge. Leaning all of his weight into it, the door resisted for several seconds before finally giving way with a loud groan. It swung inward, listing limply on rusted hinges that had pulled halfway out of the wall.

Sawyer's lips pressed into a firm line as he stepped inside, the beam of his flashlight already sweeping the interior. The putrid scent of dirty clothes and rotten food assaulted his nostrils, and he gagged, his eyes watering. He fought it back as he moved deeper into the house, stepping carefully around piles of clothing mixed with discarded trash. Flies buzzed noisily, and he swatted one away as it landed on his shoulder.

"Anyone here?" he called out.

There was no answer, and a moment later, Sawyer appeared in the doorway across from him. "Kitchen's a fucking mess, but it's clear." A scowl tugged at his lips and he shook his head. "Jesus Christ. Doesn't look much better in here, either."

Cam shook his head. "I don't know how you'd find anything in this shithole."

Sawyer tipped his head toward the stairs. "I'm going to check up here. You got the basement?"

Cam nodded and picked his way through the downstairs, checking every room on the ground floor until he found the door that led to the basement. Cobwebs clung to the switch on the wall, and he brushed them away before flicking the switch. Nothing. Cam rolled his eyes. Of course it wouldn't work.

Leveling his flashlight in front of him, he carefully descended the rickety stairs, the ancient wood bowing precariously under his weight. At the bottom of the steps, he breathed out a silent sigh of relief and swept the beam of light over the room, scanning for any sign of Lindsey.

"Find anything?" Sawyer's voice crackled through the radio.

"Negative." His gaze landed on an old metal shelving unit filled with various implements, broken glass jars, and cans of food that were beginning to rust. "You?"

"Just a lot of junk and old furniture."

Cam continued his search, his flashlight sliding over the walls and floors, revealing nothing but years of neglect and decay. The air was damp and musty, filled with the scent of mildew and rot, and water had pooled on the floor in places. He carefully navigated around the cluttered space, checking behind old shelves and inside dusty cabinets.

Suddenly, his flashlight caught the glint of something large and white tucked away in a corner. Pulse racing, Cam drifted toward an ancient chest freezer that had seen better days. Bracing himself, Cam grasped the lid and lifted, shining the flashlight inside.

Stale air assaulted him, but the freezer was empty, and the oxygen rushed from his lungs on a relieved exhale. Dropping the lid back into place, he reached over and pressed the button on the radio.

"Basement's clear. Nothing down here," he reported, more than a little frustrated.

"Copy that. I'm finishing up the second floor," Sawyer replied. "Meet you out front."

Cam propped his hands on his hips and glared at the basement. He had hoped for a clue, a sign—anything to indicate Lindsey's whereabouts. But Wade Cottrell's house was a dead end.

Cam met Sawyer back on the front porch, and the detective ran a hand through his cropped dark hair with a scowl. "Place is clean. No sign of her at all."

"It's a long shot, but let's check Parsons's place." The doctor had lived more than an hour away, but they couldn't afford to waste any more time here. The clock was ticking, and every second counted.

As they climbed into the cruiser, Cam tossed one last look at the house, dread twisting in the pit of his stomach. If Wade hadn't taken her... who had?

CHAPTER
THREE

Cam stood next to Sheriff Dare Jensen at the edge of Lake Remington, his gaze fixed on the calm, deceptively serene water. The early morning sun cast long shadows over the ground, and a light breeze rustled the leaves of the nearby trees. Despite the peaceful tranquility of the scene, tension pressed in around them.

Cam glanced at his watch. "Shouldn't they be here by now?"

Dare nodded, brows pulled slightly together. "They're running a bit late, but they'll be here."

The discovery of the body yesterday had sent shockwaves through the small community. Dare had questioned Gabby and Jared, who were still shell-shocked by the discovery. Jared had admitted to striking something beneath the water, which most likely resulted in dislodging the human remains. The deputies had retrieved the body late yesterday afternoon, and it was now with the medical examiner.

Cam paced the shoreline, his mind racing. Was it Lindsey? The deputies on afternoons had said the person was smaller, so they assumed it was a woman. "Do we have any leads on who it might be?"

Dare shook his head. "Not yet. Looks like whoever it was has been down there for quite awhile."

Not Lindsey, then. Cam exhaled deeply, the sound a combination of relief and anxiety.

The sound of an approaching vehicle drew their attention, and a truck pulled up, a boat trailer behind. The dive team had arrived.

Cam and Dare walked over to greet them, exchanging brief introductions. The team quickly began to unload their equipment, preparing for the dive.

The lead diver adjusted his mask. "We'll start at the spot where the kids found the body and work our way out from there. If there's anything else down there, we'll find it."

Dare nodded. "Be careful. We don't know what we're dealing with yet."

Dare and Cam watched as the divers slipped into the water, disappearing seamlessly beneath the surface, leaving only a trail of bubbles. The minutes ticked by slowly, each one stretching longer than the last.

Suddenly, one of the divers surfaced, signaling to the team on shore. Dare and Cam hurried over as the diver removed his mask. "Looks like there's a car down here. We need to bring it up."

"Damn." Cam exchanged a quick look with Dare, who made a call to a local towing company to have them extract the vehicle.

The atmosphere was tense as the minutes ticked by, a mixture of anticipation and dread hanging in the air. The oppressive silence was broken by the distant hum of a vehicle approaching.

Finally, the towing company arrived, their truck loaded with heavy-duty equipment. Cam and Dare moved to greet them as the crew began unloading the winch and other gear. The team worked efficiently, setting up their equipment and preparing for the extraction process.

The winch was carefully maneuvered into position, and the divers, now back on land, provided guidance. They attached the heavy-duty straps to the car, their movements practiced and precise.

As the winch roared to life, the cable tightened, and the car began to move. The silt around it swirled, creating a cloud of murky water. Cam watched intently, his heart pounding as the vehicle slowly emerged from the depths.

As it broke the surface, the silt continued to drift away, revealing a small white sedan, its once-pristine paint now marred by decades of exposure to the elements. The windshield was shattered, and the windows were opaque with decades of accumulated debris.

The crew continued to guide the car onto the shore. The winch groaned under the strain, and the vehicle creaked as it was lifted. The tension was high, and everyone watched in silent anticipation.

When the car was finally set down on the shore, Cam could practically hear the collective sigh of relief that rippled through the onlookers. The towing crew moved back, allowing Cam and Dare to approach.

"Let's get a closer look," Dare said, moving toward the vehicle. Cam followed, his gaze fixed on the sedan. The car was covered in mud, but it was clear that it had been submerged for a long time.

"We need to run the plate," Dare said, turning to Deputy Evan Landry. "See if we can track down any information about this car."

Landry nodded, then quickly retrieved the plate number and headed to his cruiser to run the information. The others set to work, documenting the find and taking photographs.

"Sheriff," Landry called out, "the car is registered to Dennis Collins."

Dare's lips pressed into a firm line as he turned toward Cam. "I'll have the car brought in for evidence. In the meantime, why don't you see what you can pull on Dennis Collins?"

With a nod, Cam strode toward his car and headed back to the station. It didn't take him long to find what he was looking for. Nearly three decades ago, Dennis Collins had filed a police report stating that his wife, Misty, had gone missing.

Cam found the case file on Misty Collins and began to read through it. A young wife and mother to her stepson, David, Misty Collins had vanished without a trace one day while Dennis was at work. Behind, she had left a typed letter, stating she couldn't go on anymore.

According to the file, no one had seen or heard from her since. Had she left of her own accord? Or had something far more sinister happened to Misty?

Dare walked in, his face grim. "Anything yet?"

"Get this." Cam sat back in his chair. "Dennis Collins reported his wife missing twenty-nine years ago. When the deputies investigated, they found a note she'd left behind."

"What about the husband?"

"He was at work at the time, and apparently there were no leads. I checked into Dennis Collins's whereabouts, but that's a dead end. He passed away a few months ago."

"Well, that's convenient," Dare muttered caustically.

Cam lifted one shoulder. "His alibi was solid. He was at work all day, and his son, David, was a junior in high school at the time. They questioned neighbors, friends... No one saw a thing."

Dare nodded slowly, his expression pensive. "Why don't you hand this off to Turner, have him do some digging?"

Cam sank back in his chair, disgruntled. "You don't want me working this?"

"I didn't say that." Dare shook his head. "But the Gill and Simms cases take priority right now, and you've already got your hands full. We're assuming the woman in the car is Misty, but we can't make any official statements until we get identification. Misty went missing decades ago; a week or two won't change anything. We need to find Lindsey while she's still alive."

Cam nodded, then closed the file and passed it across the desk. "You're right. Sorry."

Dare waved off the apology. "I get it. If Turner finds something, I'll have him follow up with you."

"Thanks." Cam dipped his head in appreciation, tossing one last look at the file as he stood. There was more to the story, he could feel it. But for now, it was going to have to wait.

CHAPTER
FOUR

Cam studied the man seated at the metal table. By all accounts, Lindsey Gill's boyfriend, Andrew Dodson, looked devastated. His eyes were bloodshot, his face gaunt with worry and exhaustion.

"What do you think?"

For the past several minutes, Cam and Sawyer had watched the footage currently being recorded in the interview room, studying the man's actions. "Emotion like that is pretty hard to fake, but..." Sawyer shrugged. "Wouldn't be the first time."

"Let's see what he has to say."

Cam entered the interview room, Sawyer at his heels. Dodson glanced up at them, his expression creased with worry.

"Mr. Dodson, thank you for coming in." Cam dropped into the chair across from him and introduced himself and Sawyer. "We understand this is a difficult time for you."

Andrew nodded, swallowing hard. "I'll help however I can. Please—I just want to find Lindsey."

Sawyer took a seat next to Cam, his sharp eyes assessing Andrew's every movement. "We'd like to start by establishing a timeline of events leading up to Lindsey's disappearance. You mentioned you were with her the night before?"

"Yes," Andrew confirmed, his voice trembling. "She came over to my place after work. We had dinner then watched a movie."

"What time did she leave?"

"Around eleven, right after the movie was over. I asked her to stay, but..." His voice cracked, and he trailed off, his eyes misting over as his gaze dropped to his hands where they rested on the table, fingers laced tightly together.

"Did she mention any plans for the next day?" Cam asked, jotting down notes in his notepad.

Andrew cleared his throat, then shook his head. "No, she just said she had to go home early because of work. I... I didn't think anything of it."

Reed leaned in slightly. "When was the last time you spoke with her?"

"That night. The night before she..." Andrew trailed off, his eyes welling up with tears. "She called me when she got home, just to say goodnight. That was the last time I heard from her."

Cam glanced at Sawyer before continuing. "She's a nurse, is that right?"

"That's right. She works in the ICU over at Danbury General."

"Did Lindsey ever mention anyone who might want to harm her? Any threats at work or unusual behavior from anyone?"

"No," Andrew said, his voice hoarse with emotion. "Everyone loves her—patients, coworkers. She's great at what she does, and she loves to help people. She has the biggest heart of anyone I know. I can't think of anyone who would want to hurt her."

Sawyer folded his arms on the table. "Mr. Dodson, we're doing everything we can to find Lindsey. Any information you provide could be crucial."

Andrew reached into his pocket and pulled out his phone, his hands shaking. "I have our conversations. You said you want a timeline. Maybe it can help?"

Cam gave him an encouraging smile as he took the phone, then scanned through the recent call log and message history. As Dodson had stated, he'd spoken with Lindsey the night before her abduction. The call had lasted a little over seven minutes, and there was no further communication between the two.

"This is helpful, thank you." He passed the phone back to Dodson. "Can you confirm where you were the morning she disappeared?"

Andrew nodded vigorously. "I was at work. My shift started at seven—my boss will confirm that."

Andrew gave them the company's information, and Cam nodded. "Thank you. Is there anything else you remember? Did she mention running into any old acquaintances recently, or experience anything out of the ordinary?"

"I don't think so." He swallowed hard. "I just can't imagine who would do this. She's..." His voice cracked. "She doesn't deserve this. Please bring her home."

Sawyer nodded. "We'll do our best. We're not giving up on her."

The man raked a hand through his hair, his eyes haunted. "What do I do now?"

That was a question Cam couldn't really answer. He understood the helplessness, the combination of fear and hope people felt when something happened to a loved one. "Keep thinking of anything that might help and let us know, no matter how small. We're looking at every option right now."

Cam saw Andrew Dodson to the door, then returned to the small office he shared with Reed. The detective turned away from the whiteboard he'd been studying and met Cam's gaze. "We need to get a search warrant for Lindsey's phone and social media accounts. Maybe there's something there that can lead us to her."

Cam nodded. "In the meantime, let's do another sweep of her house. Maybe we missed something."

Less than an hour later they pulled up to Lindsey Gill's quiet suburban home, the area still cordoned off with yellow tape that danced in the slight breeze. Cam unfolded from the driver seat, his gaze scanning the surrounding homes. Someone must have seen or heard something.

Sawyer on his heels, Cam headed up the concrete walkway to the small front porch and cracked the tape sealing the door. Inside, the house was eerily quiet. Everything remained in its place, just as it had the first time they searched. No sign of forced entry, no signs of struggle. It was as if Lindsey had simply vanished into thin air. Cam's gaze swept over the living room, taking in the small details: a framed photo of Lindsey and Andrew on the mantel, a half-finished book on the coffee table, a pair of running shoes by the door.

Sawyer had worked the scene the day of the abduction, but it had been hectic, with multiple deputies all eager to find something. "I'm going to check the kitchen again, see if I can find anything—notes, calendars, anything that might have been overlooked."

Cam nodded, then turned his attention back to the living room. The morning of the abduction, a neighbor had found Lindsey's front door wide open. When she'd called out to the woman and hadn't gotten a response, she'd notified the sheriff's office. Lindsey's purse and coffee cup were still sitting on the kitchen counter next to her keys, like she'd been getting ready to walk out the door.

There was no sign of forced entry anywhere in the house. Had someone knocked on the door to get her attention? Cam played out the scenario, walking toward the front door and pulling it open. Lindsey's driveway ran parallel to the right side of her house, and a small, detached garage sat at the end of the drive, tucked slightly behind the house. From the road, visibility to the garage was mostly obscured. It was possible the man had pulled into the driveway, then smuggled her out in his vehicle. That seemed to be the most likely option.

Lindsey's house was near the end of the street, with only two other homes to her right. Too many people lived in the neighborhood; the man would have had to work fast and efficiently to avoid being seen. The only other way to transport her would be through the woods that connected the subdivision to the back of Earl Weaver's farm. That was a long way to carry a body, and they'd seen no tire tracks to indicate an ATV had recently passed through.

Cam closed the door and moved toward Lindsey's bedroom. The bed coverings were slightly rumpled, as if she'd hurriedly tugged them back into place when she woke up. A discarded sweater had been slung over a chair in the corner, and the faint scent of her perfume lingered in the air. He searched through her dresser, rifling through neatly folded clothes and personal items, hoping to find something—anything—that would point them in the right direction.

"Find anything?" Reed's voice interrupted his

thoughts, and Cam quickly made his way back to the living room where Reed stood by the window.

"Nope. You?"

Reed shook his head. "We need to talk to the neighbors again," he said, his troubled gaze scanning the quiet road. "Someone must have seen something."

They exited the house and began their rounds, knocking on doors, showing Lindsey's photo and asking the same questions they had before. The responses were mostly the same: kind words of concern but no useful information. Finally, at end of the block, they got a potential lead.

An elderly woman who introduced herself as Helen Patterson invited them onto her front porch and offered them each a glass of iced tea.

"I didn't think much of it at first," Helen said as she replaced the pitcher on the table, "but a few days before Lindsey went missing, I noticed a dark-colored sedan parked along the curb, just over there." She pointed toward a yellow house across the street, about a hundred yards from Lindsey's home.

Cam took a sip of his iced tea. "Can you remember anything else about the car, ma'am?"

The woman shook her head. "I never saw the driver, but we don't get many unfamiliar cars around here. I thought at first maybe it was a visitor, but whoever it was didn't stay long."

"How long was the car there?"

"About fifteen minutes," she responded matter-of-factly. "I was sitting right here the whole time."

Reed nodded. "And do you know about what time that was?"

She glanced upward in thought. "It was just after my show ended, so... maybe one o'clock?"

Cam leaned in, interest piqued. "Was there anything about the car that stood out? A dent, a sticker—anything at all?"

The woman furrowed her brow in thought. "The windows were very dark. And... I believe there was a small insignia in the back window, but I couldn't tell what it was." She let out a soft sigh. "My eyes aren't what they used to be."

"Thank you, this is helpful," Cam said, handing her a card as he stood. "If you remember anything else, please give us a call."

"I will." Helen offered them a smile. "Good luck, officers. I hope you find her."

"Thank you for the tea." Sawyer dipped his chin at the older woman then fell into step beside Cam as they walked back to their car. He cleared his throat as he slid inside. "A dark-colored sedan with tinted windows and a small insignia."

Cam exhaled. "Supposedly."

He cranked the engine, his gaze sweeping the area once last time before he pulled away from the curb. Lindsey Gill was out there somewhere, and they wouldn't rest until she was found.

CHAPTER
FIVE

The man on the front porch smiled at her, but instead of putting her at ease, the gesture sent chills down her spine. There was a hostility in his eyes that made every nerve ending prickle with apprehension. Something was wrong. Very wrong.

Before she could react, he he lunged toward her, his hands closing around her throat. The clipboard she'd been holding hit the ground at her feet as she tried to scream, but no sound came out. His grip tightened, and her vision blurred, black spots dancing before her eyes. She grabbed at his hands, scratching at his forearms, kicking and twisting in his grasp, but his hold was like a vise. Fear and desperation surged through her. She couldn't give up—she had to fight.

One hand loosened momentarily, and she dragged in much-needed oxygen, dimly aware of Ainsley calling her name.

Oh, God. Ainsley. She opened her mouth to call out a warning just as the man's arm swung in a wide arc and something hard slammed into her. Pain exploded over her face, the aftershock so intense her teeth rattled.

She wavered on her feet, then lost the ability to stay upright. She couldn't move. Couldn't breathe. The last thing she saw before everything went black were his cold, dark eyes staring into hers.

Kinley jerked upright, eyes flying open wide as she dragged in a gasping breath. Her heart pounded frantically in her chest, and she clutched the sheets, her body drenched in sweat.

"Kins?"

She snapped her head toward her left, and her lungs seized up at the sight of the man in the corner. So deeply entranced in the dream, it took a moment for her mind to reconcile what she was truly seeing.

Cam sat in a chair next to the bed, his blond hair tousled, dark circles ringing his eyes. He looked exhausted, but his gaze sharpened with concern as he studied her.

"Hey. Are you okay?" he asked, his voice raspy and rough with sleep.

She took a few deep breaths, but the dream lingered, the memory of the attack replaying vividly in her mind. Everything had happened so fast; by the time she'd suspected something was wrong, the man had been inside the house, already moving toward her, wrapping his hands around her throat, squeezing until her lungs ached...

Goosebumps sprouted over her skin at the memory. "I... It was just a nightmare."

"Joel?" Cam leaned forward, his eyes never leaving her face.

Her lungs still felt tight, breathless from fear, and the words jammed in her throat. She swallowed hard and managed a small nod, though her hands still trembled.

He reached out, taking her hand in his and giving her a gentle squeeze. "You're safe, Kins. I'm right here."

Her heart rate finally began to return to normal, and she drew in a fortifying breath before speaking. "It felt so real. Like it was happening all over again."

He nodded. "I know how that feels. Your mind is still trying to process everything."

The claws of fear clutching at her throat began to loosen, and she swallowed hard. Tossing a look at the clock, she realized it was still early. She turned back to Cam. "When did you get here?"

"Last night."

Her eyes widened. "You were here all night?"

No wonder he looked dead on his feet. She hadn't seen him all day yesterday, and she hadn't expected to for quite a few days yet. A young local woman, Lindsey Gill, had been abducted from her home under mysterious circumstances the same day Joel had attacked Kinley and her sister. As far as she knew, there had been no update in the woman's case. "I thought you'd be at work already."

"Not yet." He shook his head. "I'll have to leave soon, but I wanted to see you first."

She studied him, acutely aware of the fatigue and frustration that had carved fine lines into the corners of his eyes and mouth. "Any word yet?"

"No." He grimaced. "We've been working round the clock, but..."

He trailed off, and guilt pricked her conscience. "If you need to go..."

"Not yet." He shook his head. "You were asleep when I got here last night, so I stayed the night, hoping to see you this morning before I headed back in."

"I'm glad you're here," she admitted quietly.

"Me, too." Cam stood and slid onto the bed next to her, careful not to jostle her too much. He wrapped his arm around her shoulders, pulling her gently into his side.

Ever since the attack, he had been more protective, checking in with her frequently to make sure she was safe and still feeling okay. She tipped her head against his chest, closing her eyes and breathing in his familiar scent. He was so solid and warm, and just having him next to her calmed her.

But as she lay there, a sense of shame crept over her. Though she was grateful for her family and friends who had stopped by, the person she most wanted to see was Cam. He was her best friend; she shouldn't be feeling this way, shouldn't be reveling in the feel of his strong arms wrapped around her.

He didn't have a girlfriend, so it wasn't like she was taking him away from another woman. If he wanted to be here with her, then who was she to argue? It was completely normal for friends to support one another, to be there when one of them needed help. Wasn't it?

She rubbed her temple, feeling another headache coming on. Her mind was a jumbled mess, and the past couple of days felt like a rollercoaster of volatile emotions. She was just feeling especially vulnerable right now, and Cam was there for her, like always. She had nothing to feel guilty for.

Tamping down the negative thoughts and insecurities, she allowed herself to sink deeper into the comfort of his embrace. It was easier to just enjoy the moment, to let herself be held and cared for. It would end all too soon, and things would go back to the way they'd always been.

"Are you okay?" Cam's voice was a low murmur, his warm breath stirring her hair.

She nodded, nestling closer. "I am now."

He tightened his arm around her, his fingers gently stroking her shoulder. "I'm always here for you, Kins. You know that, right?"

"I know," she replied, her voice soft. "And I really am glad you're here. More than you know."

He tipped his head so his cheek rested on the top of her head. "I'm not hurting you, am I?"

She shook her head, feeling the stubble of his five o' clock shadow catch in the strands of her hair. "Not at all."

"How's your head feeling?"

She closed her eyes. "The headache is still there, but the medicine's been helping."

He nodded, then lapsed into silence. They lay there for a while, the constant activity of the hospital a soft hum that filtered through the door. Kinley's thoughts drifted, her body relaxing as she felt the steady rise and fall of Cam's chest beneath her cheek.

The moment was shattered all too soon when Cam's alarm began to beep. He tapped his phone to turn it off and let out a hefty sigh. "I should get going."

Kinley reluctantly pulled away, and the familiar sense of guilt washed over her. She was taking up far too much of his time and attention. "Of course."

He swiveled his head to face her but didn't make any attempt to get out of bed. "You sure you'll be okay?"

Kinley felt a rush of emotion at his words. The expression on his face made it obvious that he didn't want to leave. "I'll be fine," she said, trying to reassure him. "You need to go find Lindsey. Besides, Ainsley said she'd be stopping by this morning, so she should be here in a bit."

Cam studied her for a moment before sliding off the bed. "I can stay 'til she gets here."

She forced a smile. She couldn't monopolize his time more than she already had. "You should go. Really," she said at his dubious look. She cocked a teasing brow his way. "How much trouble can I get into here?"

He narrowed his gaze at her. "I want you to promise me you'll call if anything happens. Anything at all."

"I promise," she said, a reluctant smile tugging at the corners of her lips. "And thank you. For everything."

He nodded, still looking torn. "I'll check in on you this afternoon, okay?"

Kinley nodded, giving him a small smile. "Be safe. Go find Lindsey and bring her home."

"I'll do my best." He stared at her for another long moment before taking a step toward the door. "I'll be back later."

The door swung inward, and a moment later Ainsley appeared in the space. She pulled up short and flashed him a bright smile. "Hey!"

"Glad to see you up and about." Cam pulled her in for a quick one-armed hug. "How are you feeling?"

"Much better, thanks." Ainsley tipped her head toward Kinley. "You keeping her in line?"

"Never. You know what a troublemaker she is." Kinley rolled her eyes as he flashed a quick grin. "I was actually just leaving, so she's all yours now."

Ainsley grinned. "I'll see what I can do."

He threw a wink her way, then nodded at Kinley. "See you later."

Kinley settled back against the pillows and turned her attention to her sister as she drifted closer. "Hey, Ains."

"Hey, yourself," Ainsley replied, her voice bright and bubbly. She plopped down in the chair beside the bed and ran her gaze over Kinley from head to toe. "How are you feeling today?"

Kinley studied her sister, suspicion tugging at the fringes of her mind. Even before Ainsley's relationship with her abusive ex-boyfriend, Kinley couldn't remember seeing her sister this... upbeat. She attributed some of it to Dare, Ainsley's new boyfriend, but something else was going on.

"Not nearly as good as you, apparently."

Kinley cocked an eyebrow at her sister, and Ainsley let out a tinkling laugh. "Is it that obvious?"

"Um... yeah." She stared at her older sister, completely flummoxed. Ainsley was always the reserved one of the family, and Kinley could count on one hand the number of times she'd seen her this excited.

Her gaze narrowed as she studied Ainsley. "What's going on?"

"Same as usual." Ainsley lifted one shoulder, her pretty blue eyes locked on Kinley. "How about you? How's your head?"

She rolled her eyes. "I have fourteen stitches and the headache from hell, so cut the crap and just spill it already."

Ainsley's brows drew together. "I'm sorry, I—"

"Ainsley!" An exasperated huff fell from her lips. "Seriously. I'm fine. Just tell me already."

"Are you sure?"

Kinley glared at her, and Ainsley popped up from her chair, her petite form practically vibrating with energy as she settled on the edge of the bed. "If you're sure..."

"I am." She eyed her sister. "What's going on?

"I know it seems crazy, but..." Her lips curled up in a smile that took over her whole face. "Dare and I decided that... Well, we're getting married!"

Kinley blinked, her jaw practically hitting her chest as it fell open. "But you two haven't known each other that long!"

"I know," Ainsley said quickly, her teeth cutting into her lower lip. "But he makes me so happy, Kinley. Happier than I've ever been."

Shock clung to her as Kinley studied her sister. If there was anyone who deserved to be happy, it was Ainsley. She'd been through so much recently and Dare had been her savior, in more ways than one. Still... It was awfully fast, wasn't it? How did someone fall in love in such a short period of time?

"Do you love him?"

"I do." Ainsley's face softened. "I can't imagine life without him. He's nothing like..." She trailed off and swallowed hard at the mention of her ex-boyfriend. "He loves me, too."

Old insecurities played over her sister's face, and Kinley's heart twisted. Who was she to judge their relationship? Dare obviously adored her, and she was crazy about him. As long as Ainsley was happy, that was all that mattered.

Kinley smiled. "I'm happy for you, Ains. Really, I am. This is amazing."

"Thank you," Ainsley said, her eyes glistening with happy tears.

"I mean it." Kinley grabbed Ainsley's hands and squeezed. "You've been through so much—both of you have. You deserve this."

Ainsley smiled, her eyes dreamy and soft. "It's funny in a way. I was so scared of him at first, but..." She shrugged one shoulder. "He's so good to me."

Kinley could attest to that. She'd known from the moment she'd seen the two of them together that they were a perfect match. "When did he propose?"

"Yesterday." Ainsley's cheeks flushed bright pink. "But... there's more."

"More?" Kinley lifted a brow, and Ainsley's blush intensified.

"Well, Dare and I were talking, and... I think we need something to look forward to. So we're planning to have an engagement party in two weeks."

Kinley let out a little laugh. "Well, it sounds like you have a lot to do in a short amount of time."

"It's going to be a small gathering at our place by the lake. Just close family and friends." Ainsley bit her lip. "I know it's a lot to ask, and feel free to say no, but... I was wondering if you'd be interested in helping me plan everything."

Kinley squeezed her hands. "Ains, I would love to help you."

Honestly, though she was still shocked by the news, she was glad to have something like this to focus on. The last thing she wanted was to go back to her house—the place where she and Ainsley had been attacked—and be alone day after day. Ainsley's wedding would be a welcome distraction.

Ainsley nodded, her eyes twinkling. "Perfect. I can't imagine doing this without you."

"Of course, Ains. You can count on me." Kinley's heart swelled with love for her sister. "Let's make it the best wedding ever."

CHAPTER
SIX

Lindsey's parents, John and Mary Gill, walked into the office, their movements slow, their faces etched with worry and exhaustion.

"Mr. and Mrs. Gill, please, come this way." Dare guided them to a small conference room where Cam and Sawyer were waiting.

Mary's eyes were red from crying, and she sent a pleading look their way as she slid into a seat across from Cam. "Is there any update yet?" she asked, her voice cracking on the words. "Have you found anything?"

Cam exchanged a glance with Sawyer before speaking. "We're following several leads, Mrs. Gill. We're doing everything we can to bring Lindsey home safely."

Mary's hands trembled, and she clasped them tightly together in her lap. "Have you found any clues? Anything that might tell us where she is?"

Sawyer leaned forward, his tone gentle. "We're examining every piece of evidence. A neighbor stated that she saw a dark-colored sedan parked near Lindsey's home a few days before she was abducted. Does anyone close to you drive a car like that?"

The Gills shared a quick look, then shook their heads. "No, not that we can think of. Her boyfriend, Andrew, drives a small SUV, but it's silver."

Cam knew that, of course. They'd checked extensively into Andrew before questioning him. He nodded. "If you can think of anything else, please let us know."

"We'll do whatever it takes," John said, desperation lacing his tone. "We just want our daughter back."

"We're just so worried. Especially after what happened to the Simms girl..." Mary's voice dropped almost to a whisper. "Do you think it's connected?"

Dare inhaled deeply before turning his focus to Lindsey's mother. "It's a possibility, Mrs. Gill. We're considering every option and following every lead. We can't give you all the details, but I promise you, we're doing everything in our power to find Lindsey."

Tears welled up in Mary's eyes. "Thank you," she said, her voice tremulous. "We just need to know she's okay."

Cam offered a comforting smile. "We're not giving up, Mrs. Gill. We'll find her."

As they discussed the details of the press conference,

the weight of the situation pressed heavily on everyone's shoulders. John and Mary's pain was a stark reminder of the urgency of their mission. They couldn't afford to miss a single thing.

Several miles away, the TV was tuned to local news channel in the small break room, and the room's occupants watched, enraptured.

On the screen, the sympathetic face of a reporter dominated the frame, her voice serious as she spoke. "The search for Lindsey Gill, a local woman who went missing four days ago, continues. Authorities have yet to release any significant leads. Lindsey's family is desperate for her safe return."

In the corner of the screen, a photograph of Lindsey appeared: a bright, smiling blonde woman whose eyes sparkled with life. The break room fell silent as the reporter continued, the gravity of the situation sinking in.

"Anyone with information is urged to contact the authorities immediately," the reporter said, her tone somber. The screen transitioned to a live feed from the press conference.

Mary Gill stood at the podium, her face pale and drawn. Her voice trembled as she spoke. "If anyone knows anything about where our daughter is, please come forward. We just want her home. Lindsey, if you can hear this, we love you, and we won't stop until we find you."

Sympathetic murmurs spread through the break room. "Poor family," one woman said, shaking her head. "I can't imagine what they're going through."

Another coworker nodded. "I hope they find her soon."

In the corner of the break room, a man sat alone, his eyes fixed intently on the screen. He appeared calm, almost detached, but his heart pounded with anticipation. He watched as the camera zoomed in on Mary Gill's tear-streaked face, the raw pain evident in her eyes. A fleeting pang of guilt twisted in his chest, but he quickly pushed it aside. The thought of her family's anguish, while momentarily disconcerting, was a necessary consequence of his actions.

The press conference ended, and the news anchor resumed her coverage, but the man paid no attention. He stood and straightened his tie as he walked past his coworkers, offering a polite nod and a faint smile, blending seamlessly into the everyday hum of office life.

No one would suspect that beneath his composed exterior lay a dark obsession, a twisted desire that had driven him to take Lindsey. The world outside remained oblivious to the truth, and he intended to keep it that way.

The investigation would continue, the news would

cover every development, but as long as he remained careful, Lindsey would stay hidden from those who sought to find her. And in the quiet, secluded place where he kept her, she would learn to accept her new reality.

Lindsey belonged to him now.

CHAPTER
SEVEN

Cam scrubbed a hand over his face as he sank into the ancient chair, the cracked leather poking into his skin. Five days had passed since Lindsey Gill had been abducted from her own home, and so far they didn't have a single damn lead—though not for lack of tips.

After the press conference, they'd received hundreds of calls. Dozens of people claimed to have seen Lindsey, but none of the leads had panned out. The search party's extensive sweep of Brookhaven had yielded nothing, and with each minute that ticked away without answers, the case grew colder. Her family and friends were distraught, and the hope that she'd return home alive was slowly dwindling.

The soft hum of activity around him barely registered as he stared at the photographs pinned to the whiteboard in front of him. Despite the time and effort of painstakingly researching every outlet for the past few days, they offered nothing substantial. No suspects. No evidence. No clear leads. Frustration gnawed at him, setting his teeth on edge.

"We've covered almost every inch of this city." Sawyer scowled and scrubbed a hand over his five o'clock shadow. "She's got to be here somewhere. She didn't just disappear into thin air."

Cam rubbed his temples, the weight of exhaustion and dejection settling deep in his bones. The search party had scoured Brookhaven and beyond, checking every possible hideout, every abandoned building, even combing through nearby forests.

Dr. Joel Parsons's property, though more than an hour away, had been thoroughly investigated. Cam's original theory that Parsons could have hired someone was quickly dismissed when his bank statements revealed nothing suspicious. The lack of any substantial evidence was maddening.

He momentarily closed his eyes and tipped his head back against the headrest. It felt liked they'd been going nonstop for the past week, and they didn't have a single damn thing to show for their efforts.

A scowl pulled at his mouth. There had to be something. Maybe he should go home, clear his mind and come back fresh tomorrow. But that would just make things worse. His mind refused to rest, even at home. Might as well be here, doing something useful.

He couldn't even use the excuse that he needed to check on Kinley. She'd been released from the hospital and was currently helping her sister with wedding plans. Cam was still a little shocked over the news the sheriff had dropped a few days ago.

Sawyer's chair creaked as he swiveled around and stared at the board. "For the time being, we need to rule out Parsons and Cottrell. We've exhausted every lead with those two and came up empty. So what about Jayla Simms? She and Lindsey had similar features. Let's assume their cases are connected."

It was a possibility, one they'd discussed several times over the past few days. Jayla's murder was perplexing, and the case had quickly gone cold with no DNA or solid leads. Lindsey's abduction, however, lacked the violence of Jayla's case—at least as far as they knew. But it was a thread worth tugging at. "It's possible. But we've got no evidence linking the two besides their appearance."

"If Lindsey's disappearance is tied to Jayla's murder," Sawyer said slowly, "then there's got to be something we're missing. Some connection we haven't seen yet."

Cam nodded, skimming the report compiled by the police in Milaca the previous summer. "Jayla was abducted ten months ago after her shift in Milaca," he stated. "And now we have Lindsey Gill, twenty-four, blonde, blue-eyed, abducted from her home here in Brookhaven."

Cam leaned forward, fingers drumming lightly on the armrests of the chair as he studied the photograph taken at the scene. Though they'd checked with surrounding departments, none had any cases similar to Jayla Simms's.

Official cause of death was asphyxiation, but the killer had scrubbed down every inch of her body with bleach to remove any trace of DNA. He'd then placed her in the center of town where she was certain to be found quickly. It was almost as if the killer was taunting them with his ability to slip through town, completely unnoticed.

Across from him, Reed rubbed his temples, looking equally exhausted. "There's got to be a connection, but what?"

"Why keep Jayla for so long just to kill her?" Cam pushed out of the chair and drifted toward the whiteboard. "And why pose her like this?"

The killer had transported her body in the dead of night and placed her on the park bench, carefully arranging her hands in her lap, legs crossed at the ankles. The pose appeared so natural that the jogger who'd called it in had initially thought she was alive. Only when he was up close had he noticed the blank look in her eyes.

Cam tilted his head. "It's almost like the killer had some kind of... attachment to her. Like he cared for her."

Sawyer grimaced. "If you can call that caring. But you're right. It feels personal."

Cam spun toward Sawyer. "I think we need to speak

with Jayla's family again, take another look at the people closest to her."

An hour later, Cam and Sawyer sat in the living room of Jayla Simms's parents' house. The room was filled with framed photos of Jayla, her sparkling blue eyes and sunny smile a painful reminder of the life cut short. Jayla's mother, Margaret, sat across from them, a crumpled tissue clutched in her hand. Nearby, her husband stood with his arms crossed as he stared out the window into the back yard.

For the past ten months, the Simmses had held out hope that Jayla would return to them unharmed. But that dream had been shattered just a few weeks ago when she'd been found dead in the center of Brookhaven. The local police had advised Jayla's parents of her death, but the pain was still fresh.

Funeral services had been held just last week, and several floral arrangements were scattered around the room. The blooms had begun to curl at the edges as they wilted, almost as if they too were mourning the loss of the vibrant young woman.

"Mrs. Simms, we know this is difficult, but we need to ask you some questions about Jayla," Cam began gently.

Mrs. Simms nodded, her eyes red from crying. "Of course. Anything to help."

Sawyer leaned forward, his voice soft. "Did Jayla mention anyone new in her life around the time she was taken? Anyone who seemed overly interested in her?"

Mrs. Simms shook her head. "No, she didn't. Jayla was very private. If she was seeing someone or if someone was bothering her, she never mentioned it. She seemed happy with her job; she went out on a few dates from time to time, but she mostly spent time with her friends."

Mr. Simms turned from the window. "We've been over this with the police already. She was happy, she was fine. We didn't notice anything unusual."

Cam took out his notebook. "What about her hobbies, her routine? Did she change anything in the weeks leading up to her disappearance?"

"She was busy with work, and she attended yoga class every Saturday," Mrs. Simms replied. "She was incredibly predictable."

That was good news and bad, to Cam's way of thinking. If Jayla rarely deviated from her routine, it would have been fairly easy for the killer to get to her. On the flip side, it helped to narrow down the list of places where she might have come into contact with the man.

Cam and Sawyer thanked the Simmses then left and drove to her best friend Megan's apartment. Megan greeted them at the door with a cautious smile. "What can I do for you?"

Cam introduced himself and Sawyer. "Ms. Cook, we'd like to ask you some questions about Jayla Simms."

"Please, come in," she said, holding the door wide. She led them to a small, cozy living room and dropped into an armchair, leaving the men to occupy the couch. "I was sorry to hear about Jayla. I'd hoped…" Her face pulled into a grimace. "Well, you know. It's been so long."

Cam nodded. "We appreciate you taking the time to see us. I'm sure this has been hard on you."

"It still doesn't feel real." She gave a slow shake of her head. "I'm just glad she was finally laid to rest."

Sawyer glanced at Megan. "If you can, I'd like to talk about the last few days before Jayla was abducted. Was she seeing anyone that you're aware of?"

Though Jayla's parents weren't aware of Jayla dating anyone around the time of her disappearance, Cam was hoping that Megan might have more information. Friends were often privy to details that parents weren't, and they desperately needed a lead to find Jayla's killer.

Megan thought for a moment, then shook her head. "Not that she mentioned. She'd broken up with her boyfriend, Josh, a couple months before. I think she'd been on a few dates, but no one that really stuck out."

"Do you know their names?"

She made a little face. "I'm sorry, I never met them so I'm not sure who they were. I think she met one guy online, so maybe start there."

Cam nodded and made a mental note to double

check her social media accounts and phone records. The local police hadn't listed anyone of interest in her disappearance, but he would double check to make sure anyone Jayla had dated was questioned.

Sawyer tipped his head. "What about work? Did she mention anything odd to you? Anyone new or strange hanging around?"

"No. She was her usual self. We talked about work, our plans for the weekend, but nothing seemed off."

Sawyer pressed further. "Did she ever talk about the men she'd gone out with? Maybe someone who made her uncomfortable?"

"Not that I can remember," Megan said. "If someone was bothering her, she would have told me."

"Thanks for your time." Cam pushed to his feet, and Sawyer followed suit. "We're sorry for your loss."

Next, they visited the bank where Jayla worked. The manager, a middle-aged woman named Tina, welcomed them into her office.

"Jayla was one of our best employees," she said, her eyes sad. "She was always so cheerful."

"Did she ever mention feeling uneasy here?" Cam asked. "Was she involved in any altercations with customers or other employees?"

Tina shook her head. "Not that I'm aware of. Any formal complaints would have come to me, and I checked to make sure nothing was ever filed. She had a few unhappy customers from time to time, of course, but nothing that ever escalated."

"Anyone who might have paid too much attention to her?"

"Sorry." An apologetic grimace pulled at the corners of her mouth. "No one that I can think of."

It was a dead end, but not unexpected. Cam dipped his chin in acknowledgment. "Thanks for your time, ma'am."

Her coworkers echoed the same sentiments—Jayla was friendly, reliable, and didn't seem troubled by anyone. She also never mentioned any men of interest to her coworkers.

Their next stop was Serenity Yoga Studio. The receptionist, a young woman with short brown hair, greeted them. "Can I help you?"

Cam flashed his badge. "We're investigating a homicide. Do you remember Jayla Simms?"

The receptionist's face paled, and her hand flew to her throat. "I remember her. She was a regular. I still can't believe she's gone."

"Did you notice anything unusual? Anyone who seemed out of place or too interested in her?" Sawyer asked.

Her lips curved down in a frown. "Not really. The studio is pretty quiet. People come in for their classes and leave."

The receptionist didn't have anything to add, so the men thanked her and headed back to the station.

"Well that was a waste of time," Sawyer said, slumping into his chair.

Cam stared at the board filled with photos and notes. "Not entirely. Megan said she'd been on a few dates before she was abducted. Let's double check those reports again and see if the locals up in Milaca found the men and interviewed them."

Diving into Jayla's social media account, Cam found messages she'd exchanged with a man named Devon. According to the transcript, they'd flirted for a couple of weeks, gone out on one date, then decided they weren't a good fit.

Sawyer was busy highlighting passages from her text messages. "I've got her here talking about going on a date with someone—Henry Greico."

Cam added both men's names to the list. "We'll question them, see what they have to say. Maybe we'll get lucky and one of them will lead us to Lindsey."

Sawyer sighed. "Wishful thinking. The only thing they seem to have in common is their features. What still bothers me is—why keep Jayla for so long if the plan was to kill her eventually?"

Cam shook his head. "I don't know. But there has to be a connection here somewhere."

Jayla's killer was still out there, and Lindsey's life hung in the balance. They needed a lead—before Lindsey became the next victim.

CHAPTER
EIGHT

They'd hit another dead end. Henry Greico was a bartender who'd been at work, surrounded by dozens of people. The other, Devon Mills, had been out of town, attending a friend's bachelor party in Vegas.

A knock sounded on the door, and both men glanced up at their dispatcher. "Sorry to interrupt," Yvonne began, "but I just got a call from Earl Weaver. Says he was out fishing and found something you might want to see."

Reed studied her. "He say what it was?"

"A woman's shoe." Yvonne lifted one shoulder. "Said it got his attention because it hardly had a speck of dirt on it. Not too common out in the woods."

No, it wasn't. Cam nodded as he and Sawyer pushed from their chairs. "Thanks, Yvonne. Send the coordinates to my phone and tell him we'll be there soon."

Earl Weaver operated a small sporting goods store in town and owned a good chunk of land that abutted the subdivision where Lindsey lived. They'd questioned him several days ago but his wife, who was retired, hadn't seen or heard anything at the time of her disappearance. Earl himself had just opened the shop and was the only person on duty until eleven that morning.

Cam's phone pinged with a message as they slid into the cruiser, and Sawyer plugged the location into the GPS. According to the directions Weaver had given them, the location was approximately one mile northwest of Lindsey Gill's home.

"Wasn't the search party out this way already?" Reed asked, his brow furrowed as he stared out the windshield.

"I thought so." Cam bit back a curse. "Must have missed it on the first pass."

Cam wanted to be pissed, but the volunteers had worked tirelessly for several days before coming up empty-handed. Though they'd collected a handful of evidence, nothing had been linked conclusively to Lindsey's disappearance. To find the shoe now seemed more than a little suspicious.

When they arrived, the scene was already being secured by two uniformed deputies. Yellow tape fluttered in the breeze, marking off the area where the shoe had been found.

Earl Weaver stood to the side, and Cam made a

beeline toward him. "Thanks for calling us, Mr. Weaver."

"Cam." Earl extended a hand for a firm shake.

"Have you met Detective Reed yet?" Cam gestured toward Sawyer. "He's new to Brookhaven."

Earl dipped his chin at Sawyer and shook his hand. "Sorry to meet under these circumstances, Detective."

Sawyer nodded. "Can you show us where you found the shoe?"

Weaver nodded and led them a few yards into the underbrush. The shoe lay there, partially hidden by leaves and dirt.

Sawyer crouched down, examining the shoe without touching it. "We need to get this to the lab ASAP."

Cam nodded in agreement. "Let's secure the area, see if we can find anything else."

Sawyer carefully collected the shoe, along with any other potential evidence. A few yards away, Cam noticed some broken branches, and he wandered in that direction. The ground had been disturbed, the leaves kicked up as if something—or someone—had recently passed through.

"Reed." He gestured with his chin toward a slight depression in the earth. "Looks like someone might have been through this way."

Sawyer joined him a moment later, his eyes scanning the ground. "Footprints."

Cam nodded. "Someone tried to obliterate them, but the ground must have been too soft."

Sawyer glanced over at Cam. "When did it rain last?"

"Two days ago."

"And before that?"

Cam immediately picked up on his train of thought. "Shit. We need to check to see whether it rained the night before her disappearance."

Maybe the search party hadn't missed the shoe at all. Maybe the perp had circled back and planted it after he'd absconded with Lindsey.

"Let's spread out, see if we can track them."

Sawyer nodded, his eyes scanning the ground. "Looks like the footprints lead that direction," he said, pointing toward a faint trail of impressions in the soft earth. He lifted his gaze to Cam, brows drawn together. "Wait. Isn't Lindsey's subdivision that way?"

Cam glanced toward the woods and nodded grimly. "Yep."

They moved carefully, eyes trained on the ground as they set off toward Lindsey's house. The sporadic footprints led them deeper into the woods, the dense canopy overhead casting dappled shadows on the forest floor. They followed the trail for what felt like an eternity, the forest growing quieter around them, until they reached a small creek that cut through the backside of Earl's property.

The creek babbled softly, its clear water flowing over smooth stones. The footprints led straight to the edge of the creek and then... disappeared. Cam and Sawyer stood at the water's edge, staring at the spot where the trail seemed to vanish.

"My guess is he waded into the creek," Cam said, his brow furrowed. "But which way did he go?"

Sawyer scanned the area, considering the possibilities. "Let's split up."

Cam nodded. "Keep looking over here. See if he followed the water. I'll check the other side."

He waded through the shallow water to the bank on the opposite side, then clambered out, his eyes scanning the ground for any sign of footprints. But the ground here was as clean as the forest—no footprints, no broken branches, nothing.

"Goddamn it." Cam propped his hands on his hips. "Either he obliterated the rest of the prints, or—"

"He was in the water," Sawyer finished for him, his expression grim. "Fuck."

Cam looked down the length of the creek. "If he waded through the creek, he could have gone either north or south."

"I'll take the north, you head south," Sawyer replied. "If we don't find anything, we'll regroup back here."

Cam nodded, then slowly made his way south along the creek. The water gurgled softly beside him as he kept his eyes peeled for any sign of the perpetrator. A few hundred yards away, he noticed an outcropping of rock jutting out over the water, the surface slick and covered with moss.

He climbed onto the rock, examining it closely. If the man was trying to avoid leaving a trail, the rocks would be a good place to climb out. Carefully, Cam made his way up the rock, searching for any sign that someone else had been there. His heart raced as he reached the top, but his excitement quickly faded. There were no footprints, no signs of disturbance. It was as if the rock itself was the end of the line.

Pulling out his phone, he called Sawyer. "I found an outcropping where he could have climbed out without leaving a trail," he said. "But there's nothing here."

"Nothing on my end either," Sawyer replied, his voice tinged with frustration. "Let's search the area around those rocks. Maybe there's something we missed."

While Cam waited on Sawyer, he began to methodically search the area around the outcropping. A few moments later Sawyer arrived and together they combed through the underbrush, turning over fallen logs and scouring the rocky ground for any clue that might have been overlooked. But the forest remained stubbornly silent, giving up none of its secrets.

After more than an hour of searching, they stood together on the outcropping and stared out over the creek. Sawyer raked one hand through his hair. "It's like he vanished into thin air."

Fury pulsed through Cam's veins. The asshole was taunting them. He'd taken Lindsey, and now he was deliberately leaving clues, trying to throw them off their game.

He met Sawyer's gaze. "There's a trail here somewhere, and we're damn well going to find it."

CHAPTER
NINE

The squeal of rubber against asphalt broke the stillness of the calm afternoon, startling Kinley. Halfway across the street, she tossed a look over her shoulder just as a car whipped around the corner.

Her gaze locked on the vehicle as it grew closer, the roar of the engine filling her ears. Bright sunlight reflected off the windshield, obscuring her view of the person inside. The sedan was dark, and the space on the front bumper that would normally accommodate a license plate was conspicuously bare. Apprehension washed over her, and goosebumps broke out along her skin despite the heat of the afternoon.

Seconds felt like hours as the car bore down on her, and Kinley realized with sickening dread that it was headed straight for her. For a moment, she couldn't move. The box in her arms felt like it weighed a thousand pounds as she forced her muscles to cooperate.

Her heart jumped into her throat as she dropped the box and threw herself out of the way, aiming for the parking lot several feet away. Kinley tumbled to the pavement between two vehicles, head spinning and limbs aching from the hard landing. But instead of speeding past, the car followed her trajectory.

Metal screeched as the driver in the sedan sideswiped the red car closest to her, pushing it against the other car. Protected within the V of the two damaged cars, she dared a look under the white car to her right, watching as the driver took off down the road. The sedan made a sharp left at the intersection, heedless of oncoming traffic, sending up a cacophony of blaring horns.

Her palms ached as she pushed to a sitting position and rested her back against the fender of the car next to her. Her breath came too fast, and her pulse still thrummed so rapidly she could hear the rush of blood in her ears.

She gingerly scraped the bits of gravel and dirt from her palms, then brushed at the torn knees of her jeans.

Footsteps pounded against pavement, and a middle-aged man appeared in front of her. "Hey, are you all right? That guy didn't even try to stop."

Kinley grimaced but managed a small nod. "I think I'm okay, just a little banged up."

"That looks like it hurts."

His sympathetic gaze moved over her face, and she automatically lifted a hand to her forehead. The gash near her hairline had reopened and sullenly oozed blood. She swiped it away before it could drip into her eye.

"Hold on." The man disappeared, then reappeared less than a minute later. He extended a handful of fast-food napkins her way.

"Thanks." Kinley gratefully took them and pressed them to the wound.

"No problem. The cops are already on the way. I'll have the stores page the owners' license plates. My name's Jim, by the way."

"Kinley." Using the car as leverage, she pulled herself unsteadily to her feet. "I appreciate you sticking around."

"No problem." He gave a slow shake of his head. "The nerve of some people. Who does that?"

That was a good question. "Did you get a look at the driver?"

"Not really, no." The man shook his head ruefully. "He had on a baseball cap and sunglasses, so it was hard to tell for sure. But he looked about your age."

Kinley nodded. She hadn't gotten a look at him, either. The sunlight had glinted off the windshield, obscuring her view. She'd been far more worried about getting out of the way than looking at the driver. "That's okay. I'm sure the cops will figure it out."

Less than ten minutes later, a cruiser pulled into the parking lot and the patrolman unfolded from the car. Jim lifted his hand in a wave, directing him to their position.

Cooper Klein approached, concern etched deep in his expression. "Kins? What happened?"

Cooper had been one year ahead of Kinley in school, and she shot him a weary smile. "Hey, Coop."

She and Jim took turns relaying the story. Cooper took notes, intermittently asking questions, before turning to Kinley. "Are you okay, Kins? We should get you to the hospital so they can fix those stitches."

His gaze moved to her forehead, and she self-consciously ducked her head. She hated the injury that drew everyone's attention. "I don't need an ambulance or anything."

"Are you sure?" His brows drew together. "I can drive you if you're not feeling up to it."

She forced a tight smile. "I'll be okay, I promise."

He nodded. "I have everything I need for now. Make sure to get that looked at."

"Thanks."

Cooper helped her clean up the damaged vases, salvaging what they could, which was precious little. She fired off a quick text to Ainsley letting her know she was running late, then climbed into the car and headed toward the hospital. Dr. Patel fixed her stitches, administered painkillers, and sent her on her way. By the time she was released, Kinley was exhausted.

She needed to see Ainsley, though she wasn't looking forward to it. Bracing herself, she headed toward Dare and Ainsley's house on the lake.

Her sister greeted her at the door, worry clouding her features. "Is everything okay?"

"It is now. There was an accident downtown, so I got held up." She followed Ainsley inside and settled in the kitchen. "I have some bad news, though. Most of the vases for your centerpieces didn't make it."

"Don't worry about that." Ainsley's gaze swept over her face. "I'm just glad you're okay. What happened?"

The sound of heavy footsteps drifted toward the kitchen, and Kinley braced herself as they drew closer. She swiveled on the chair and offered her sister's fiancé a tight smile. "Hey, Dare."

His brows pulled together as his gaze landed on her face. "What happened?"

"Just an accident."

"The hit and run downtown?"

She supposed it had been a hit and run, considering the driver had damaged two vehicles then fled the scene. "Yeah. I was just in the wrong place at the wrong time."

"I heard the call come across," Dare spoke up, "but they never mentioned your name. Had I known, I would have been there."

"It's no big deal—really. The driver was just in a hurry, and I wasn't fast enough." Even as she said the words, a chill slithered down her spine.

It was almost eerie how the driver had seemed to steer right toward her even as she dove between the two cars. She shook off the odd sensation. More than likely he was on his phone or something and just wasn't paying attention.

Dare's intense gaze moved to her forehead and she fought the urge to cover the injury. "Well, I'm glad you're okay. You sure you don't need anything?"

"No, I'm good." She shook her head and turned her attention back to Ainsley. "But if you don't mind, I'm going to head home. Can we work on the party stuff later this week?"

Her head ached as it had often for the past week, and all she wanted was to lie down and relax. The effects of the fall had begun to kick in, and she felt bone-tired.

"Of course. Don't worry about the centerpieces, we have plenty of time to get them done." Ainsley pulled her in for a hug. "You just get some rest and call me tomorrow."

"Will do." Kinley gave her sister one last squeeze, then headed toward home.

Ten minutes later she steered the car into the small detached garage behind the house, then climbed out. Her gaze drifted toward the house, and a scowl pulled at her mouth. She propped her hands on her hips and glared at the pile of wood that, just a couple of weeks ago, had been her back deck.

It was just one more thing on her ever-growing list of things to fix. The rotted, splintering wood boards had been ripped away, along with a good section of siding from the lower portion of the house. The old metal siding was dented and rusting, and the previous owners had pieced the home together, or updated as needed, because it didn't match the newer vinyl siding at the top of the house at all.

Now, it wasn't likely to ever get fixed. With absolutely no experience with these things, Kinley had hired a local handyman a few weeks back. As it turned out, that hadn't exactly been her greatest idea.

Hayes had asked for cash up front and, naïve idiot she was, she gave it to him. He'd shown up for all of a day, just long enough to rip the deck and siding down, toss it in a pile, then take off without another word.

She'd tried calling a dozen times, but each had gone unanswered. His voicemail was full, too, probably from the messages she'd continued to leave for the past week and a half since he'd skipped out on her. She tried to give him the benefit of the doubt for the first few days, but she now had to admit that he was never coming back.

Now she was out the money she'd paid him, and she couldn't afford to hire someone else. Though she could've asked her parents for the money, Kinley would rather die than admit she needed help.

Her gaze slid to the pile of tools lying next to the shed. She'd stupidly assumed he would at least come back for those, but they didn't seem to be of much value to him. Although, now he had an extra twenty-five-hundred bucks in his pocket that he could use to replace them.

A lengthy sigh escaped before she could stop it. Well, if he ever did come back for tools, she wasn't going to make it easy on him. He'd damn well have to talk to her if he wanted his things back. Scooping up an empty box as she passed, she strode determinedly toward the shed, then tossed the stray hammers, saws and other paraphernalia, inside with a little more force than necessary.

He was supposed to have taken the siding to be scrapped, but apparently the few extra bucks he'd have made weren't worth the trip. Angry at Hayes but even more mad at herself, she snatched up the box and stormed back into the garage.

Too many bad things had happened recently, and Kinley no longer wanted any part of living here. Hence hiring the handyman. With student loans coming due, on top of the monthly mortgage and utility bills, she was strapped for cash. But after what had happened to Ainsley right here in this house, she couldn't bear to stay here any longer than necessary.

She'd originally planned to make this her starter home, stay here for a few years until she—maybe—got married. That prospect was dying a slow death, though, too.

Shaking the thought away, she slid the heavy box onto the counter and headed for the house, pushing all the negative thoughts away. Just once, she wished things would work out the way they were supposed to.

CHAPTER
TEN

Cam's temper hadn't cooled by the time he stormed back into the office. Yvonne tossed him a questioning look but wisely stayed quiet.

He dropped into his chair and logged into the system, then printed off a picture of the shoe they'd found at the scene. Grabbing it off the printer, he pinned it to the board next to Lindsey's photograph.

The soft squeak of rubber on tile alerted him to Sawyer's presence. "The lab will prioritize the shoe, see if we get a match."

After the trail of footprints had gone cold, they'd returned to speak with Earl Weaver and his wife, Jeannette. According to the older man, he couldn't recall seeing or hearing anyone on his property after the search party had come through.

Jeannette liked to putter around the large garden behind their house, but she hadn't seen or heard anything, either. Earl promised to keep an eye out and let them know if he noticed anything out of the ordinary.

Sawyer nodded slowly. "What are you thinking?"

"About the footprints..." Cam turned to face the detective and propped a hip on his desk. "Or the shoe?"

Sawyer lifted one shoulder. "Both."

"Honestly?" He scrubbed a hand over his face. "My gut says he's toying with us, trying to throw us off the trail."

"It's not a coincidence those footprints just disappeared, or that the shoe showed up as soon as the search party was gone."

Something tickled at the back of Cam's mind, and he strode back toward the whiteboard. The footprints seemed to lead away from the creek and move toward the subdivision where Lindsey's house was located. Helen Patterson, the elderly woman who lived a few houses down from Lindsey, had recalled seeing a strange dark-colored sedan in the neighborhood just a few days prior to Lindsey's disappearance.

What if the person had returned to the subdivision and cut through the back of Earl's property to leave the shoe for them to find? It was risky, but the man—if it was, in fact, the same person who'd killed Jayla Simms—was clearly adept at blending in and moving throughout town undetected.

The sound of footsteps approached the office, and

Cam tossed a look over his shoulder at Cooper Klein. "Hey."

"Gentlemen," Cooper said, nodding to each of them.

"Hey, Coop," Sawyer replied, barely looking away from the report in his hands. "Anything new on your end?"

Cooper turned to Cam, a wry grin twisting his lips. "You could say that. Your bestie has a knack for getting into trouble, doesn't she?"

Cam tensed. Cooper had teased him about Kinley for years, always asking when he was going to ask her out. Cam had always brushed it off, but after her recent injury, the jokes stung more than usual. "Why?"

Coop straightened, his smile slipping away. "You didn't hear?"

"Hear what?" Every cell of his body went hyperalert as he focused his full attention on the deputy. "What happened?"

Sensing the shift in Cam's mood, Cooper turned serious. "She was almost hit by a car downtown. Crossing the street near the florist."

Cam's heart stuttered to a stop. "Is she okay?"

"Yeah, she's fine," Cooper said quickly. "Shaken up, but no injuries. Lucky for her, the driver swerved just in time."

Jesus Christ. What else could go wrong? "Thanks for letting me know, Coop."

He needed to check on her, but... His gaze was

drawn back to the whiteboard. His plate was already overflowing, damn it.

Cooper glanced at the photos on the wall. "You two still working on the Gill abduction?"

"Yeah," Sawyer said, tossing the report on the desk. "We've got a few leads we're following up on."

Cooper clapped Cam on the shoulder. "I'll leave you to it then."

Reed waited until Cooper disappeared from the room then flicked a glance Cam's way, one dark brow lifting in concern. "If you need to go..."

He was conflicted. He needed to find out what the hell had happened to Lindsey. On the other hand... He threw a look at Sawyer. "Keep me posted if anything comes up?"

Sawyer dipped his chin. "Go. I'll keep digging here."

Grabbing up his files he hurried out of the office, his mind racing. The drive to her house passed in a blur, Cam barely registering the familiar streets and landmarks as he navigated through town. He couldn't shake the image of Kinley, vulnerable and scared, narrowly escaping another brush with danger.

Leaping up the rickety porch steps, he gave a quick triple knock. He felt anxious and jittery, and he could feel his restlessness increase as ten seconds passed, then thirty. He scowled at the slab of wood. If she thought she could avoid him, she had another thing coming. Cam pounded the side of his fist on the door, his heart hammering in his chest.

"Hold on!" came an exasperated voice from the inner recesses of the house. A moment later the door was yanked open and he came face-to-face with a very irritated Kinley.

She rolled her eyes when she saw him waiting on the other side. "I was wondering how long it would take you to find out."

"Yeah, well, news travels fast in a small town." His gaze flew over her face as he stepped into the house, forcing her backward. "What the hell happened?"

Kinley repressed a sigh as she turned and strode back toward the couch, then flopped into the corner. "It's not as bad as it looks."

Cam shut the door then stormed forward, a scowl pulling at his lips. "You sure? Because it looks pretty damn bad."

"Thanks, asshole."

"Seriously." Kneeling in front of her, he took her chin in his hand and tipped her face one way, then the other. Her forehead now sported a dark contusion, and flecks of dried blood adorned the fresh stitches. He stroked his thumb lightly over her cheek. "How did this happen?"

"I fell."

"You fell." Disbelief tinged his tone as he peered at her. His gaze swept lower, and he grabbed up her palms, holding them up for inspection.

They'd been best friends for years, and he'd always kept her safe. But ever since Ainsley's ex had attacked

Kinley, leaving her with a head wound that required more than a dozen stitches, he'd felt more protective of her than ever.

"I'm fine. Really." She tugged her hands free, but Cam continued to glower at her. She relented with a hefty sigh. "I stopped to pick up the vases Ainsley wanted to use for the party. When I left, some idiot came whipping around the corner. I jumped out of the way, but..." She shrugged. "I wasn't fast enough."

He gently touched her forehead. "You hit your head again, didn't you?"

"I said I was fine." She made an aggravated sound in the back of her throat. "I appreciate your concern, but the doctor already took a look at it. I have six new stitches to match the others."

She was too damn independent for her own good. Cam dropped his hand away and regarded her for a long moment. "Did you see who it was?"

"No. I couldn't see anything through the windshield. Like I said, it was just an accident."

"A hit and run isn't an accident," Cam said, his tone hard.

Kinley rolled her eyes. "It wasn't like he was intentionally trying to hit me."

So she said. His lips pressed into a firm line. He hated seeing her hurt. Not to mention, the recent murder and abduction worried him incessantly. He shifted onto the couch next to her and changed his tack. "How are you feeling?"

She shrugged, trying to brush off his concern. "Aside from the new bumps and bruises added to my collection? Fine."

Cam bit back a growl. Goddamn her for being so flippant about the whole thing. It was no laughing matter. She'd been attacked a week ago; now some idiot had nearly run her down with their car.

"Kins, I'm serious."

"So am I." She turned that defiant blue gaze on him. "I said I'm fine."

He wanted to shake some sense into her. Wanted to pull her against him and kiss the life out of her. She was so damn infuriating, but he loved her for it.

He studied her face, noting not for the first time the dark circles under her eyes, the strain at the corners. She looked exhausted... and in pain. "Your head's still bothering you, isn't it?"

"Nothing a painkiller won't fix."

"Stay here." Cam pushed off the couch and grabbed the medicine and a bottle of water from the kitchen, then was back less than a minute later. He passed her two tablets and she swallowed them down, briefly closing her eyes as another frisson of pain flashed across her face.

"You need to rest. Come here." He pulled a pillow into his lap, then waved her over. Her entire body tensed as he guided her down so she was lying across his lap. He began to massage her head and neck, his fingers moving in slow, comforting circles.

She leaned into him, her tension gradually melting away. "I'm sorry."

A smile pulled at his lips. "You don't have to apologize. I've known you too long to take offense to your grumpy ass."

She smacked his thigh, and he laughed. His fingers sifted through her hair, the long golden locks sliding along his skin like silk. He lightly rubbed her temples, easing the pain away.

"You don't have to do this, you know," she murmured, though her eyes were already drifting closed.

"I want to," he replied softly. "Just relax."

Within minutes, she was asleep against him, her breathing deep and even. He watched her sleep, her features soft and peaceful, and the sight punched him in the chest. Blonde hair, blue eyes... She looked remarkably like Jayla and Lindsey.

His throat grew tight. What if the hit and run downtown wasn't an accident at all? The eerie similarity between the victims and Kinley sent chills down his spine. It could have easily been her who'd ended up dead or missing.

The thought had the power to rock him to his core. Nothing like that would ever happen to her—he'd make sure of it.

CHAPTER
ELEVEN

Cam was pissed. So far, he didn't have a single damn lead. None of the three stores he'd visited had camera footage from yesterday's incident.

A few employees he'd interviewed said they'd heard a loud crash but hadn't witnessed the accident. The only person who could account for the incident was Jim Hogan, who had apparently helped Kinley after she'd fallen.

According to Jim, the driver of the car had never slowed down, even after swiping the two cars parked along the street. As Kinley had said, the car was a silvery gray sedan, but Jim hadn't gotten a look at the license plate.

Cam shook his head as he climbed back into the cruiser and steered toward the station. With today's technology, how in the hell had no one seen anything?

He headed inside, pausing briefly to pet Sarge before

heading into the sheriff's office. Dare pulled his attention from the computer and glanced up at Cam as he dropped into the chair opposite him. He lifted a brow before turning back to the screen. "Make yourself at home."

"I will, thanks."

Dare didn't respond, and Cam let out a little growl. "No one saw a damn thing."

"We already knew that. Coop wrote that into his report."

"I was hoping someone would remember something."

Dare sighed and leaned back in his chair. "I asked Turner and Webb to patrol downtown. If someone does something stupid, they'll nail him."

"And what about Kinley? You saw her." Cam's blood practically boiled at the memory of the worry clouding her eyes, fresh bruises and scrapes decorating her skin.

It brought to mind the scene he'd walked in on just over a week ago, where Kinley lay unconscious on the floor of her living room, blood pooling around her head.

There had been so much blood. He'd never felt fear like. He'd seen worse injuries, of course, but it had never affected him so deeply before. Because none of the previous victims had been Kinley. His best friend. And the woman he'd loved for years.

Cam couldn't regret that the asshole who'd hurt her and Ainsley was dead. But the fact remained that Kinley had been hurt not once, but twice. Her wound hadn't even had a chance to heal before it had been torn open again because of some idiot who couldn't keep his eyes on the road.

Dare propped his elbows on the arms of the chair and steepled his fingers together as he regarded Cam. "You spend a lot of time with Kinley. Tell me something."

Cam lifted a brow in question, and Dare inhaled before speaking. "Has she seemed different since the attack?"

He shrugged. "She's been getting headaches, but the doctor says that's normal. Otherwise, she says she's okay."

"My question is," Dare said slowly, "is it possible that maybe she just misjudged the distance between her and the car?"

He held up a hand when Cam opened his mouth to snap back in her defense. "I'm not questioning the hit and run. Two vehicles were damaged, but... Kinley was in the parking lot when the witness found her."

"She wouldn't lie about something like that," Cam ground out. "If she said the car almost hit her, then that's what happened."

Dare stared at him for several long moments. "Then I trust you to find out who it was."

"Damn right I will." Cam pushed from the chair. Though that was easier said than done.

Cam McCoy pulled into the parking lot of the Medical Examiner's Office, his mind racing with the implications of the submerged vehicle and the skeletal remains. The building was small and unassuming, but it held the answers to questions that had haunted the town for decades.

Inside, the cool air provided a stark contrast to the heat outside. Cam approached the front desk and nodded to the receptionist. "I'm here to see Dr. Tom Seidel. He's expecting me."

The receptionist gave a quick smile and gestured down the hallway. "He's in his office. You can go right in."

Cam walked down the hall, his footsteps echoing in the quiet space. He found Dr. Seidel's door ajar and knocked lightly before entering. The medical examiner looked up from his desk, his expression weary.

"Cam, come in. Have a seat," Dr. Seidel said, waving him over.

Cam settled into the chair, leaning forward. "You have the autopsy results?"

Dr. Seidel nodded. "Yes, we do. The remains are most likely Misty Collins, but we won't know for sure until we can compare the dental records. However, the signs are pointing in that direction."

Cam felt a mix of relief and dread. "What can you tell me about her injuries?"

Dr. Seidel picked up a file and flipped it open. "There are ridges on her ribs consistent with wounds from a sharp object, most likely a knife. I can't be certain unless you have the weapon to compare, but the pattern is indicative of stab wounds."

Cam's stomach churned. "So she was murdered."

"It appears so," Dr. Seidel confirmed. He flipped to a photograph of what was once a blue shirt. "She was wearing this the day she disappeared. See these?"

He pointed to several gaping holes in the fabric. "There's been obvious decay over the past thirty years, but look at the edges. See how straight these are?" He lifted his gaze to Cam. "I would guess she was stabbed at least a dozen times."

A dozen stab wounds was a lot—and it would have been messy. According to the report, the house had been clean, and there was no indication that she'd been stabbed inside the car. What the hell had happened?

Cam absorbed the information, his mind racing. "We pulled up the car, but there was nothing inside except a suitcase full of clothes."

"There are also signs of blunt force trauma, which could have occurred before or after death. It's hard to say without more evidence." Dr. Seidel nodded, leaning back in his chair. "Based on the state of the remains, she's been underwater since the day she disappeared."

The weight of the revelation settled heavily on Cam. Misty Collins hadn't left on her own accord; she'd been murdered and hidden in the lake, her fate unknown for nearly thirty years.

"Do you have any idea who could have done this?" Dr. Seidel asked, his eyes searching Cam's face.

Cam shook his head. "We're still piecing it together. The car was registered to Dennis Collins, Misty's husband. He never remarried, and from what I've gathered, he lived alone until he passed away a few years ago. But there's a lot we don't know."

Dr. Seidel closed the file and placed it on his desk. "Well, I'll keep you updated as soon as we have more information. The dental records should give us a definitive answer soon."

"Thanks, Tom," Cam said, standing up. "This case is turning out to be more complicated than I ever imagined."

Dr. Seidel nodded. "That's often the way with cold cases. Just keep digging, and eventually, the truth will come to light."

Cam left the medical examiner's office, his thoughts consumed by the new information. As he drove back to the station, he couldn't shake the image of the skeletal remains and the realization that Misty Collins had been murdered. Someone in Brookhaven had committed a heinous crime and had lived with that secret for nearly three decades.

The investigation was far from over, and Cam knew he had to find answers not just for Misty, but for the entire community. The truth had been buried for too long, and it was time to bring it to the surface.

CHAPTER
TWELVE

Cam paused in the doorway of the living room, his assessing gaze sweeping over Kinley where she sat curled up in the corner of the couch flipping through the channels.

His worry had only grown over the course of the day. What if Dare was right? The tests had come back clear, but head wounds were a tricky thing. What if she was more injured than she was letting on?

She gestured with the remote. "If they really wanted these shows to be realistic, they'd have someone like me out there scraping paint off the siding and patching eight thousand holes in the drywall."

His brow furrowed at her words. "I thought you hired someone."

Kinley bit her lip and shifted uncomfortably, and dread rolled through him. "What happened?"

With a sigh, she rolled her head his way. "I did hire someone…"

His gut clenched with foreboding. "But?"

"He skipped out on me," she finally admitted.

Cam shook his head. Why the hell couldn't people ever stay true to their word? "Can't you hire someone else?"

"Not exactly." The way she hesitated put him on edge. "I kind of don't have the money right now."

Before she even said the words, he knew what was coming. "He asked for an advance and I figured it was only fair, so…" She lifted one shoulder. "He estimated all the work to be about five grand. I gave him half for materials and everything, then never heard from him again."

Fury rolled over him, and he bit back the urge to curse. "Who is this guy, anyway?"

She dropped her head back. "His name is Hayes."

His gaze narrowed. "Is that his first name or last?"

Another sigh filtered from her lips. "I don't know."

Goddamn it. The man had swindled her out of thousands of dollars, and she didn't even know his real name. Getting her money back would be damn near impossible, but if Cam knew his name, he could pay the guy a visit, drop a word or two in his ear.

He thought he could take advantage of her after everything she'd been through already? Hell, no. Not on his watch.

"Where did you find him?"

She rolled her eyes. "You know the bulletin board at the coffee shop where local businesses pin their cards and advertise stuff? I saw his paper and called the number. He seemed nice enough at first, but..."

She trailed off, and Cam turned toward her. "You still have the ad?"

She shook her head. "I didn't take the ad, just his number. But it's in my phone."

"Let me see."

She swiped it off the coffee table, scrolled through her contacts, then passed it his way. Cam shared the contact info with himself, then handed the phone back to her. Tomorrow he would do a little research, see if he could track him down.

Kinley glanced his way, brows furrowed. "What are you thinking?"

"I'll run the number, see if I can find him."

"You don't have to—"

"Don't worry." He shook his head. "I just want to see if I can find out who it is."

"All right," she said dubiously, "but he's probably long gone by now."

Cam tipped his head her way. "Why don't you talk to a realtor?"

After what happened to Ainsley, he'd have put the damn thing on the market the next day. She wanted out of that place, and he would do anything he could to help her. Kinley had been killing herself trying to renovate the place so she could turn a decent profit.

"I don't know." Her lips turned down in a frown. "There's still so much I want to do. And if I sell it half-finished, the way it is now, I won't get nearly as much."

After the incident with Joel, Cam and Dare had tried to clean up the blood left behind. It had taken hours to scrub it out of the grout in the kitchen, but the carpet in the living room was a lost cause. No matter how many times they went over it, the stain refused to come up. In the end, they'd pulled up the carpet, deciding it was better to get rid of it entirely.

"If you're just flipping it anyway, put something inexpensive in there. Then just get out."

She dropped her head back. "Where would I go?"

"Right here."

Her eyes went wide as she swiveled to look at him. "What?"

"Move in here." He lifted a shoulder. "You're here all the time anyway."

Her mouth opened and closed several times before she finally forced out a coherent thought. "What about... you know?" Her cheeks flared bright red.

"Dates?" He lifted a brow her way.

"Yeah, I mean..." She licked her lips and dropped her gaze to the floor. "Wouldn't it be awkward?"

Unless it was the woman beside him, he didn't plan on bringing anyone to his home. "I'm not seeing anyone. Are you?"

"Not at the moment..."

He studied her. He'd met Kinley several years ago

when Brookhaven Elementary had invited Cam to speak at career day. The beautiful teacher had immediately caught his interest. Of course, she'd been seeing someone at the time, so he kept his distance. But they'd run into one another several times over the next few weeks, and they'd become fast friends.

They discovered they had the same dark sense of humor, similar tastes in movies and music. Now, they spent most of their time together. Though he'd dated other women over the past couple of years, no one had come close to making him feel the way Kinley did. One of these days he was going to grow a pair and tell her exactly how he felt. But first he needed to find a way to push her out of the comfort zone they'd established years ago.

"Just think about it. I think we'd be good roommates."

Her nose scrunched up, and a tiny smile curled her mouth. "You say that now."

He shook his head. "I won't change my mind. But it's not my decision to make. You're always welcome here, you know that."

He'd given her enough to think about for one night. He just hoped he could convince her to take the plunge. It was time to move on and put the past behind her.

CHAPTER
THIRTEEN

Kinley opened her eyes and blinked against the soft glow of morning light streaming through her bedroom window. She stretched, wincing slightly as a faint, dull ache pulsed through her head. The headaches had been less frequent lately—a sign, she hoped, that she was finally beginning to heal.

Throwing back the covers, Kinley swung her legs over the side of the bed and stood up. She slipped on her robe and padded down the hallway, the old wooden floors creaking under her bare feet. As she descended the staircase, a cool draft washed over her, sending apprehension skittering down her spine.

She froze on the steps, her gaze drifting over the living room. A blanket had been draped haphazardly over the arm of the couch, and a book she'd left unfinished rested with pages spread face down rested on the coffee table. Everything appeared to be in its place. So why did it feel... off?

Pulse thrumming wildly in her veins, the hairs on the back of her neck lifted in warning, and she crept cautiously toward the kitchen. When she reached the threshold, she stopped dead. The back door stood wide open, the morning air drifting in, carrying with it the sounds of chirping birds and distant traffic. A wave of confusion and fear washed over her. She was certain she had locked it last night. She always did.

Heart pounding in her chest, she slowly approached the door, half-expecting to see someone hovering just outside. Memories from the previous week swamped her, intensifying the already-pounding headache that plagued her. She pushed them away, swallowing down the bile that had risen in her throat.

Moving closer, she kept her back to the wall as she approached quietly, then peeked around the doorjamb. A relieved breath rushed from her lungs as her gaze swept over the lush green grass, sparkling with dew. The yard was empty, the world outside seemingly undisturbed.

She stepped forward and cautiously closed the door, turning the lock with a decisive click. For a moment, she stood there, staring at the lock, her mind racing.

She had locked the door last night... Right?

It was late when she'd gotten home from Cam's house, and she'd entered through the back door as she

always did, since it was closest to the driveway. Then...
Then what?

Her gaze slid toward the kitchen. Her purse lay on the counter next to her keys where she'd dropped them the night before. She was almost certain she'd closed and locked the door behind her, but she couldn't be sure.

She thought about calling Cam but almost immediately, she dismissed the idea. He was already overprotective as it was. And she refused to tell her family. Her parents and sisters were worried about her head injury already. The last thing she needed was their pity—or worse, the subtle hints that maybe she should stay with them for now, like she couldn't take care of herself.

Maybe that was why Cam had offered to let her move in. Was he worried that she wasn't thinking clearly? If she told him about this, he would insist on taking her back to the hospital to have more tests run.

No. She'd had enough of hospitals to last her a lifetime. This was one problem she would handle on her own.

She took a deep breath in an attempt to steady her nerves. Pushing away from the door, she wound her way through the bottom floor of the house, checking to make sure everything was secure. Nothing appeared to be out of place and, aside from the door standing wide open, there was no sign of anyone having been inside the house.

She moved toward the stairs, keeping to the edge of

the living room. The dark spot on the floor near the door stood out in the bright morning light, and her stomach twisted. She ripped her gaze away, like if she ignored it, all the memories would disappear. Though Cam had pulled up the carpet, the blood had penetrated all the way down to the subfloor, leaving a large brown spot where she'd been attacked.

Kinley swallowed hard, hands shaking as she grasped the banister and climbed the stairs to the second floor. She checked both bedrooms and the bathroom, but everything was exactly as she had left it. She paused, leaning against the vanity, and closed her eyes as she tried to draw back on the events of the previous night.

She remembered leaving Cam's house, remembered pulling into the driveway, coming inside and getting ready for bed. But the small details eluded her.

Kinley shook her head. She'd checked every inch of the house; no one was inside. Everything was fine. She couldn't afford to let her imagination run wild. From now on she would just have to be more careful and make sure to double-check the locks before she went to bed.

She could admit that she'd been on edge ever since the incident with Joel last week. Maybe she was just overthinking things, seeing trouble where there was none. The house was old; maybe the door hadn't latched properly, and a breeze had blown it open. That made her feel better. A small laugh escaped as she pushed away from the vanity and headed for the stairs. Of course there was a rational explanation.

Back downstairs, Kinley moved toward the coffee pot, losing herself in the familiar morning routine. She leaned against the counter and sipped the warm liquid, pushing the unsettling thoughts from her mind.

Her gaze strayed toward the living room—to the place where she'd been attacked. The coffee turned to ash in her mouth as bile filled her throat. Her heart raced as memories washed over her, and tremors worked their way through her body. She quickly set the cup down and wiped her clammy hands on her robe.

Closing her eyes, she drew in a deep breath and willed her pulse to slow. It still felt so fresh, like it had happened just yesterday.

She swallowed hard. How did Ainsley do it? How did she just go on like nothing had ever happened? She seemed so happy, so excited for the future. Every time Kinley closed her eyes, all she could see was Joel forcing his way through the door, wrapping his palms around her throat and squeezing...

She dragged in a shuddering breath and shook her head. Ainsley had gotten good at hiding her true feelings; maybe she chose to focus on the good rather than the bad. She had nothing to worry about anymore. The man who'd hurt her was never coming back.

Kinley straightened away from the counter. Enough was enough. Cam was right; it was time to take charge and move on.

An hour later, she stood in the home improvement store, surrounded by rows of carpet samples. She ran her fingers over various textures, contemplating her choices. She needed something nice but inexpensive.

After making her selection, she headed to the counter to pay for the carpet. After the snafu with Hayes, she was still a little strapped for cash, but thankfully she had a credit card she kept in case of emergencies. This definitely counted as an emergency.

She swiped the card through the machine, then scheduled the installation for the following day. As she walked back to her car, she considered what Cam had said about needing a fresh start. He was right. She did deserve this. She needed to move on from the memories tied to her home, both good and bad.

The idea of moving in with him had crossed her mind more than once over the past twenty-four hours, but she wasn't ready to make that decision just yet. Regardless of where she ended up, she knew she needed to put the past behind her. This was her chance to wipe the slate clean and start fresh, to create a future unburdened by the past. She was ready to move on—and this was the first step.

Brynlee leaned in close. "So what happened with Ted?"

"He's an asshole." She didn't know why they were whispering. Maybe because the beautiful bridal salon seemed like a sanctuary in its own right.

"Language," their mother quietly admonished.

"Sorry," she automatically responded.

Kinley dipped her head next to her sister's. "Ted wasn't really interested in me." She fiddled with the swatch of material in her lap. "What he really wanted was a built-in nanny for Addie, not a girlfriend or a wife."

For the two years Kinley and Ted had been together, she'd loved Addie like she was her own. Addie had attended Kinley's Kindergarten class several years ago, and she'd first met Ted at parent-teacher conferences. At the time, he'd seemed like an amazing father—caring and concerned, loving and trustworthy. Those qualities had quickly disappeared.

The shift had been gradual, so much so that she didn't notice until it was almost too late. He'd begun leaving Addie in her care more and more often, relying on Kinley to transport Addie to and from school. From there it only got worse. Kinley ended up staying at their house more often than not, tucking her into bed while Ted "worked late." She'd been such a fool.

"Don't you worry, sweetheart." Her mother gently patted her knee. "You'll find the right man."

Tears pricked her eyes as the mirrored door swung open and Ainsley stepped out in a cloud of tulle. The soft material draped beautifully over her sister's slender form, making her look like an angel.

Ainsley stepped up on the small, round dais and gazed in the mirror before turning toward them. "What do you think?"

Kinley's throat clogged as she stared up at her sister. For the past hour, Ainsley had tried on dress after dress, all of them beautiful—but none like this.

"Honey, it's beautiful," their mother said, happy tears glistening in her eyes.

"Agreed," Brynlee spoke up. "You look gorgeous."

"You think so?" Ainsley bit her lip and glanced back in the mirror. "It's not too much, is it?"

"It's... perfect." Kinley swallowed hard and shook her head. Seeing her sister now, looking like a bride, made things seem so much more... final.

Logically, she knew Ainsley wasn't going anywhere. She and Dare would still live right outside of town, and she'd be able to see her whenever she wanted. But the knowledge didn't stem the rush of emotion that streamed through her, squeezing her chest. Kinley couldn't help the tears that slipped down her cheeks.

Ainsley deserved every bit of happiness this world had to offer. Kinley had seen firsthand how much Dare adored her, and she knew he would never take her for granted.

"Are those sad tears or happy tears?" Ainsley's voice cracked as her gaze slid over them, not a dry eye present.

Kinley launched herself out of her seat and threw her arms around Ainsley in a tight hug. "I'm so happy for you."

"Could've fooled me." Ainsley laughed brokenly against her shoulder. "Do you think it's crazy, what we're doing? Is it too soon?"

Kinley pulled back to look at her sister. "I think everything is working out exactly the way it's supposed to."

"Really?"

"Really. You two are perfect for each other. I'm so glad to see you happy," she whispered.

"Thanks."

Ainsley pulled her into another hug, and Kinley closed her eyes as she held on tight. Despite what her mother and Brynlee said, she had to wonder if her true love was actually out there somewhere. Ted was only one in a long line of failed relationships.

Pushing the thought aside, Kinley leaned away from her sister. "So is this it? Is this the gown?"

A huge smile spread over Ainsley's face as she turned toward the mirror. "I think so."

"Good." Kinley returned the smile.

It felt so good to see Ainsley smile again, and hope expanded through Kinley's chest. Everything happened for a reason. She just needed to be patient and hope that good things would come her way.

CHAPTER
FOURTEEN

Kinley waved goodbye to her family, then made a beeline for the coffee shop in the plaza across the street. She was exhausted, the persistent ache in her head slamming against her skull like a drum. Caffeine likely wouldn't help, but at this point she needed the boost of energy.

The bell over the door jingled as she stepped into the cozy little coffee shop. The soft murmur of conversation and the clinking of ceramic mugs filled the air as the invigorating aroma of freshly brewed coffee wrapped around her, instantly lifting her mood.

Kinley took a step toward the counter, then stopped dead in her tracks when her eyes landed on Ted, who stood less than a dozen feet away. Her breath caught in her throat as her gaze skimmed over his handsome face, then lower, to the expensive dress shirt and blazer—and his arm wrapped around the tiny waist of the beautiful woman next to him.

His mouth kicked up in a smirk when her eyes jumped back to his. The brunette turned toward her as well, her perfectly shaped eyebrows rising in curiosity.

Kinley was dimly aware of the door opening behind her, and the noise jolted her out of her introspection. She shuffled forward, out of the way of the incoming patron, and forced a smile to her face. "Hey, Ted. How are you?"

"I'm doing well, thank you." He tightened his grip on the brunette's waist and tipped his head toward Kinley. "This is Lauren. Lauren, this is Kinley Layne. She was Addison's Kindergarten teacher."

Her heart twisted at the blow. They'd dated for nearly two years, but in the span of just a few weeks, her status had been reduced to nothing more than his child's teacher.

Kinley forced her muscles to move and managed to stick out her hand. "Lovely to meet you."

"You too." The woman's smile was insincere, her palm barely sliding into Kinley's before she pulled away again and rested her hand on Ted's chest.

Kinley felt sick to her stomach. She should be glad things had ended—and she was, truly. But that didn't mean it didn't hurt. They'd spent nearly two years together, and Kinley thought they would get married. But she'd discovered that they not only weren't on the same page—Ted had been in an entirely different book.

Ted's gaze locked on the stitches that cut across her forehead, and one eyebrow lifted almost mockingly. His mouth opened, but Kinley quickly cut him off before he could speak. "Well, it was great seeing you."

She turned on a heel, ready to flee back out the front door, when she slammed face-first into a wall of muscle. The man glanced down at her, his expression morphing from concern to understanding before he pasted on a bright smile.

"Hey, babe. Sorry I'm late."

Kinley blinked up at him, utterly blindsided by the man's arrival. Who the hell was this guy? Her gaze quickly swept over his face, taking in his dark brown hair and vivid blue eyes. Did she know him? She didn't think so.

"Uh..."

"I got caught up at work," he continued smoothly as he slipped an arm around her waist, then pulled her close. "Did you order yet?"

The man's arm around her felt strange, but she quickly realized what he was doing. Playing along, she leaned into him slightly as they faced the other couple, hoping her face wouldn't betray her.

"Not yet." She smiled. "I was actually just getting ready to step outside to call you when you walked in."

Ted cleared his throat, and Kinley jumped a little. "Uh... This is Ted," she said, motioning to her ex.

"Nice to meet you," the man said with a charming smile, extending his hand to Ted, who shook it with a bewildered look. "I'm Lance."

"And this is..." Kinley's mind went blank as she

turned her gaze toward the brunette. She was still too taken aback by the abrupt turn of events, and her synapses weren't firing properly.

The woman's lips curled down in a frown before she switched her attention to the stranger. "I'm Ted's girlfriend, Lauren."

"Right. Lauren." Kinley winced internally as an awkward, high-pitched laugh escaped before she could stop it.

"Nice to meet you," Lance said with a charming smile, extending his hand to Lauren. "Sorry if I'm interrupting anything."

"Not at all," Ted murmured, clearly caught off guard. "We were just catching up. Small world, huh?"

"Yeah, it is," Lance said with a grin. "Well, it was great to meet both of you. Are you ready to order, sweetheart?"

"Uh... sure," Kinley replied, grateful for the lifeline. She flashed a quick look at Ted and Lauren. "Nice to see you."

She allowed Lance to guide her to the counter, where the barista greeted them with a smile. "What can I get for you?"

Kinley could feel Ted and Lauren's eyes on them, and the dull ache in her head intensified. She forced herself to focus on the menu, but the words seemed to dance on the board in front of her. She closed her eyes against the glare of the lights overhead and drew in a slow, deep breath in an attempt to steady her racing heart. Seeing Ted and Lauren together had thrown her completely off balance.

The stranger—Lance—tossed a sideways look at Kinley. Sensing she needed a moment to gather herself, he placed his order first. All the while he kept his arm around her as if he were waiting for her to pass out at any second. By the time he was done, Kinley had recovered enough to place her order. When she reached into her bag to pull out her wallet, Lance gave an abrupt shake of his head, his eyes flicking behind them.

Her gaze followed his to where Ted and Lauren stood close by, still watching them intently. Of course. She smiled up at Lance, conveying her understanding. He'd committed himself to being her fake boyfriend, and he was going to play this whole charade out 'til the end.

She brought out her phone instead, pretending to check something on the screen before stowing it away again. Lance smiled down at her, and she grinned unrepentantly as she leaned into his side.

Once they had their drinks, Lance led her to a quiet table at the back of the coffee shop. They sat down, and he finally let go of her, shooting her an apologetic smile.

"I'm sorry if I overstepped," he said, his voice low. "I saw the look on your face and figured you could use some help."

Kinley took a deep breath, feeling the tension slowly drain from her body. "No, actually I really appreciate it," she said. "The whole thing caught me off guard. Thank you for stepping in. That was... awkward."

Lance nodded. "I could tell. Ex-boyfriend?"

"Yeah," she admitted, absently swirling the spoon through her chai latte. "We just broke up a few weeks ago. Seeing him with someone else so soon..."

"I can imagine," Lance said sympathetically. "He sounds like a dick."

"He kind of is." Kinley laughed. "I'm glad we're not together anymore, but... it still hurts, you know?"

"Well, if it's any consolation, I think seeing us together rattled him." Lance grinned. "I've known a lot of guys like him, and trust me—you can do better."

Kinley blushed. "Thanks."

Lance shrugged modestly. "No problem. I'm just glad I was here at the right time."

She studied the man across from her, as if really seeing him for the first time. He had a kind face and bright blue eyes that crinkled at the corners, as if he liked to laugh. His hair was dark with just a touch of salt and pepper at the temples, but he was in great shape.

More than once, Lance's gaze strayed to the stitches on Kinley's forehead, but he politely chose not to bring it up, instead making small talk.

"So, what do you do for work?" Kinley asked, genuinely curious.

"I'm a realtor," Lance replied easily. "I work for a small brokerage over in Danbury."

"That sounds fun," Kinley said, her smile widening. "I'm a Kindergarten teacher."

Lance's eyebrows raised in admiration. "Wow, that's incredible. I don't think I'd have the patience for that."

Kinley laughed softly. "It has its challenges, but I love it. The kids make it all worth it."

As the conversation continued, Kinley felt a strange sense of serendipity. Just yesterday, she and Cam had been discussing the possibility of selling her house. It felt like a sign that she had run into Lance so soon after that conversation.

"You know," Kinley began slowly, "my friend and I were just talking about selling my house yesterday. It feels like a stroke of luck meeting you here."

Lance's eyes lit up. "Really? Well, if you're considering listing your home, I'd be more than happy to help."

"That would be amazing." Kinley smiled, giddiness spreading through her chest. "I'll warn you though—I have a few things I need to do yet before it'll be ready."

"No problem at all." Lance reached into his pocket and pulled out a business card, then slid it across the table to her. "Here's my card. Give me a call if you're interested, and we can set up a time to discuss everything in detail."

Kinley took the card, glancing at it before slipping it into her purse. "Thank you, Lance. I'll definitely be in touch."

They sat in comfortable silence for a few moments,

sipping their drinks. Kinley glanced surreptitiously around the room, but it appeared as though Ted and Lauren had left.

"Looks like they're gone," Lance said, following her gaze. "You okay?"

"Yeah," Kinley said, feeling a weight lift off her shoulders. "I'm good now. Thanks again for all your help. I really appreciate it."

"Any time." As they finished their coffee, Lance stood up and offered her a warm smile. "It was great talking with you, Kinley. I hope to hear from you soon."

"You too," she replied, watching as he left the coffee shop.

Meeting him might have been a coincidence, but it felt like an amazing opportunity had just been dropped in her lap. With the prospect of selling her house and moving forward, Kinley felt a glimmer of excitement for the future. She couldn't wait to tell Cam.

Kinley stepped out of the cozy warmth of the coffee shop, a spring in her step as she adjusted her purse on her shoulder. The early evening air was crisp, and a gentle breeze tugged at her hair as she made her way toward the parking lot. She'd almost reached her car when a familiar—and very unwelcome—figure emerged from the row next to her.

Ted's presence hit her like a slap to the face. He sauntered toward her, his face twisted into a mask of smug disdain. Every muscle went tense as she turned to face him, the pleasantness of the evening quickly evaporating.

"All alone again, Kinley?" Ted drawled, his voice dripping with sarcasm. "Did the new guy leave you already?"

She clenched her fist so tightly that the keys cut into her flesh. Somehow she managed to force her lips into a smile. "He has a long day tomorrow, so we decided to make it an early night."

Ted laughed, the sound sharp and mocking. "You think I don't recognize a lie when I see it? What was this —your first date?"

Kinley's cheeks burned with a mix of anger and humiliation, but she refused to give Ted the satisfaction of knowing he was right. "It's none of your business. Besides, I don't know why you act like you care. You've moved on. Why shouldn't I do the same?"

He lifted one shoulder in an insouciant shrug. "I just think it's funny that you've already scared him off."

"You don't know anything about my life," she shot back. "And frankly, I don't care what you think. You lost the right to tell me your opinion when we broke up."

"I know enough." Ted stepped closer, his eyes gleaming with malice. "Must be tough, huh? Knowing you're not enough for him, either. I'm heading home with Lauren tonight. Meanwhile, you'll be all alone, as usual."

Her heart ached at the mention of the woman who'd been hanging on his arm. Kinley felt a sharp pang of hurt, but she refused to let Ted see how his words affected her. She lifted her chin and sent a frosty glare his way. "In case you've forgotten, I was the one who walked away from you," she stated coldly. "And quite frankly, I'd rather be alone than be with someone like you."

"Fuck you, Kinley." He took a step closer, his voice dropping to a whisper. "You may have walked away, but I was done with you a long time ago. Maybe if you'd paid more attention to what was happening between us, you'd know that I've been seeing Lauren for months. You were just too stupid to notice."

The sting of his words was like a physical blow, but Kinley stood her ground. "I might be alone right now, but at least I'm not afraid of it. You? You can't stand to be alone because you're terrified of facing who you really are."

Ted's face twisted with anger, but before he could respond, Kinley turned on her heel and slid into the driver seat, her heart pounding.

As she pulled out of the parking lot and made her way down Main Street, her bravado faded away. The hurt she'd been holding back rose to the surface and tears burned across the bridge of her nose.

The stop sign in front of her blurred before her eyes and she brushed the tears away. Damn Ted for making her feel like she wasn't good enough.

She hesitated for a moment before flicking on her

turn signal and steering the car toward the one person she could always count on.

CHAPTER
FIFTEEN

The chime of the doorbell cut through the silence, and Cam glanced out the window into the fading twilight. Who the hell could be here?

Had they found new evidence in the Gill case? Almost as quickly as the thought came to him, he pushed it away. If there'd been a break in the case, dispatch would have contacted him instead of sending someone to the house.

That only left a handful of people who would show up at... He glanced at the clock. Eight o'clock. Lead settled in his gut, apprehension sweeping up the back of his neck as he yanked open the door. On the other side, Kinley's tear-streaked face greeted him.

Without thinking, he looped an arm around her and yanked her toward him. Threading his fingers through the silky waves of her hair, he tucked her face against his chest and kicked the door closed with his foot.

Her arms slipped around his waist as a sob broke free, slicing through him like a knife. God, he hated seeing her upset.

He wrapped his free arm around her back in a fierce embrace, holding her tight as sobs wracked her slight frame. Hot tears soaked his shirt and he gently rocked her side to side, whispering against her hair. "Shh. Everything's gonna be okay."

He'd held her plenty of times over the past couple of years during her relationship with that asshole, Ted. But she'd finally broken things off with him a few weeks ago. So if it wasn't Ted... What the hell had happened?

"Talk to me, sweetheart. What's wrong?"

Kinley was quiet for several moment before finally inhaling a hiccuping breath. "Ainsley's getting married."

Her words were muffled against his shirt and he hesitated for a long moment, not entirely sure what to say. Was she sad? Jealous?

Her head lifted away from his chest and her eyes searched his, heartbreaking in their vulnerability. "What's wrong with me?"

Christ. The pieces of the puzzle fell into place, and red filled his vision. He was going to kill that asshole for making her think she wasn't good enough.

Cam pulled back and framed her face with his hands. "Nothing," he said fiercely. "There's not a goddamn thing wrong with you—not one damn thing. You are smart and beautiful and perfect. Ted was an idiot for letting you go. Don't you dare shed one more tear for that prick, because he doesn't deserve it."

The bleakness in her eyes threatened to gut him. His arms slipped down around her back like a vise and he held her tighter. "You mean the world to me, Kinley. You know that, right?"

She lowered her head to his heart and nodded. He rested his cheek on the top of her head. "I'll always be here for you. I don't care if it's the middle of the night, you can always come to me."

"Thank you," she whispered.

He pulled back a bit and lifted her chin. He waited for her to meet his gaze, then offered a small smile. "You know what'll make everything better?"

A watery smile curved her lips as he tipped his head toward the kitchen. "Come on. I've got your favorite. Go sit and I'll bring it to you."

He released her and made his way to the kitchen where he pulled the container of cookie dough ice cream out of the freezer. He always kept it on hand, because it was her favorite. He crossed the room and grabbed a spoon before heading to the living room.

Kinley had settled on the couch, legs tucked beneath her, arms wrapped around a pillow in her lap. Remnants of tears streaked down her face, and he gave a slight shake of his head.

Instead of sitting next to her, he plopped down on the coffee table directly across from her and grasped her chin. Directing her attention to his, he studied her for a long moment. "You good?"

She swallowed once then gave a slight nod. "Yeah. Thanks," she whispered.

Leaning forward, he briefly brushed his lips over her forehead. "Good."

Before she could overthink the kiss, and before he would do anything he'd regret later, he ripped the lid off the carton of ice cream and tossed it on the table beside him. Digging the spoon into the soft, creamy confection, he scooped up a bite and held it to her lips.

With a tiny smile her mouth closed around the metal, and she tugged the spoon—and the carton—from his grasp.

He grinned, glad that he'd lightened her mood, then slid off the coffee table and onto the cushion beside her. They sat just like that for several minutes until she abruptly dropped the spoon into the carton, then reached over and set them on the table.

"I thought we would get married."

It was the last thing he expected, and it took every ounce of control to school his expression. He had no idea what to say, and a million questions whirled through his mind. Was that why she was so upset? Did she miss him—still want to be with him?

He dreaded the answer to those questions. "What happened?"

She quirked a small smile. "Isn't it obvious?"

Her smile fell away when he didn't respond, and she

fiddled with the corner of the pillow. "He didn't want me."

A combination of bitterness and sadness tinged her voice as she continued. "Well, that's not true. He wanted me—but only for Addie."

He tipped his head in question. "What do you mean?"

"He really just wanted a babysitter, a built-in nanny for his daughter."

He'd had his suspicions about that. Kinley adored kids, and Addison was no exception. She'd loved that little girl, had gone to every recital, play, and ballet practice. She was more of a parent to Addie than Ted was.

"I knew things weren't great," she started. "but I thought we could get through it. You know he took me to his favorite Italian place for our anniversary?" He nodded at her rhetorical question, and she continued. "Over dinner, he pulled out a small box and slid it across the table."

She gave a little shake of her head. "It caught me off guard, and I asked if it was a ring. He just laughed and said 'hell, no!', like I wasn't even worth asking."

Anger churned in his gut. "Why didn't you say anything before now?"

She turned her despondent gaze his way. "I know you've never liked him."

"No, but I would have supported you if that's what you'd wanted." Even if it killed him. "But I'm not sad things ended. You deserve better than someone like him."

She gave a little nod. "I know."

Her eyes were slightly puffy from the earlier tears, but there was a hint of resolve in them now. She took a deep breath and began to speak. "I picked out carpet today," she said softly.

"Really?"

She nodded. "It's scheduled to be installed tomorrow."

Cam smiled. "That's great, Kins. I'm really happy for you."

"And... I met a realtor this evening," she continued, looking up at him with a mixture of hope and uncertainty. "He offered to list my home."

Cam shot her an encouraging smile. "It sounds like everything's falling into place."

"It is, isn't it?" Kinley smiled, but it didn't reach her eyes.

"You're welcome to stay the night, if you want," he offered softly, brushing a strand of hair away from her face.

Kinley shook her head slowly and pushed to her feet. "Thanks, but... I should be there tomorrow when the workers get there."

"If you need anything, let me know. I can't wait to see it," he said as he stood.

He couldn't begin to imagine what she was dealing

with at the moment. As much as he wanted to push, he knew he shouldn't.

Instead, he walked her to the door and held it open for her. "Call me tomorrow."

"I will."

As she walked away, Cam watched her go, a mixture of emotions swirling in his chest. He was happy for her, glad that she was taking steps to move forward, but he couldn't help the worry that gnawed at him.

He lifted a hand to wave as she pulled out of the driveway, and he watched her car until the taillights disappeared from view. Closing the door, he let out a sigh and scrubbed a hand over his face. She needed time and space to deal with everything, and he had to respect that.

She'd come to him tonight. It was a start, and for now, that was enough.

CHAPTER
SIXTEEN

Kinley woke with a start, her heart pounding in her chest. She lay still for a moment, listening to the sounds of the early morning that filtered through the window. She took a deep breath, trying to tamp down the unease that had settled in the pit of her stomach.

The faint headache that had become her constant companion pulsed lightly, but she ignored it as she sat up and swung her legs over the side of the bed. Pulling on her robe, she moved toward the stairs, the wooden floorboards creaking softly under her feet.

The memory of the previous morning flashed in her mind, and her skin prickled with apprehension. She descended the stairs slowly, her muscles like lead as she drew closer to kitchen. When she reached the doorway, her heart dropped to the floor and icy dread flooded every cell of her body.

The back door was wide open.

Again.

Kinley froze, her breath catching in her throat. A dizzying wave of fear washed over her, and she stretched out a hand, grabbing onto the doorframe to balance herself.

What was happening here?

Her gaze skimmed the kitchen and dining room, but everything was quiet and still. As she stepped forward to close the door, she peeked out into the yard, half-expecting to see someone watching her.

It was empty.

Kinley closed the door, then turned the lock with a trembling hand. A rush of air left her lungs as she closed her eyes and tipped her head against the door, the glass panes cool against her overheated skin.

She stood there for a long moment, her mind a blank void. She hadn't left it unlocked last night—and she most certainly hadn't forgotten to close the door after she'd returned from Cam's.

So what the hell was going on? There had to be a rational explanation.

Jerking upright, Kinley grabbed the handle and twisted, then yanked the door open. It swung open easily, and she studied the frame. Nothing was broken, and the striker plate appeared to be fine. She slowly closed the door, watching carefully for any spots where the door might be catching the frame and preventing it from closing the whole way. It shut easily enough, and when she turned the lock, it caught easily as it slipped into place.

What the hell? Furious, she gave the lock a vicious twist and jerked the door open again. She stepped outside and closed the door once more, then studied it from the outside. She ran her fingers around the seal, but everything appeared to be in working order. She pressed a hand to the door, testing it, but it refused to budge.

Goosebumps sprouted over her flesh despite the warmth of the morning sun washing over her. Her gaze flitted down to the doorhandles, and she inspected the keyhole. No scratches, no damage...

What was going on?

Kinley dropped back a step and ran a hand through her hair. Staring at the door, she dragged in a deep breath in an attempt to steady herself. Everything looked fine. Nothing could explain why the door had been open—again.

Maybe she really was losing her mind, because there was definitely nothing wrong with the door or the lock.

Deeply unsettled, she made her way back inside, locking the door behind her and double-checking to make sure it was secure. Drifting toward the counter, she brewed a cup of coffee on autopilot, her gaze occasionally darting across the room to the door.

The familiar scent of coffee did little to soothe her, and she briskly ran her hands over her arms to dispel the chill that seemed to have settled in her bones. The coffee pot beeped as it finished its cycle, and she gratefully grabbed up the mug, reveling in the heat that emanated from the porcelain. Forgoing her usual sugar and milk, she lifted the mug to her lips and sipped, her hands shaking slightly.

Something was very wrong. But the question was— was it the house... Or her?

Disturbed, Kinley dropped into a chair at the small breakfast table, her eyes glued to the door just a few feet away. There had to be a logical explanation for whatever was happening here. Maybe there was a draft, a malfunction in the lock, something she hadn't considered. The house was old; maybe the wood swelled, or—

A sudden sharp knock at the front door startled her, causing her to jump. The coffee sloshed precariously over the rim, splattering her skin. She sucked in a breath at the sudden burning sensation and let out a swift curse. "Damn it!"

Her attention splintered and her heart leaped into her throat. For a moment, she was caught off guard, but then she remembered—the carpet installers were scheduled to arrive today. She quickly set her mug down and hurried toward the front door, wiping her hand on her robe.

She peeked through the side window and saw two workmen standing on her front porch. A large white van was parked in the driveway, the home improvement logo printed on the side. She grabbed the doorhandle then froze, her cheeks flaring with heat when she realized she was still clad in her pajamas.

"Just a minute!" she called through the door, then bolted upstairs, yanking off her robe as she moved. She grabbed the closest things at hand and pulled them on, stumbling as she hurriedly stepped into a pair of shorts. Tugging a tank top into place, she ran a hand through her hair to restore some semblance of propriety, then headed back downstairs.

"Good morning," she greeted the men breathlessly as she swung the door open. "Come on in."

"Good morning, miss."

The installers nodded and stepped inside. One of the men tipped his head her way. "If you don't mind, I'll have you check this over and make sure everything looks good."

He extended a clipboard her way, and the sight of it momentarily took her breath away. Barely a week ago, Joel had stood right there in that very spot, clipboard in hand... Right before he'd wrapped his hands around her throat and squeezed.

Her throat closed up and black spots danced before her eyes. Her hands clenched into tight fists as she swallowed hard, fighting to push the memories away. It was over; he was gone. She couldn't continue to allow one isolated incident to control her life.

She dragged much-needed oxygen into her lungs and forced a smile to her lips. "Of course. Thanks for coming."

She glanced over the details, then nodded and passed the paperwork back to him. "Everything looks good. Feel free to move anything you need," she said, gesturing to the furniture.

The men set to work, efficiently moving the furniture to clear the space, and Kinley drifted back toward the kitchen. She tried to keep herself busy, wiping down counters and organizing cupboards, but her mind kept wandering back to the door that had been left open not once, but twice now.

Kinley rested her elbows on the counter and stared out the window over the sink, her mind racing. She needed to do something, needed to feel safe in her own home again. And her first order of business was to replace the existing locks—just in case.

Pulling a pen and notepad from a kitchen drawer, she dropped into a chair at the table and began a list. The lock on the front door had been there since she moved in, and the once shiny brass was now dull and scratched. She added door knobs and deadbolts for both doors to her list, then pushed from the chair and turned her attention to the windows.

She methodically checked each one, beginning with the kitchen. She slid the windows open and shut, testing the latches to make sure they engaged properly. In the laundry room, she tightened a loose latch. Satisfied with the windows, she moved on to the last part of her inspection—the basement.

Kinley descended the stairs to the basement, the

cool, damp air assaulting her as she approached the bottom. It was at least ten degrees cooler down here, and a shiver moved down her spine as she crossed the room toward the exterior door.

The thick slab of wood stood out against the cinder block walls. Testing the knob and deadbolt, she found them both securely locked. The doorknob appeared to be an older style she hadn't seen in years. She vaguely remembered her grandparents having the skeleton key-style locks on their home.

She never came in through the basement since it was built into the ground, originally part of an old storm shelter. The Barkers must not have used it either, because even the realtor didn't have the key when Kinley had purchased the house. She briefly considered tackling the locks on the basement door but decided against it for the time being. The ancient door had held up for decades; it could wait a little longer.

She returned upstairs feeling a bit more at ease. She glanced at her list, mentally planning a trip to the store. The house felt more secure already, though the new locks would be the final touch. She placed her notepad on the counter with a smile, satisfied with her morning's work.

A few hours later, one of the installers called out to her. "Miss? We're all done!"

"Thanks," she said, a smile spreading across her face. "It looks amazing."

The installers nodded, pleased with her reaction.

They gathered their tools and headed out, leaving Kinley alone once more. She sank into the sofa, toes curling into the soft, clean carpet. This was the fresh start she needed.

Though the house still held memories of the past, it was now ready for a new chapter. And so was she.

CHAPTER
SEVENTEEN

Cam stared at the lab results in front of him, frustration gnawing at his insides. The woman's shoe found in the woods was definitely Lindsey Gill's—there was no doubt about that. But it was another dead end. No prints, no DNA, nothing that could point them toward her abductor.

He leaned back in his chair and rubbed his temples. The shoe had been found in an area that had already been combed by the search party, solidifying the suspicion that someone had placed it there after the initial search. Whoever took Lindsey was still out there, watching, taunting the police with every move.

The idea that someone was out there, enjoying this game of cat and mouse, made Cam's blood boil. He was determined to find Lindsey's abductor and bring him to justice. The thought of Lindsey, alone and scared, gave him a renewed sense of urgency.

There had to be something they were missing. He spread out all the evidence on the conference room table. Photos, reports, timelines—everything they had gathered since Lindsey's disappearance. This was the work of someone meticulous, someone who knew how to cover their tracks. The shoe was a deliberate move, a way to mock their efforts.

He needed to speak with Lindsey's friends and family again—see if they'd remembered anything. He pushed from his chair and grabbed up his keys. They needed a lead, something to break the case open.

A half-hour later, Cam knocked on the front door of the well-kept house. It swung open and Mrs. Gill greeted him, her eyes red-rimmed from sleepless nights and endless tears. She ushered him inside without a word, leading him to the living room where Mr. Gill and Lindsey's boyfriend, Andrew, were waiting.

"Thank you for seeing me again," Cam began, taking a seat. "I know this is difficult, but we need to find who did this to Lindsey. Has anyone remembered anything that might help us? Anyone who had a grudge or seemed suspicious?"

Mrs. Gill shook her head, her voice barely above a whisper. "We've gone over everything so many times. She was such a good girl. No enemies, no trouble."

Mr. Gill's face was stony, his grief manifesting as anger. "We'd have told you already if we knew something. This is killing us."

Cam's gaze shifted to Andrew, who had been silent,

staring at the floor. "Andrew, you spent a lot of time with Lindsey. Was there anything at all that stood out? Even something that seemed minor at the time? Anyone new she might have come into contact with?"

Andrew looked up, his expression stark. "Not really. I mean..." He trailed off, looking pensive. "There was one thing... She was in a minor car accident a couple of months ago. Just a fender-bender, but it shook her up a bit."

Cam leaned forward, adrenaline coursing through his veins. "Do you know who was involved in the accident? Or where she got the car repaired?"

Andrew nodded slowly. "Yeah, she told me about it. The other driver was some guy, not sure of his name. But I remember she took her car to a local repair shop. Benson's Auto Repair, I think."

"That's right," Mary said. "But we've used Joe Benson's shop for years."

Cam nodded. "It's a place to start. Maybe she ran into someone there, or he's hired someone new recently." He turned back to Andrew, his mind racing with possibilities. "Did she mention if the other driver was angry or upset?"

Andrew frowned, trying to recall. "The guy ran a stop sign, but he blamed her for it. I think he was just in a hurry and upset he got caught. But it was just a small accident, you know? We didn't think much of it."

Cam stood, a sense of purpose igniting within him. "This is good, Andrew. Very good. We'll check out

Benson's Auto Repair and find out who the other driver was."

Mr. Gill rose, his expression softening slightly. "Thank you, Lieutenant. Please, find who did this to our girl."

Cam nodded then headed straight to his car, dialing Sawyer's number as he walked. The phone rang twice before the detective picked up.

"It's Cam. I'm just leaving the Gills place now." He briefly explained what Andrew had told him. "We've got two new leads—Benson's Auto Repair and the other driver involved in Lindsey's fender-bender. I'm heading to the repair shop now."

"Got it," Sawyer replied. "I'll start digging into the accident report, see if I can find out who the other driver was. Let's hope this gets us somewhere."

Cam hung up and drove toward Benson's Auto Repair, a small, rundown building on the outskirts of town. Inside, his senses were assaulted by the pungent smell of motor oil and the sound of clanging tools.

A middle-aged man in greasy overalls approached him, wiping his hands on a rag. "Can I help you?"

"Lt. Campbell McCoy," he said, flashing his badge. "I'm looking for information about a car that was repaired here a couple of months ago. A woman named Lindsey Gill brought it in after a minor accident."

The man, Joe, scratched his head, thinking. "Yeah, I know her—Mary and John's girl. Her car had a busted bumper and a few dents. Took me a couple of days to fix it up."

"Do you have any records of the repair?"

Joe nodded as he headed toward a cluttered desk in the corner and rifled through a stack of papers before pulling out a file. "Here it is. Lindsey Gill's car."

Cam took the file, quickly scanning the contents. "Can I get a copy of this?"

"Sure thing."

As the man made a copy of the file, Cam's mind raced. He had a starting point, and now he needed to find the other driver. This lead felt promising, like the first crack in the case that could bring the whole thing down.

"Here you go." Joe passed the paper to Cam, then dropped into his chair.

"Thanks." He glanced up at the white board listing the vehicles next in the queue, and the mechanics' names next to them. "Last thing—Who worked on Lindsey Gill's car?"

Joe leaned back, his chair creaking. "That'd be Ray. Good mechanic. Does most of the bodywork around here. He's off today, though."

Cam nodded. "Do you have Ray's full name and contact information?"

Joe scribbled down the details on a piece of paper and handed it over. "Ray Mitchell. You can call him, but he's usually out fishing on his day off. Won't get much from him until tomorrow."

Cam pocketed the note. "What's Ray's usual schedule? Was he here the day Lindsey was abducted?"

Joe frowned, thinking back. "Let me check the time sheets." He shuffled through another pile of papers and pulled out a logbook. "Yeah, he was here. Clocked in at seven forty-two and left a few minutes after six."

Relief and disappointment swept through Cam in equal measure. Another lead checked, another dead end. Ray could be ruled out.

"This helps a lot." Cam gave a tight smile. "I'll get in touch with Ray tomorrow, just to cover all bases. Thanks for your help."

Joe tipped his chin. "Good luck, Detective. I hope you find who did this."

As Cam walked back to his car, he dialed Sawyer's number again. The line connected, and Sawyer's voice filtered through a moment later. "Reed."

"Sawyer, it's Cam. Got the mechanic's name—Ray Mitchell. He was at work during Lindsey's abduction, so we can rule him out."

"Good," Sawyer replied. "One less suspect to worry about."

"Any luck on the other driver?"

"Boyd Ellis," came Sawyer's reply.

"I'm heading back to the station now," Cam said as he cranked the engine. "We need to talk with this guy. He might be our break."

Back at the station, he scanned the accident report.

There was an address and phone number listed, and a glimmer of hope flashed through his chest.

Cam dialed the number, heart pounding. It rang three times before a voice answered, gruff and impatient. "Hello?"

"Mr. Ellis, this is Detective Cam with the Brookhaven Sheriff's Department. I need to ask you a few questions about a car accident you were involved in a couple of months ago with a woman named Lindsey Gill."

There was a pause on the other end, a hesitation that made Cam's pulse quicken. "Yeah, I remember. What about it?"

"I'm not sure if you're aware, but Ms. Gill was recently abducted from her home."

The man paused. "I didn't realize that was her. Sorry to hear that."

"Thank you, Mr. Ellis. We're checking with everyone she's come into contact with recently. Can you tell me your whereabouts that morning?"

Cam rattled off the date and time, and Boyd Ellis made a low sound on the other end of the phone. "Let me check my calendar."

Cam fidgeted restlessly, listening to the soft shuffling in the background, until the man finally came back on the line. "I was in Denver that week for work."

Goddamn it. Cam clenched his molars together before speaking. "I assume someone can verify this?"

"My boss—Cindy Broussard."

Cam took down the woman's information, then thanked the man and disconnected the call. A few moments later, having confirmed Boyd Ellis's alibi with his boss, Cam hung up and tossed his phone on the desk. Another fucking dead end.

He sat back, exhaustion and frustration creeping over him. They needed something—anything—that could point them in the right direction. Tomorrow, he hoped, would bring the breakthrough they needed.

CHAPTER
EIGHTEEN

Cam hopped up the steps to Kinley's house and gave a quick triple knock. Muffled movement came from inside, and he watched a shadow slide across the wall as Kinley strode toward the door. It swung inward a moment later, and she greeted him with a smile.

"Hey."

"Hey, yourself." He stepped inside and closed the door behind him, his gaze already roving the living room. "This looks great."

"I know, right?"

He turned his focus back to her. "How are you feeling?" he asked, his gaze sweeping over her.

She looked tired, the circles under her eyes more pronounced, and her hand automatically moved to the stitches on her forehead, a habit she'd developed since the accident.

"I'm okay," she replied, though the shadows in her eyes told a different story. "Still getting headaches, but they're not as bad as they were."

She dropped into the corner of the couch and pulled a blanket over her lap. Cam moved next to her and draped an arm over the back of the couch. "Long day?"

She heaved a sigh. "Kind of. Just... There's so much to do, you know?"

He definitely did. This place needed a lot more TLC before it would be market ready, and they were getting there, slowly but surely.

"So." He propped his feet on the coffee table and nudged her with his elbow. "Tell me what's going on."

"With what?" She tipped her chin up to him and searched his face.

He dropped his head back against the couch. "I don't know. Just talk to me."

"Well..." She fingered the hem of her shorts between her fingers before abruptly turning to face him. "Can I tell you something?"

"Of course."

"I'm not really that upset about Ted."

Considering the way she showed up on his doorstep a complete mess last night, he wasn't sure he believed her. "Why's that?"

She shrugged. "I feel like the idea of him was better than the reality. I know he didn't really love me, and I don't think I ever loved him. I just..." She drew in a deep breath. "I just wanted to be loved."

He turned toward her, his eyes holding hers for a second before speaking so she understood the sincerity of his words. "Kinley, sweetheart, You are loved. Your family loves you. Your friends love you." He paused for a moment, debating the wisdom of his next words. "I love you."

"Thanks." She smiled, but her eyes were clouded with worry.

He studied her for a long moment. His fingers dangled just inches from her shoulder, and he gently touched her arm. "It's not just Ted. Something else is bothering you, isn't it?"

She hesitated, her gaze dropping to the floor. After a moment, she let out a deep sigh. "There's something I haven't told you," she began slowly. "I didn't think much of it at first, but now..."

She trailed off, her fingers unconsciously tracing the stitches on her forehead. Cam reached out, gently taking her hand to stop the anxious movement. "What is it?"

"I know it's going to sound crazy, so just bear with me." Her teeth dug into her lower lip, and she took a moment to gather herself before continuing. "Yesterday I woke up and went downstairs, like I always do. Before I even got all the way down the stairs, I knew something was wrong."

Dread swirled in his stomach and he bit back the myriad questions that jammed on his tongue as she gestured toward the living room. "I can't really explain it —it was just a feeling I had. Nothing appeared to be out of place, exactly, but I felt this cool draft, and it immediately put me on edge."

"What happened?" he asked quietly.

"When I walked into the kitchen... the back door was wide open."

His brows lifted. "But nothing was moved? Nothing missing?"

"Not that I can tell."

He tipped his head to the side. "Why didn't you call me?"

"I don't know. I guess I didn't want you to worry. After everything that's happened..."

She trailed off with a shrug, and he turned slightly to see her better. "Of course I worry about you. But you know you can always come to me. Even if you think it's no big deal, I want to know about it."

"Well... That's not all." She licked her lips nervously before continuing. "It happened again this morning."

The hairs on the back of Cam's neck lifted in warning. "And you're sure nothing is missing?"

"I don't think so." She shook her head. "At first, I thought maybe I had forgotten to lock it. But then it happened again. I double-checked it last night—I'm sure of it."

Cam squeezed her hand, trying to offer some comfort. "I'm sure there's a logical explanation. Have you checked the lock?"

"The lock, the door, the frame..." She swallowed

hard and gave a little shake of her head. "Everything looks fine, but I'm going to replace all the locks tomorrow—just in case."

"Good idea. Better safe than sorry." Dare's words from the other day crept back to him. Kinley had just been released from the hospital a week ago. Though the tests showed that everything was fine, head wounds were tricky. Maybe Dare was right; maybe she was still recovering.

"I was going to do it today, but I lost track of time after the installers left." Kinley's fingers once again brushed against her stitches and her breath hitched. "Cam... What if it's me? What if my injury is worse than we thought and I'm... forgetting things?"

The worry in her voice cut through him like a knife, and he curled his arm around her, pulling her close and holding her tight. "Hey. You're not losing your mind," he reassured her. "You experienced a traumatic event, and you're doing incredibly well. The doctors said your scans were clear. Physically, you're healthy."

She leaned into him, a shudder racking her small frame. "I want to believe that. But it's happened twice now. What if I'm forgetting things or doing things without realizing it?"

He pulled back slightly and met her worried eyes. "Listen to me. You've been through a lot, and it's natural to feel unsettled. But I believe you. Something's going on here, and we're going to figure it out."

She nodded slowly, her gaze searching his for reassurance. "Thank you."

"You don't have to thank me," he said softly, brushing a stray hair from her face. "You know I'm here for you, no matter what. We'll figure out what's going on."

She offered a small smile, her muscles relaxing a fraction at his words. "In fact," he said, "I'm going to stay here tonight, keep an eye on things. We'll see if anything happens."

"Are you sure?" she asked, her voice tinged with both relief and worry.

"Absolutely," he replied. "I'm not letting anything else happen to you."

Cam shifted her slightly away as he scooted toward the edge of the cushion. "Why don't you grab me a pillow? I'm gonna check the back door."

Cam slid off Kinley's couch and wound his way through the kitchen to the back door. The soft sound of Kinley's footsteps on the stairs drifted toward him, and determination swept through his veins. He wasn't sure what was going on, but he would do whatever it took to make sure she felt safe.

He reached for the knob and found it locked. So far, so good. Unlocking the door, he pulled it open and inspected the lock and striker plate. Everything appeared to be in working order.

He crouched down, his fingers tracing the edges of the lock. No signs of forced entry, no visible tampering.

It was almost as if the door had been left open deliberately. But why? According to her, nothing had been taken. Nothing was out of place.

Rising to his feet, Cam's mind raced with possibilities. He turned his gaze back to the living room, where Kinley stood next to the couch, a fluffy pillow clutched in her arms. He tossed a reassuring smile her way. She'd been through so much already; the last thing she needed was another source of stress.

"Well?" She dropped the pillow in the corner of the couch and stared up at him expectantly. "What do you think?"

Cam hesitated for a moment, choosing his words carefully. "It doesn't look like the lock has been tampered with, and everything is working properly from what I can tell. Looks like someone might have left it open on purpose."

Her face paled, and she wrapped her arms around herself as if to ward off a sudden chill. "I swear I checked—"

"Not you." He shook his head, cutting her off. "Have you seen or heard anything from that handyman you hired?"

Her eyes went wide. "You think it was him?"

"It's a place to start," Cam replied, trying to sound reassuring. "I just want to rule out any possibilities. Did he have access to the house when you weren't here?"

"No." She shook her head. "He was only here the

one time, when I paid him. He did a little bit of work, then I never saw him again."

"We'll figure this out," he promised. "I won't let anything happen to you."

He hadn't had time over the past couple of days to look into Hayes, but the man had just moved to the top of his list.

CHAPTER
NINETEEN

Cam pushed open the heavy station door, the familiar scent of coffee and paperwork enveloping him. Inside, the station was just beginning to wake up, with deputies and clerks moving about in their early morning routines.

Sheriff Dare Jensen was already at his desk, poring over a stack of reports. He looked up as Cam approached, noting the dark circles under his eyes. Dare arched a brow his way. "Rough night?"

Cam sank into the chair across from Dare and rubbed his temples. "You could say that. I spent the night at Kinley's.

At Dare's surprised look, Cam elaborated. "When she woke up a few mornings ago, she found the back door standing wide open."

Dare's brows dipped low. "We didn't get a call."

"No." Cam shook his head. "She didn't call it in. She said she let it go because we would think she was crazy."

Dare opened his mouth to speak, but Cam lifted a hand to stall him. "I know. I told her the same thing. But that's not all." He ground his teeth together. "When she came downstairs yesterday morning, it was wide open again."

Dare leaned back in his chair and regarded Cam for a long moment. "And? What do you think?"

"Hell, I don't know. All her scans were clear, but..." He let out a sigh. "I just don't know. She's upset, because she thinks it's her. But she swears she doubled checked it the night before. There's nothing wrong with the door or the lock—I checked those myself. But the door being open twice now? It doesn't make sense."

Dare steepled his fingers and rested them against his lips for a moment before speaking. "You think someone's messing with her?"

Cam shook his head, frustration welling up inside his chest. "I don't know. Maybe you're right about the head injury. Maybe it's affecting her faculties. But we can't ignore the possibility that something else is going on."

Dare sighed, running a hand through his hair. "I understand where you're coming from, but..."

Cam knew exactly what he was thinking. Unless they got some concrete evidence that it was, in fact, someone trying to cause trouble for her, their hands were tied.

"I was thinking," Cam said slowly, leaning forward in his chair, "maybe you could send Ainsley over to spend some time with her. She could go over and ask Kins for some help planning the wedding. It'll help take her mind off everything. Plus, Ainsley knows her sister—she can let us know if anything seems off."

Dare nodding slowly, considering the suggestion. "That might work. Ainsley's been wanting to involve Kinley more in the wedding plans anyway. She'd be happy to go over there and keep an eye on things."

"Great," Cam said, relief washing over him. "I just want her to be safe."

"I'll talk to Ainsley," Dare promised. "She'll be over there by this afternoon."

Cam leaned back in the chair, feeling a weight lift off his shoulders. "Thanks, man. I appreciate it."

"Don't thank me." Dare waved one hand dismissively. "I know that feeling better than most. Trust your gut."

And he did; Ainsley had survived a hell of an ordeal with her ex, and Dare had witnessed it unfold. Cam gave a little shake of his head. "That house has caused her nothing but stress. I need to get her out of there sooner rather than later."

"And into yours?" One eyebrow ratcheted toward Dare's hairline, but Cam couldn't find it in him to feel the least bit abashed. Before he could speak, the sound of footsteps approached the office.

Yvonne, obviously eavesdropping on their conversation, moved closer, coffee cup in hand, and gave a slow shake of her head. "That house is bad luck. I'd hoped it turned around, but..."

She trailed off, and Cam turned to look her way. "What are you talking about?"

"The woman who disappeared." She tipped her head his way, an expectant look on her face. "You know—Misty."

Cam tossed a look at Dare who shrugged, and Cam turned back to Yvonne, brows furrowed. "What about her?"

Seeing Cam inside the office, Sawyer had drifted toward them and now stood in the doorway.

Yvonne slid into the chair next to Cam. "The Collins family lived there at the time—David Collins, his father, Dennis, and his stepmother, Misty."

Cam swiveled her way. "Wait. They lived in Kinley's house?" How had he not known that? "Did you know them?"

She nodded. "My aunt Agnes lived across the street at the time, so I would see them once in a while when I visited." She shook her head sympathetically. "Not every day something like that happens."

"What did happen?" Sawyer asked from where he lounged against the doorjamb.

"No one's really sure." Yvonne took a sip of her coffee. "Misty just up and disappeared one day. Dennis came home and found her gone."

Her lips turned down in a frown. "Such a nice

family. They always seemed so happy together. Dennis was devastated. He loved Misty somethin' fierce."

"She just left?" Sawyer lifted a brow in disbelief. "People usually don't just take off like that without a good reason."

"I seem to remember her leaving a note. Told them she couldn't do it anymore." She gave a slow shake of her head. "Old Sheriff Johnson and his men did what they could, but there was never any sign of foul play."

"When did they move?" Sawyer asked.

Yvonne glanced up at the ceiling, presumably drawing back to that particular period of time. "Maybe a week or so after she went missing?"

Dare's jaw went slack. "Johnson just let them leave?"

"Not much he could do." Yvonne lifted one shoulder. "There was no evidence, and Dennis had an alibi. He was at work when she supposedly disappeared. Neighbors saw her that morning picking up the paper. Next think you know, Dennis gets home and she's long gone."

Dare grimaced. "So they think she skipped town while Dennis was at work and David was in school."

"That's right." She gave a little nod. "Sheriff Johnson questioned everyone, but no one had seen anything. It was like she'd just disappeared into thin air."

"Odd," Cam murmured. The story left him feeling unsettled and anxious.

"I think Dennis went a little crazy that day," Yvonne said slowly. "Aunt Agnes said Dennis quit his job, packed up the house and was ready when David got home from school one afternoon. They took off and never came back."

"Strange," Cam murmured. He didn't know how it played into the current situation—if at all—but it was intriguing.

"Crazy to think she might have been murdered." Yvonne shivered. "You really think Dennis could have had something to do with it?"

"I'm not sure, but it's possible. Maybe he killed her the night before and dumped the car in the lake." Cam shrugged. "Misty stayed at home during the day, so no one would have missed her."

"I guess." Yvonne's didn't look convinced. "I just never would have suspected it of him. They seemed so great together."

"They usually do," Dare said drily.

"You think any of this is tied into what's been happening at Kinley's house?" Cam asked.

Dare shot him a dubious look. "Misty died thirty years ago. Why would someone start causing trouble now?"

"What about that older couple who lived there..." Yvonne snapped her fingers. "The Barkers. Aren't they the ones who sold Kinley the house a couple years back?"

Cam nodded. "I never heard of any trouble with them, but it's worth checking out."

"Maybe see if they filed any complaints, or if they have ties to anyone who might want to cause trouble."

Cam arched a brow. "They were like... eighty."

Dare lifted a shoulder. "I've seen stranger things. Just gotta find the right motive."

Cam made a face. "Fair point. I'll see what I can dig up."

He left the office, mind whirling. It was a strange coincidence, and definitely worth looking into. But right now, he had another target in mind.

CHAPTER
TWENTY

Kinley took a deep breath, trying to calm her racing heart. She wasn't going to let the events of the past few days control her life. She would handle this, just as she had handled everything else. She wouldn't let fear or uncertainty dictate her actions. She was stronger than that.

The local hardware store was a short drive away, and as Kinley navigated the familiar streets, she allowed herself to relax a little. The sky was a brilliant blue, the sun shining brightly overhead. It was the kind of day that made anything seem possible.

She pushed the unsettling thoughts to the back of her mind and focused on the task at hand. Grabbing a cart, she steered it into the store toward the aisle full of door handles. She was so lost in thought that she didn't notice the man right in front of her. She jolted in surprise as her cart slammed into his. "Oh, God, I'm so sorry!"

His surprise melted away as he did a kind of double-take. "Oh, hey. Hi."

"Hey." She couldn't help but smile at Lance, whose bright blue eyes bored into hers. "Good to see you again."

He grinned. "You, too. Hope things are going better for you."

She gave a little flick of her wrist. "Not really, but it's nothing I can't handle."

"I'm sorry." His smile slipped away. "Another run in with your ex?"

"No, thank God." She made a little face. "There's just been a lot going on recently, and I've been a little... stressed."

"I can understand that." His gaze flicked once more to the stitches that cut across her forehead, and she fought the urge to cover them.

She felt compelled to change the subject, and her gaze dropped to his cart. "Looks like you're working on a project, too."

He tipped his head toward the various tools. "Replacing some tile in the bathroom. What about you? What are you working on?"

"I'm actually replacing the locks on my doors." She gestured to the wall of locks and doorhandles. "My place is pretty old. Just want to feel a bit more secure, you know?"

Lance nodded, his expression turning serious. "I get that. Well, if you need any recommendations, I can help. I've done a bit of this myself." He reached for a lock on the shelf, examining it before handing it to her. "This one's pretty solid. It's a bit more expensive, but it's worth it for the peace of mind."

Kinley took the lock, looking it over. "Thanks, Lance. I appreciate the help."

"Anytime," he said, his smile returning. "Hey, if you're ever feeling up to it, I'd love to take you out sometime. Maybe dinner? No pressure, of course."

Kinley felt a warmth spread through her at his words. "That sounds nice. I'll let you know, okay?"

"Great. Just let me know when you're ready." He gave her a friendly wave as he headed toward the checkout.

Kinley finished her shopping, her mind still on Lance's invitation. It was nice to have something positive to think about, something that wasn't overshadowed by fear or uncertainty. She made her way home with her new locks, feeling more hopeful than she had in days.

Once home, she set to work replacing the locks. She started with the front door, following the instructions meticulously. A sense of giddy accomplishment washed over her as she tested the new door handle and lock. When she was certain everything was working properly, she moved on to the back door, repeating the process a little more quickly this time.

A smile broke over her face as she stared at her handiwork. It felt as if a weight had been lifted off her shoulders. As she sat down to relax, she smiled to herself, feeling a spark of anticipation for the future. Everything was finally falling into place. There was still a lot to be done—but for now, she just wanted to enjoy the feeling of being secure in her own home again.

CHAPTER
TWENTY-ONE

It didn't take long to reverse track the phone number Kinley had given him. Corey Hayes, forty-two, lived just outside of Brookhaven. And it appeared that this wasn't the man's first brush with the law.

A list of petty crimes associated with Hayes appeared on his screen: fraud, minor theft, and a few counts of breaking and entering. It was no surprise, considering Hayes had just swindled Kinley out of thousands of dollars. Cam's jaw tightened as he read through the offenses. The man was a professional scam artist, preying on unsuspecting victims.

Cam grabbed his keys and headed out the door, his mind churning as he drove toward the outskirts of town. Was Hayes the one who'd been in Kinley's house, leaving the door open? And, if so, what was his motive? Was he just trying to scare her? Cam couldn't come up with any other rational reason. Why not just take whatever he wanted and leave?

Of course, that was assuming Kinley hadn't mistakenly left the door open herself. But twice seemed like too much of a coincidence. She truly believed something was going on, and Cam owed it to her to find out. Even if Hayes wasn't responsible for breaking into her home, he'd stolen money from her under the guise of securing work.

When Cam arrived at the address listed in the man's file, he parked a few houses down and observed the property for a moment. The paint on the small run-down house was peeling, and the yard was wild and overgrown. It was clear that Hayes wasn't particularly concerned with appearances.

Cam approached the front door and knocked, listening intently for any sounds of movement inside. He waited nearly a full minute, but everything remained quiet and still. He knocked again, harder this time. Another thirty seconds passed with no response. He peered through a front window, but the curtains were drawn and he couldn't see inside.

He decided to look around the property, hoping to find any clues as to where Hayes might be. As he walked around the house, he peeked through the windows, but everything inside seemed normal, if a little messy. Beer cans and an empty pizza box littered the coffee table in the living room, and clothes appeared to be haphazardly strewn over the furniture and floor.

Cam glanced around the yard, noting the signs of neglect. It looked like Hayes hadn't been home for a while. Frustrated, he made his way back to the front yard.

As he rounded the corner, he noticed a neighbor watching him from the yard next door. An elderly woman watering her garden eyed him curiously, and Cam lifted a hand in greeting. He flashed his badge as he approached. "Good afternoon, ma'am. I'm Lt. Campbell McCoy with Brookhaven Sheriff's Department," he said politely. "I'm looking for the man who lives here, Corey Hayes. Have you seen him around recently?"

The woman squinted at him, then shook her head. "No, I haven't seen him for a while now. A week or more, maybe. He comes and goes at odd hours. Keeps to himself mostly."

Cam nodded, taking in the information. "Thank you. If you see him, could you let him know I'm looking for him?"

She nodded, her curiosity piqued. "Will do."

Cam returned to his car, frustrated with the lack of progress. Hayes's absence was suspicious. If he was behind the incidents at Kinley's house, perhaps he had gone into hiding. Or maybe he was planning something more sinister.

Determined to find answers, he decided to drive by a few local places in hopes that someone recognized Hayes and could point Cam in the right direction. He checked a couple of bars, a hardware store, and even a local diner, but there was no sign of him. It was as if Hayes had vanished.

His thoughts turned to Kinley as he climbed back into the car and steered toward her house. She was strong, but she had been through so much. The idea that someone might be targeting her made his blood boil. Maybe Hayes preyed on single women, using his access to their homes to intimidate or manipulate them.

More than ever, he wanted Kinley to get out of that house. She needed to be somewhere safe, away from the memories and the potential danger.

Cam pulled into the driveway and parked next to Ainsley's car, then jogged up the walkway to the front porch. He'd just lifted his hand to knock when the door swung open. Ainsley greeted him with a wide smile. "Hey. Good timing."

She turned and gave Kinley a little wave. "See you later!"

Cam waited for Ainsley to pass then stepped inside. Kinley grinned as she held the door wide and waved back. "Bye, Ains!"

Kinley watched her sister for another moment before she carefully closed the door and turned to face Cam. Her smile slipped away, her expression morphing from happiness to anger, and Cam let out a grunt as she drove her fist into his midsection.

"What the hell, Kins?"

"Don't give me that shit." She started to stomp away

then thought better of it and whirled back to him. He jerked back to avoid getting punched again as her eyes flashed with fire. "Seriously? You sent my sister over here to babysit me?"

He opened his mouth to speak, but she cut him off. "I'm just fine. I don't need someone watching over me, so you can go home, too. Asshole."

He grabbed her wrist as she stormed off again. "Kins—"

"No." She slapped her free hand against his chest and shoved. "Fuck you. Everything you said last night was a lie. You made me think—"

"I did not lie to you," he spoke over her. "I just—"

"What? Think I'm crazy?" She glared at him. "Is that it?"

"No," he said harshly. "I just want you to be safe."

She crossed her arms over her chest, her face set in a mulish expression. Cam sighed, knowing nothing less than the truth would appease her. "Something is off," he said. "For right now, I don't want you alone. I figured it was better to have your sister here."

"Why?"

She refused to budge an inch, and he sighed. "I couldn't find Hayes. He's not at home, not at any of the local hangouts. His neighbor said she hasn't seen him for a while. I don't want you alone until we figure out what's going on."

The tension in Kinley's shoulders began to relax,

and she dropped her defensive pose. "I understand. I put new locks on the doors, just in case."

Cam nodded, walking over to inspect the locks. He trusted Kinley, but his instincts compelled him to check anyway. Satisfied with her work, he turned back to her. "You did a good job. These should hold."

She smiled, but it didn't reach her eyes. "Thanks. I do feel safer."

"Let me stay the night again, just to be sure," Cam offered, his tone more pleading than he intended.

Kinley shook her head gently. "I appreciate it, really, but I'll be fine. You need to get some rest, too. You've got a lot going on right now. This"—she waved one hand toward the door—"isn't a huge deal. We'll figure out what's happening, but for now everything is fine."

He frowned, the idea of leaving her alone gnawing at his insides. "If anything happens—anything at all—call me. Understand?"

She offered a small smile. "I will. Promise."

Reluctantly, Cam stepped back toward the door, his chest tight with worry. "All right. I'll be back first thing in the morning to check on you."

As he left the house, a sense of unease settled over him. Something about the situation didn't feel right, and his instincts screamed at him not to leave her alone. Yet, he forced himself to respect her wishes, a sinking feeling in his gut as he left her house and headed home.

Back at his place, Cam paced the floor, unable to

relax. Hayes's disappearance was troubling, but the nagging worry for Kinley overshadowed everything else. He checked his phone repeatedly, half-expecting a call from Kinley. But the phone remained silent, and the night dragged on, each passing minute amplifying his anxiety.

"Damn it," he muttered to himself, sinking into the couch. He tried to distract himself with television, but his mind kept drifting back to Kinley.

In the quiet of his apartment, Cam made a decision. He would head back to Kinley's place before dawn, unable to wait until morning. He needed to be sure she was safe. Until then, he would remain vigilant.

As he finally drifted into a fitful sleep, one thought echoed in his mind: something was very, very wrong.

CHAPTER
TWENTY-TWO

The hot sun beat down on her shoulders as Kinley shifted the box of supplies in her arms. The front door swung open before she could knock and Ainsley stood there, a smile lighting up her face. "Hey! Come on in, we're just about to start on the centerpieces."

Inside, Brynlee was already seated at the dining table, surrounded by a sea of flowers, ribbons, and glass vases. She looked up and grinned. "Hey, Kins!"

Kinley returned the smile, her heart feeling lighter just being around her sisters. "Hey, yourself."

They settled around the table, the familiar rhythm of their chatter and laughter filling the room. Kinley tried to immerse herself in the task at hand, but the persistent throbbing in her head made it difficult to concentrate. She reached up, subtly rubbing her temples, hoping her sisters wouldn't notice.

Unfortunately, Ainsley did. "You okay, Kins?" she asked, her brow furrowed with concern.

Brynlee glanced over, her expression mirroring Ainsley's worry. "Are you still having those headaches?"

Kinley forced a smile, trying to sound more confident than she felt. "I'm fine. The doctor says they'll come and go. Nothing to worry about."

The truth was, she'd considered multiple times telling them about the back door being open the last few mornings, but she knew what they would say. Ainsley and Brynlee would insist she get therapy or go for more tests. Kinley wasn't ready for that kind of scrutiny, so she kept it close to her chest.

Instead, she took a deep breath and shifted the conversation. "Actually... I do kind of have some news, though. I've been thinking about selling my house."

Ainsley and Brynlee looked surprised. "Really?" Ainsley asked. "What brought that on?"

Kinley fiddled with a piece of ribbon, avoiding their gazes. "After what happened two weeks ago... the attack... It's just hard to be there now. The house holds more bad memories than good."

Her sisters' expressions softened with understanding. "We get it," Brynlee said, reaching out to squeeze Kinley's hand. "That must be really tough."

Ainsley nodded. "If selling the house will help you move on, then we're all for it. And we'll help in any way we can."

Kinley felt a wave of gratitude wash over her. "I

know," she murmured. "It's just... It's important that I do this on my own, you know?"

Ainsley laid a hand on Kinley's shoulder. "No one would ever accuse you of taking advantage of something or someone. But, Kinley, it's okay to ask for help."

She hesitated for a long moment, her gaze sliding toward the window. Her voice was quiet when she spoke again. "I wish I'd asked for help sooner, you know?"

Her words broke Kinley's heart. "You did the best you could. You know that, right?"

"I just wish..."

"Whatever happened is in the past," Brynlee jumped in. "You did what you had to do. You got out of a bad situation, and look at you now." She gestured widely. "You got a fresh start, and you're getting married to the man of your dreams soon. It doesn't get much better than that."

Ainsley smiled, her eyes glazed with tears. "You guys are the best, you know that?"

Kinley forced herself to focus on something—anything—else so she wouldn't break down and cry. She couldn't bear to think of what Ainsley had been through.

As the last of the centerpieces were carefully arranged, Ainsley turned to Kinley. "You know, Kins, if you really do decide to sell your house, you can always move into the suite—the one I used to rent from Dare."

Kinley smiled. "Thanks, Ains. That's really nice of

you, but you guys are just settling in and getting used to being a couple. I wouldn't want to intrude."

Brynlee chimed in, her expression apologetic. "I'd offer my place, but it's just a tiny one-bedroom in a duplex. Plus, my neighbor is the spawn of Satan."

Ainsley let out a choked laugh, and Kinley bit her lip to control her own as Brynlee grinned unrepentantly. "But my couch is always available if you need somewhere to crash."

Kinley chuckled, the familiar banter between her sisters a comforting distraction from her worries. "Thanks, Bryn. I appreciate it."

Ainsley glanced at Brynlee before turning back to Kinley. "So, have you thought about where you might go?"

Kinley hesitated for a moment, then took a deep breath. "Actually, Cam offered to let me move in with him."

Ainsley and Brynlee exchanged a quick look, a silent communication passing between them. Ainsley leaned forward, her tone gently probing. "How do you feel about that? Moving in with Cam, I mean."

Kinley bit her lip, her thoughts swirling. "We've been best friends for years. He's always been there for me. But... I don't know. What if things don't work out? We have such a good friendship, and I don't want to ruin that."

Brynlee's eyes sparkled with curiosity and her head

tipped slightly to one side. "Why would that ruin things?"

Kinley felt a blush creep up her cheeks. "Oh, I don't know, I just... don't want it to be awkward or anything."

Brynlee's gaze turned speculative. "Do you think you might have feelings for him? Like, more than just friends?"

Kinley swallowed hard, her gaze fixed on the table. "There have been a couple... moments. I just don't know."

Ainsley propped her chin in her hand. "Have you said anything to him?"

"God, no!" Kinley looked up, horrified. "I'm sure he's just being nice."

"I don't know," Ainsley said dubiously. "I don't think you see the way he looks at you sometimes."

She slid a look at her sister. "What do you mean?"

"She means," Brynlee put in, "that we think he feels the same way about you. But he's probably afraid to push you too much, especially right now."

Kinley arched a brow. "But moving in together? That's a big step."

Ainsley nodded, her expression thoughtful. "It is a big step, but it could also be a wonderful opportunity. If you're already feeling an attraction, maybe it's worth exploring those feelings."

Kinley sighed, feeling the familiar pounding of stress at her temples. "I just don't want to lose him as a friend.

What if things get awkward or don't work out? I'd hate to jeopardize what we have."

Brynlee reached out, placing a comforting hand on Kinley's arm. "It's a risk, sure, but every relationship is. And if anyone can handle a situation like this, it's you and Cam. You two have such a strong foundation."

Ainsley nodded in agreement. "Whatever you decide, we'll support you."

Kinley felt a swell of gratitude for her sisters. Moving in with Cam could be the fresh start she needed, a chance to heal and perhaps discover something deeper between them.

"Thanks, guys." Emotion swept through her and Kinley hugged her sisters tightly. "I don't know what I'd do without you two."

Ainsley smiled. "Good thing you'll never have to find out. We're here for you."

Brynlee nodded in agreement. "Always."

CHAPTER
TWENTY-THREE

The woman in the car was Misty Reynolds. Official ID had come back just this morning, and Cam had immediately reached out to Misty's sister, Lorraine, to let her know. He'd tried calling David Collins, but it went to an automatic voice message. He would give it some time and try again later.

The old case file, yellowed with age, lay open before him. Cam traced the worn edges of the paper, feeling the weight of nearly three decades pressing down on him. Misty's name stood out in bold letters, a ghost from the past demanding his attention.

Misty Collins had disappeared nearly thirty years ago, vanishing in the middle of the day while her husband, Dennis, was at work, and her stepson, David, was at school. No signs of struggle, no items missing from the home, just a typed letter left behind. And then... nothing. No further communication, no sightings. She had simply vanished.

Cam skimmed the report, the details etched into his mind. Misty's case had been cold almost from the start. Dennis and David had been thoroughly questioned, their alibis solid. Friends and neighbors had been interviewed, but no one had seen anything unusual. The police at the time had chalked it up to a woman overwhelmed by her circumstances, deciding to leave everything behind. But now they knew better.

He leaned back in his chair, glancing at the photo of Misty clipped to the top of the report. She was a beautiful woman, her smile radiant even in the grainy photograph. Cam couldn't shake the feeling that there was a connection between Misty's disappearance and the disturbances Kinley was experiencing.

He flipped through the pages, looking for any detail he might have missed. There had to be something. His eyes landed on the interview with Dennis. He had described Misty as perpetually happy, content with her life as wife and mother. There had been no signs of depression or distress. And yet, the letter...

The letter. Cam's mind raced. It had been typed. That was unusual for a variety of reasons. Most people in emotional distress would write something by hand. The typed letter felt cold, detached. Could someone have forced her to write it? Or worse, could someone have written it for her?

The question remained—why? Something wasn't

right, and he was damn well going to figure out what the hell was going on.

He pushed from the chair and strode toward Dare's office. Sawyer was following up on a few leads from Jayla Simms's case—a friend had just returned from vacation, and he wanted to question her about the few weeks leading up to Jayla's disappearance.

Cam paused in the doorway and gave a quick knock before moving forward and dropping into the chair across from Dare. The sheriff barely glanced up from the mound of grant paperwork in front of him. "Anything new on the Gill case?"

"No." Cam barely repressed a growl. "We've checked every lead, questioned every single person she came in contact with, but no one knows a damn thing."

Dare frowned. "Something will turn up; it always does."

Cam drummed his fingers on his desk. Lindsey's case wasn't the only thing bothering him. "I've been thinking about what Yvonne said the other day—about the Collins family home."

A single dark eyebrow lifted, and Cam leaned forward in his chair. "Maybe there's a connection there."

Dare stared at him for a long moment. "Did you look through the old case file?"

Cam nodded. "Not a damn thing worthwhile in there. They treated her like a runaway."

"She was an adult," Dare pointed out. "Maybe there was something going on between her and Dennis that no one knew about. If he killed her, we're never going to know. He probably took that secret to the grave."

It was possible, but something about the whole situation just didn't sit right with him. There had to be something. "I'd like to go talk with Sheriff Johnson."

Though the man had been retired for half a decade, everyone still used the title out of deference of his dedication to the community.

Dare nodded slowly. "Couldn't hurt. I'll come too."

Giving Sarge a quick pat on the way out, they piled into Dare's SUV and headed to the Johnson place on the outskirts of town. A half hour later they pulled up to a quaint farmhouse, windows glowing cheerily in the fading afternoon light.

Dare cut the engine and glanced at Cam. "Hopefully Sheriff Johnson remembers something useful."

They climbed out of the car and approached the front door. Before Dare could knock, the door swung open. Harold Johnson stood there, his tall frame slightly stooped with age but his eyes sharp and alert.

"Jensen, McCoy," he greeted, stepping aside to let them in. "Come on in. Coffee's on the table."

The inside of the house was cozy, and the scent of freshly baked bread lingered in the air. Cam's stomach rumbled, reminding him he'd forgone lunch today, so completely enveloped in Misty's old file.

Dare and Cam followed Johnson to the kitchen, where Edith Johnson greeted them warmly, wrapping them each in a hearty hug. "It's so good to see you both!" Her full cheeks glowed pink with cheer. "Can I get you some coffee?"

"That would be great, ma'am, thank you."

Cam slipped into a seat at the table next to Dare, and soon two steaming cups slid in front of them. Edith promised to check back with them again soon, then left them to speak with Harold alone.

Sheriff Johnson turned a sharp eye their way. "What brings you boys by?"

Dare got straight to the point. "Thanks for seeing us, Harold. I'm sure you've heard about Misty Collins."

Harold's face tightened, and he gave a slow shake of his head before speaking. "Sure did. She was such a sweet girl. Feels like it was just yesterday."

"Can you tell us what you remember?" Cam asked, leaning forward.

Harold took a sip of his coffee. "Misty was a good soul. Beautiful, friendly. Seemed to have everything going for her. Then one day she just... up and left."

"Dr. Seidel said she sustained wounds that appeared to be from a knife or sharp object," Dare said quietly. "From what he can tell, Misty didn't leave—she was murdered."

"I had a bad feeling about that," Harold murmured. "She left a note saying she was leaving town. Nothing suspicious about it on the surface, but something never sat right with me. Dennis was distraught—said it wasn't like her to just up and leave without a word."

Dare nodded. "Where did you find the note?"

"Right there on the kitchen counter," Harold replied. "Said she needed to get away, said not to worry and that she'd be in touch."

"Did you ever get any leads?" Cam asked.

Harold shook his head. "At the time we were treating it as a missing persons. We checked her credit card activity, but it was like she vanished into thin air." He paused. "We even checked with her friends, coworkers... No one remembered anything."

"What about her family?" Dare pressed. "Did they mention anyone who might have wanted to hurt her?"

Harold slowly shook his head. "Everyone seemed to love her. She used to work in the office at the old paper mill, but she quit when she got married. Dennis was sure she wouldn't just leave. He was convinced Misty was taken, but we never found any evidence to support that."

Dare exchanged a glance with Cam. "Anything else you remember? Anything at all?"

Harold leaned back in his chair, his gaze distant. "Just that damn note. It felt staged, like someone wanted us to believe she just ran away. But I could never prove it."

Dare nodded slowly. "Thanks, Harold. We'll take a look at those files again. Maybe there's something in there we missed."

Harold stood up, moving with surprising agility for

his age. "I have some notes from back then, too. I'll get them for you."

As Harold disappeared into another room, Dare turned to Cam. "What do you think?"

Cam frowned. "We know Misty didn't leave on her own. Someone made her disappear—but who?"

"More to the point," Dare said, "why?"

Harold returned with a box of files and set it on the table. "Here you go. Everything I had on Misty Collins."

Dare and Cam thanked the retired sheriff and gathered the files. With a last goodbye to Edith, they headed out into the twilight. Back in the cruiser, Cam flipped through the files. "You think I'm crazy, don't you?"

Dare was silent as he started the engine, then steered the car toward Brookhaven. "What does your gut tell you?"

A heavy sigh filtered from Cam's mouth. "I think they're connected. I don't know how or why, but..."

"Go through Harold's notes, see if anyone else remembers anything," Dare said firmly. "If there's a connection, we'll find it."

Cam nodded. The past had its secrets, and he was determined to bring them to light.

CHAPTER
TWENTY-FOUR

The scream bounced off the walls, reverberating in his ears. The woman's face contorted in pain and she groaned, her legs curling up.

He rushed forward, his gaze roving over her swollen belly, the muscles taut. "What's wrong? What's happening?"

"The baby..." she gasped, her eyes fluttering open, wide with fear. "It's... Oh, God!"

Her back arched violently and she gritted her teeth against the pain racking her body. "The baby is coming," she panted out.

Panic surged through him and he shook his head. No. It was too soon. She was only a few months along; this couldn't be happening.

Sweat broke out along her forehead and chest as her lungs heaved with effort. "Do something!" she begged. "I need—"

Pain rippled across her face again, and another ear-shattering shriek broke free.

"Help her!" screamed the second woman from her place in the corner. "She needs a doctor!"

That wasn't possible. He tried to remain calm, to think clearly. This happened sometimes, didn't it? Surely there were just false contractions. "Take a deep breath," he said, though his own breathing was becoming erratic. "Just breathe through it."

Minutes turned into an agonizing eternity. Her cries grew louder, her body writhing in pain. His mind raced, trying to recall any fragment of first aid or emergency birth procedures he might have heard or read.

Then, the bleeding started. A dark, ominous stain spread across the blanket. His heart thudded painfully in his chest. This wasn't right. This was too much blood.

"You're bleeding," he said, his voice barely more than a whisper. "Oh God, you're bleeding."

"I can't... I can't stop it," she gasped, tears streaming down her face.

His stomach pitched violently. He had to help her. He had to do something. Wadding up the sheets, he pressed them between her legs.

Her cries turned to whimpers, her grip on his hand weakening as red saturated the dingy white sheets.

She looked at him, her eyes filled with a mixture of pain and fear. "I can't..."

"No," he choked out. "You're going to be okay. You have to be okay."

But deep down, he knew. He knew this was beyond his control, beyond his ability to fix. Her body convulsed, then went limp. Panic gave way to cold, hard fear.

"No, no, no," he repeated, his voice breaking. "Stay with me. Please, stay with me."

He felt her pulse, weak and fluttering like a trapped bird. He tried to remember CPR, tried to do anything that might keep her with him. But the blood kept coming, soaking through the sheets and pooling around them.

He was losing her. He was losing both of them.

Hours felt like seconds. He held her, sobbing, as the life ebbed from her body. Then, she was gone. Her body went slack in his arms, her breathing stopped. He clung to her, rocking back and forth, his heart shattered into a million pieces.

CHAPTER
TWENTY-FIVE

Cam raised his beer bottle to toast Ainsley and Dare, then took a healthy sip as a smattering of applause broke out from their family and friends gathered in Dare's backyard.

A new song drifted from speakers set up in the corner of the patio, and his attention was drawn to Kinley, seated next to him. He pushed back his chair and extended a hand to her. "Come dance with me."

She slipped her hand into his and he pulled her out to the makeshift dance floor. Placing one hand on her hip, he pulled her as close as he dared. Her gaze flitted around the yard before meeting his, full of pleasure and pride. "This turned out really well, didn't it?"

He smiled. "It did. I can't believe you put this together so fast."

"Where there's a will, there's a way." Her dreamy gaze drifted toward her sister and soon-to-be brother-in-law. "You know, I don't blame them for not wanting to wait. They've both been through so much..."

Cam agreed. Almost losing the love of your life had a way of putting things in perspective. Though Dare and Ainsley had only been together for a short period of time, Cam had never seen the sheriff so damn content. They were meant to be together.

"They deserve to be happy." Cam glanced down at her. "Does it make you wish for your own wedding?"

Her gaze once again strayed over his shoulder, and a sad smile flitted across her lips. "I'd have to find a decent guy first."

Their conversation about Ted from the other night came back with brutal force. That asshole had never appreciated her, and she deserved so much better than some asshole looking for a nanny to take care of his kid. Forcing his anger down, he took a tiny step forward, shifting Kinley so she was even closer.

"You know... I might have a solution for you."

"What's that?" Her head tipped to one side.

He peered down at her. "You could just save yourself the trouble and marry me instead."

Her eyes widened fractionally, and her chest hitched as she drew in a sharp breath. Several beats passed as she stared up at him and his shoulder blades tightened nervously. He was just about to make a joke about it when she broke the silence. "Maybe I should."

Her expression suddenly turned serious, unsure, her teeth digging into her bottom lip. He knew that look.

He'd pushed far enough for one night. She'd been hurt far too much recently, and she needed time for things to settle down. If he pressed any more, she would bolt.

Cam dipped his head and spoke next to her ear. "In case I haven't told you already, you look absolutely stunning."

A shy smile curves her lips. "You clean up pretty well yourself, mister."

The song drew to a close, the final notes lingering in the air like a whispered promise. Cam reluctantly let his hand fall away, but not before squeezing Kinley's hand, a silent message he hoped she understood. She smiled up at him, a hint of something unreadable in her gaze.

"Kinley, I—"

"Mind if I cut in?"

Kinley stiffened at the sound of the other man's voice, and Cam drew back, frustration pulsing through his veins.

Cam turned to face Cooper Klein, and his stomach swooped violently. Klein was a great cop, and Cam enjoyed working with him. But now, watching him stand next to Kinley, he couldn't help but hate the man just a little.

Kinley smiled warmly, her face lighting up at the sight of her old friend. "Hey. Glad you could make it."

"Wouldn't have missed this for the world." An easy smile stretched his face as he extended a hand toward Kinley. "Dance with me?"

"Of course," Kinley replied, her voice cheerful. She glanced back at Cam. "Thanks for the dance."

He nodded and forced a smile as he stepped away. "Any time, Kins."

He made his way to the bar, trying to push down the swell of jealousy rising in his chest. Ordering a whiskey, he glanced back at the dance floor just in time to see Kinley laughing at something Cooper had said. They moved together effortlessly, a testament to their shared history, and it stung more than he cared to admit.

"Damn, McCoy," a voice drawled beside him. "Keep scowling like that and you're likely to clear the place out."

Cam turned to see Sawyer Reed leaning casually against the bar, a teasing glint in his eye. "Shut up, Reed," Cam muttered, taking a gulp of his drink.

Sawyer swiveled toward him. "Seriously. What's up with you and the Layne girl?"

"Why?" The question came out far more hostile than he'd intended, and the corner of Sawyer's mouth kicked up.

"Don't shoot." He held up a hand in Cam's direction. "It was just a question."

Cam rolled his eyes and glanced back at Kinley. She was smiling up at Cooper, but Cam couldn't tell how genuine it was. Was she really into him?

"You're friends, right?"

Cam nodded. "Yep."

"And?"

He glanced over at the detective. "And what?"

Sawyer rolled his eyes and gestured between Cam and Kinley. "How long have you been doing this?"

Cam turned his attention back to the whiskey in his hand. "Don't know what you're talking about."

Sawyer chuckled. "Don't bite my head off. If I can see it, so can everyone else."

Cam sighed, setting his glass down with a little too much force. Reed was a relatively knew addition to Brookhaven. The man had moved here a few months ago, but he was right about one thing. If the new guy could sense his interest in Kinley, then he had it bad.

He shook his head. "It's not that simple."

"It never is," Sawyer agreed, his tone losing some of its teasing edge. "But glaring at her while she dances with Klein isn't going to win you any points."

Cam took another sip of his drink, savoring the burn as it slid down his throat. "I know."

Sawyer's gaze drifted across the dance floor, and his easy smile faded, replaced by something entirely different. Following Sawyer's line of sight, Cam's eyes landed on Brynlee Layne, Kinley's younger sister. She moved gracefully among the guests, her peal of laughter mingling with the music.

A mirthless laugh escaped before he could stop it. "Hypocrite."

Sawyer's eyes snapped back to Cam. His eyes went wide for half a second before he smoothed his expression into a blank mask. "Not sure what you mean."

"Right."

For a moment, they stood in companionable silence, both lost in their thoughts. Happy party goers buzzed around them, filled with joy and celebration, yet they were both keenly aware of the two women who seemed just out of reach.

"You gonna do something about it?" Sawyer asked finally, breaking the silence.

Cam shrugged, his gaze returning to Brynlee. "Someday. When the time's right."

The final notes of the song drifted out, and Cam pushed to his feet. If Kinley wanted another dance, it sure as hell wasn't going to be with Cooper Klein.

CHAPTER
TWENTY-SIX

Cam ignored the phone buzzing insistently in his pocket, but a moment later, he watched as Sawyer pulled his own phone from the inner pocket of his suit jacket. Cam's heart sank.

Fuck. The synchronized buzzing was a bad sign.

Cam slowed his movements but didn't release Kinley. His gaze was firmly fixed on Sawyer, hoping like hell it wasn't what he suspected.

Sawyer lifted the phone to his ear. "Reed."

"Copy that," Sawyer said into the phone, his face growing more serious with each passing second. "We're on our way."

Sawyer tipped his head toward Cam, indicating he follow, and Cam bit back a sigh. Goddamn it.

He squeezed Kinley's waist. "I'm sorry. I've gotta go."

"Is everything okay?"

Her big blue eyes were full of concern, and he wanted so badly to reassure her. He brushed a long lock of hair behind her ear. "Duty calls."

Dare's laser-like gaze met his from across the dance floor, and Cam shook his head. He wasn't going to allow this to interrupt Dare's celebration. He and Ainsley deserved one night to themselves.

"Tell Dare and your sister congratulations for me and not to worry about anything. Sawyer and I will handle everything."

"All right." She bit her lip. "If you need anything…"

"Thanks." He offered a tight smile before pulling away from her. "I'll talk to you later."

He forced himself to put one foot in front of the other as he dragged himself away from Kinley and met up with Sawyer at the edge of the driveway.

"We've got a situation," Sawyer said as Cam slid into the car. "A young woman was found dead just outside of town. Posed—just like the first one."

Foreboding slithered down Cam's spine. "Shit."

Sawyer grimaced as he put the car into gear and pulled away from Dare's house. "Yep."

The location given to them was a secluded spot near the edge of the forest, a place not commonly frequented by locals. When they arrived, the area was already cordoned off with yellow crime scene tape. Uniformed officers were scattered around, and the flashing lights of police cruisers painted the scene in an eerie blue and red glow. Cam and Sawyer ducked under the tape, moving toward the center of the activity.

The body lay in a small clearing, surrounded by trees that seemed to close in protectively. It was a young woman, no more than twenty-five years old, with long blonde hair fanned out around her head like a macabre halo. She had been posed carefully, her arms folded over her chest and her legs straightened.

Cam's breath caught in his throat. The scene was almost serene, a stark contrast to the brutality of the crime. "Who found her?" he asked one of the deputies.

"A hiker, sir," Tony Webb replied. "He called it in about an hour ago."

Sawyer crouched beside the body, examining the careful placement. "Whoever did this took their time. This isn't a spur-of-the-moment kill."

"Any ID on the victim?" Cam asked.

"Not yet," Webb replied. "We're running her fingerprints now, but it might take some time."

Cam looked around the scene, taking in every detail. The way the body was posed, the location—all of it felt deliberate. "We need to canvass the area," he said. "See if anyone saw or heard anything unusual."

They began their meticulous work, photographing the scene and collecting evidence. Cam and Sawyer spoke to Marty, the hiker who had found the body, but he hadn't seen anyone else around and had stumbled upon the scene by accident.

"Did you notice anything unusual on your hike?" Cam asked.

Marty shook his head. "No, nothing. I come this way every day."

Cam thanked the man and let him go. As he turned back to the scene, his phone buzzed with a message from the station. They had identified the victim.

"Her name is Hilary Swanson," Cam said to Sawyer, reading the message. "Twenty-two years old, lived in Cloverdale. Reported missing seven months ago."

Sawyer sighed. "We need to talk to her family and friends. Find out who she was, if she had any enemies, or if there was anyone in her life who might have wanted to hurt her."

They continued their examination of the scene until the medical examiner arrived. Dr. Seidel nodded in greeting as he approached to began his preliminary assessment.

"What can you tell us, Doc?" Sawyer asked after several moments.

Dr. Seidel gestured toward the woman's prone form. "Possibly asphyxiation. There are no obvious signs of struggle, and no visible external injuries."

"Same as the first victim," Cam noted with a frown. "Asphyxiation, careful posing. This is definitely our guy."

Dr. Seidel nodded. "It looks that way. I'll know more after the autopsy, but based on what I'm seeing here, it fits the pattern."

Cam and Sawyer exchanged a grim look. They had hoped the first murder was an isolated incident. A second woman killed in the same manner within a short period of time was far too coincidental.

"Thanks, Doc," Cam said. "We'll need your full report as soon as possible."

Dr. Seidel nodded. "I'll get it to you as soon as I can."

As the medical examiner continued his work, Cam and Sawyer stepped aside to discuss their next steps.

"We need to start running leads," Cam said. "Talk to her family, her friends, anyone who knew her. We need to figure out who had access to her and who would want to do this."

"And we need to look into the first victim again," Sawyer added. "There might be a connection we're missing."

Cam agreed. "Let's head back to the station and see what we can find."

They headed back to their car, the scene still a flurry of activity behind them. The sun was beginning to set, casting long shadows across the clearing. It was going to be a long night.

CHAPTER
TWENTY-SEVEN

Cam guided the car into the lot of the sheriff's department, pulling into the spot next to Dare's familiar SUV. They stepped out almost in tandem, and Cam's brows drew together as he glanced over at Dare. "You didn't have to come."

Dare waved him off. "I heard there was another homicide and wanted to be here to help."

Sawyer moved next to them. "We can handle it if you want to be with Ainsley."

Dare lifted one shoulder. "The engagement party was winding down anyway. Besides, she understands."

Cam's brows knit together with worry at the thought of Kinley being alone. Dare seemed to read his thoughts, because he clapped a reassuring hand on Cam's shoulder. "The ladies are hanging out at my place for now."

Cam slid a look at Sawyer, who appeared faintly

relieved to hear that Brynlee was safe with her sisters. Sawyer had been uncharacteristically quiet since they found the body.

Cam spoke as they walked inside the station. "Marty Ballard went for a hike and found a woman on the trail. We got a hit on her prints—Hilary Swanson, abducted seven months ago from Cloverdale."

Dare cocked a brow. "Asphyxiation?"

Cam shook his head. "No clear cause of death yet."

Dare made a low humming noise in the back of his throat as he turned into his office and dropped into the chair behind his desk. Cam and Sawyer followed suit, sitting across from him.

"The body was posed, just like Jayla Simms," Sawyer spoke up, "and victimology is similar. Both had blonde hair and blue eyes—same as Lindsey."

Dare stroked his chin. "Assume for now they're all connected. Let's see what we can find out from the scene photos and initial reports. We need to get ahead of this before it spirals."

Cam nodded. "Agreed. We need to talk to her family and friends, see if anyone can give us a direction to go in."

"Sir?"

The men turned toward Tony Webb, who hovered in the doorway, blue folder in hand. "I have the information you requested."

"Thanks." Dare pushed from his seat and extracted the file from the man's outstretched hand, then passed the file to Cam. "Her address and next of kin information. Her parents still live in Cloverdale. I'll contact the officers over there so they can notify them, but you'll need to follow up. I've requested a copy of the original police report, so I'll pass that along as soon as I get it. We need all the cooperation we can get."

"We're on it." Cam dipped his chin and left the office, Sawyer at his back. He tossed a look at the detective as he dug his keys from his front pocket. "Let's hit her place first, see if her roommate is home. Maybe she'll be able to tell us something."

They piled into the cruiser and headed toward the apartment Hilary had shared with her friend, Lisa. The apartment was located in a modest building on the edge of town. They climbed the narrow staircase to the second floor and knocked on the door.

A moment later, it opened to reveal a young woman with dark, questioning eyes. "Can I help you?"

"Lisa Morales? I'm Lieutenant Cam McCoy," he introduced himself gently. "This is Detective Sawyer Reed. Do you mind if we come in for a moment? We'd like to talk with you about Hilary Swanson."

"Sure, of course." Her brows drew together as she closed the door behind them and gestured toward the living room. "Can I get you something to drink?"

"No, thanks." Cam dropped onto the couch next to Sawyer and glanced at Lisa, who settled gingerly on a plush armchair across from them.

"You said you wanted to talk about Hilary?" She

wrung her hands nervously in her lap, hope and fear mingling in her dark eyes. "Did… did you find her?"

The details of Hilary's death had been released to the media this morning after her parents had been notified, but apparently Lisa hadn't yet heard the news.

"Actually, ma'am." He rested his elbows on his knees as he leaned forward. "That's what we'd like to speak with you about. I'm sorry to tell you this, but Ms. Swanson passed away."

Her eyes went round and she jerked back as if he'd slapped her. Shock flitted over her features, immediately followed by despair, and her face crumpled.

Cam glanced around the room, searching for a box of tissues, and found one just a few feet away. He held it out to Lisa, who silently slipped it from his fingers, tears sliding down her cheeks.

Cam and Sawyer exchanged a look, giving Lisa a moment to compose herself. Finally, she cleared her throat enough to speak. "W-What happened?"

"We're not entirely sure yet," Cam replied softly. "But I'm hoping you can help with that."

Lisa nodded a little but didn't speak, and Cam continued, "I know this is a difficult time, but we need to ask you some questions about Hilary."

Lisa nodded again and swiped at her eyes. "Of course. Anything to help."

"Can you tell me about Hilary? What was she like?"

"Hilary was… amazing," Lisa said, her voice trembling. "She was kind, always helping others. She volunteered at the animal shelter and was studying to be a teacher. She didn't have any enemies. I can't imagine who would do this to her."

"Did she have a boyfriend? Anyone she was seeing recently?"

Lisa shook her head. "Not really. She dated a few guys, but nothing serious. She was focused on her studies and her volunteering."

"Did she mention anyone who made her uncomfortable? Any unusual behavior or people she was worried about?"

Lisa thought for a moment. "Not that she ever mentioned. She was always so outgoing and nice to everyone. I always warned her that she came off as flirtatious sometimes, but..."

She trailed off, and Cam gave her a gentle smile. "Thank you, Lisa. This helps a lot. You said she volunteered at a shelter—Do you have the name?"

Lisa relayed the information and Cam jotted it down.

"Please find who did this." Lisa's voice cracked on the heartfelt plea. "Hilary didn't deserve this."

"We'll do everything we can," Sawyer promised, standing up. "If you think of anything else, please call me."

Sawyer passed her a card, and Cam nodded to the young woman before making his way to the door. Outside, he tossed a look Sawyer's way. "No boyfriend, but I wonder if she was seeing anyone."

"I'll put in a request for her phone records, see if we can find anything."

Sawyer dug his phone from his pocket as Cam slipped behind the wheel and cranked the engine. Cam entered the name of the shelter into the GPS, then pulled into traffic.

When Sawyer ended the call, he turned back to Cam. "With any luck, we'll find some correlation between the women."

Cam's lips pressed into a firm line. "We need something, because so far we don't have jack shit. There's no overlap. Jayla worked at a bank. Lindsey was a nurse. Hilary was studying to be a teacher. Aside from their looks, what the hell do they have in common?"

Nothing, as far as he could tell. They'd been digging into every aspect of the women's lives and had come up empty. They were all from different cities, all had different professions and hobbies...

So far, there wasn't a damn thing tying them together. They'd checked everything they could think of from yoga studios to hair salons to stores they'd frequented.

Cam drove to the shelter, the sky darkening as low-hanging clouds settled over them. The sign on the shelter door read that it was closed, but a middle-aged woman lingered behind the counter.

Cam knocked on the door and her head snapped in his direction, her brow furrowing. She gave a little shake of her head, her mouth forming the words "We're closed."

Cam flashed his badge through the large glass window. "Ma'am? It'll just take a minute."

She bustled out from behind the counter, then unlocked the door to let them in just as the rain overhead let loose.

"Just in time," the woman said before closing the door against the driving rain. "What can I do for you, officers?"

"I'm Lt. Campbell McCoy," Cam introduced himself before tipped his head toward Sawyer.

"Detective Sawyer Reed."

"I'm Karen Mills, the manager here."

He nodded toward the woman. "Thank you for staying late. I was hoping we could ask you some questions about a volunteer who used to work here—Hilary Swanson."

The woman's face fell. "I just heard the news. Poor thing. Hilary was a wonderful volunteer. We were all devastated when she went missing."

"I'm sorry for your loss," Cam said sincerely. "I'm hoping you can help us with our investigation. Hilary's roommate mentioned she worked here. Did you ever notice anything strange when she was here—anyone who might have had an interest in Hilary?"

Karen thought for a moment, then led Cam to a small office. She rifled through a stack of visitor logs and pulled out a few pages. "We've had a few people come by regularly. There was one man… He didn't give his name, but he seemed particularly sweet on Hilary."

Cam took the pages and examined the entries. "Do you have any security footage or anything that might help us identify him?"

Karen shook her head. "I'm afraid not. We're a small operation and don't have the budget for that kind of security."

"Anything else you can tell me about him? Physical description, behavior?"

"He was tall, maybe six feet, with dark hair. He seemed very interested in the animals, but not in a way that felt genuine. More… detached, if that makes sense."

Cam nodded. "Thank you, Karen. This helps a lot. If you think of anything else, please contact me."

Back in the car, Sawyer frowned. "It's not much, but it's a start. Let's head back to the station and see if we can cross-reference this with any known suspects or similar cases."

Back at the station, they spread out the visitor logs and began the painstaking process of cross-referencing the descriptions and patterns with their database of known offenders and suspects. Hours passed as they sifted through the information, looking for any connection that might lead them to their killer.

"This guy is careful," Cam said, rubbing his tired eyes. "He takes his time, plans everything out. We need to find a pattern, something that links his victims."

Sawyer nodded, his own exhaustion showing.

"Agreed. We need to look at similar cases, even ones outside our jurisdiction. This guy could have done this before."

"We'll get him," Cam said, his voice filled with conviction. "We have to."

Sawyer nodded in agreement. "Yeah. We will."

As they prepared for the day ahead, their minds were already racing with the possibilities, the clues, and the relentless pursuit of justice for Hilary and the other victims who might be out there.

CHAPTER
TWENTY-EIGHT

Kinley reached into her purse, her fingers brushing against various items until she found the business card she had been looking for—Lance Barton, Realtor. Today was the day she would visit the realty office and finally take the leap toward listing her home.

She grabbed her keys and headed out the door, her heart racing with a mix of excitement and nervousness as she drove to the brokerage. Inside the office, the atmosphere buzzed with activity. Agents spoke animatedly on phones, discussing listings and negotiations. Kinley scanned the room, searching for Lance. It didn't take long for her to spot him at his desk, a welcoming smile spreading across his face as he caught her gaze.

"Kinley! Good to see you!" Lance exclaimed, standing up to greet her. His enthusiasm was infectious, easing some of her nerves. "What brings you in today?"

Kinley returned his smile, the tension in her shoulders gradually receding. "Actually, I've been thinking a lot, and… I'm ready to list my home."

Lance's smile widened. "I'm glad to hear that. Let me walk you through the process."

Just then, a second man walked by and stopped when he saw them. "Hello there, I'm Max," he introduced himself, extending a hand to Kinley.

"Kinley," she introduced herself, offering her hand for a quick shake.

"I couldn't help but overhear that you're listing your home?"

She grinned. "I am."

Max nodded emphatically, a spark of enthusiasm in his voice. "I hear you live in Brookhaven. What a beautiful place. I had some friends who lived there, and they always raved about it. You're very lucky."

Kinley smiled at the compliment. "Thank you. I actually grew up there, so I'm probably biased, but it's a great neighborhood."

"Well, it was great meeting you."

Max wished her luck and moved on, leaving Kinley and Lance to continue their conversation. Lance led her to a small conference room where they could discuss the details privately. They began to talk about her property—its features, any recent upgrades, and her expectations for the sale. They dove deeper into the logistics of the listing—discussing pricing strategies, staging tips, and scheduling an appointment for Lance to come over and take photos of the house.

"Let's aim for tomorrow afternoon if that gives you enough time," Lance suggested, pulling out his calendar. "I want to make sure we showcase your home in the best light."

"Sounds great," Kinley replied, heart racing with anticipation. "I can't believe this is finally happening."

After they finished scheduling the appointment, Lance looked at her earnestly. "If you have any questions or concerns during the process, don't hesitate to reach out. I'm here to help."

She smiled. "Thanks. I really appreciate it."

As she left the office, Kinley felt lighter, as if a burden had been lifted from her shoulders. She stepped out into the bright sunlight, her mind racing with possibilities. This was the first step toward a new chapter in her life, and she was determined to embrace it fully.

Kinley moved through the house in a frenzy, her mind whirling as she mentally checked items off her list. She'd been at it for hours, ensuring that every surface gleamed and every item was in its rightful place. The house had to be perfect.

She passed through the living room and ran the cloth over a spot she'd missed on the coffee table, then straightened the cushions on the couch. Bright sunlight streamed through the freshly cleaned windows, casting a warm glow over the beige carpet that still had the distinct, slightly chemical smell of newness.

In the kitchen, she double-checked the appliances, making sure there were no smudges or fingerprints. She arranged a bowl of bright green apples on the counter, their crispness and color a deliberate choice to add a touch of vibrancy to the room. The counters were spotless, the backsplash gleamed, and the faint scent of lemon cleaner lingered in the air.

She moved upstairs, checking the bedrooms. In the master, she fluffed the pillows and straightened the bedspread. She made sure the closets were neat, the floors vacuumed, and the curtains drawn back to let in as much natural light as possible. The bathrooms were her final stop. She ensured the mirrors were streak-free, the sinks and tubs scrubbed, and the towels neatly folded.

The doorbell rang, the cheerful chime echoing through the quiet house. She took a deep breath, trying to calm the flutter of nerves in her stomach. It was time.

Kinley stowed the cleaning supplies then crossed to the door, peering through the peephole to find Lance standing on the front porch. She nervously swiped her hands over her jeans before swinging the door open.

"Morning." Lance greeted her with a wide smile as he stepped inside, his gaze sweeping the room. "The house looks fantastic."

"Thanks," Kinley replied, fighting down the nerves

threatening to creep into her voice. "I hope it's good enough."

"It's perfect," he assured her. "Ready to get started?"

Kinley nodded and watched as Lance set up his camera and tripod in the living room. She hung back, not wanting to get in his way. She leaned against the kitchen counter, watching as he meticulously framed each shot, adjusting the lighting and angles to capture the house in its best light.

He moved methodically from room to room, occasionally muttering to himself or adjusting something slightly. Kinley followed at a distance, anxious but hopeful. Each click of the camera felt like a step closer to a new beginning.

After what felt like an eternity, Lance finally lowered his camera and packed up his equipment. He turned to Kinley with a satisfied smile.

"All done," he said. "The photos turned out great. I'll have these edited and get the listing created. It should be up on the market by the end of the week."

Kinley let out a breath she didn't realize she'd been holding. "That's great news. What happens now?"

"Now," Lance replied, "we wait for the offers to come in. The new carpet and the updates you've made will definitely help. Buyers love move-in ready homes. I'm hopeful we'll see some interest quickly."

Kinley nodded, feeling a mix of relief and anticipation. "I hope so. It's been a lot of work."

Lance gave her a reassuring smile. "It'll pay off. I'll be in touch as soon as we have any news."

As he left, Kinley closed the door behind him and leaned against it, closing her eyes for a moment. The house was ready, the photos taken, and the listing would be up soon. All she could do now was wait and hope for the best.

She glanced around the house, taking in the spotless rooms and the faint smell of fresh carpet. She had done everything she could. Now, it was in fate's hands.

CHAPTER
TWENTY-NINE

Cam glanced up at the clock on the wall, his foot tapping an impatient rhythm on the tiled floor. Hilary Swanson's autopsy was scheduled for this morning, and he was champing at the bit to figure out if this was in any way tied to the open cases they had. He likely wasn't finished yet, but maybe Doc Seidel had some information that might help them, and he wanted to get a jump start.

Cam slid into the cruiser and headed toward the medical examiner's office. Inside, he was directed down the stark gray hallway that smelled of disinfectant and death. A metal door brought him to a halt, and he glanced through the window. Doc was bent over the exam table, his attention fixed on the human remains in front of him.

Cam gave a soft triple knock, then quietly pushed

the door open. He waited patiently until the doctor jerked his chin in acknowledgment. "Lieutenant."

Cam glanced across the metal table at Dr. Seidel. "Official cause of death?"

Dr. Seidel gestured toward the young woman on the table. "Severe blood loss."

"Blood loss?" Cam's brows drew together. "I don't remember seeing any wounds."

"No wounds." Doc Seidel shook his head. "I found elevated levels of HCG in her system. Hilary was pregnant at or around the time of her death."

"Pregnant?" Cam jerked back at the news. "Where's...?"

The doctor made a face. "That, I can't answer. She experienced severe hemorrhaging, which ultimately led to exsanguination. She could have miscarried, or she could have experienced the heavy blood loss after giving birth."

Cam squirmed a little, deeply uncomfortable. "So we don't know if it was intentional?"

"From what I can tell, there was no other trauma. Aside from a few scratches and minor dehydration, she appeared healthy."

That was disturbing on multiple levels. Where was the baby? And how far along was Hilary when she'd died? "Is there any way to tell how far along she was?"

"My guess would be in her second trimester, although I can't be certain. The pregnancy was never recorded in her medical history. In fact, she had a birth control implant installed just a few months prior to her abduction. So, it either failed or was removed. How long ago, I can't tell."

Cam tipped his head toward the young woman. "Did you find anything else? Any DNA?"

Dr. Seidel shook his head. "No hair or fibers, no skin cells under her nails. There's a faint impression around her throat, but it wasn't a contributing factor to her death."

He gestured to a light abrasion that ringed the woman's neck. "The wound doesn't appear to be consistent with damage from a rope, and I didn't find any fibers. It looks more like she wore a choker of some sort."

Christ, that was revolting. "You think he gets off on it?"

He lifted one shoulder. "I'm not a psychologist, but I would say yes. More than likely he gets off on the power aspect, having the women completely at his mercy."

Cam grimaced. "Anything else?"

"Bleach." The doctor shook his head. "Just like the others, there's evidence of sexual assault but no bodily fluids. He scrubbed her down afterward to obliterate any evidence."

The man was practiced at this, which didn't bode well. It also meant he'd done extensive research before killing these women, or he'd been doing it long before the first victim had been found.

At least it answered one question, though—the murders appeared to be connected, despite the different manners of death. While Jayla had been asphyxiated, Hilary had died of what appeared to be natural causes. The Sheriff's Department had never leaked the full details of the women's deaths, so the general populace had no idea that he'd used bleach to obliterate any evidence.

"Thanks for your time, doc. Send me a copy of the report when you get a chance, and let me know if you find anything else."

The doctor nodded his assent, and Cam headed out of the medical examiner's office, thoughts swirling through his mind. How was the man choosing his victims? How did he know they didn't have family, no boyfriends, or roommates?

He could only assume that meant he knew the women, at least in passing. The killer probably watched them, studied their every move for days if not weeks before approaching them.

This case was becoming more disturbing by the moment. Had Hilary miscarried early in her pregnancy, or had she given birth? There was no sign of a baby at the scene, so it was possible that whoever had abducted Hilary had done something with the child.

It was possible the person had kept the child, but it was just as likely that the pregnancy had come as a surprise to them. Maybe she'd given birth and the perpetrator had given the baby away. Cam made a mental note to check with local agencies to see if an infant had recently turned up anonymously.

His stomach twisted as he pulled away from the ME's office. They needed to find the women's abductor, and fast, before Lindsey became the next victim.

CHAPTER
THIRTY

The trees lining the street swayed gently in the breeze, and birds chirped merrily from their perches overhead. He parked his cruiser in front of the living facility, his gaze scanning the surface. Yvonne had told her Aunt Agnes he was coming—he just hoped like hell she could give him some answers.

Inside the facility, the receptionist directed him to the correct room, and Cam made his way down the winding hallways to room 46. He knocked, and after a few moments, the door creaked open. A petite, elderly woman with kind eyes and a welcoming smile stood in the doorway.

"Lt. McCoy, right?" she asked, her voice slightly thready with age.

"Yes, ma'am," Cam replied, offering a reassuring smile. "Thank you for agreeing to speak with me, Mrs. Duncan."

"Please, call me Agnes," she said, stepping aside to let him in. "Come in, come in. Would you like some tea?"

"Tea would be great, thank you," Cam said, stepping into the cozy living room. Agnes shuffled into the kitchen to prepare the tea, and Cam took the opportunity to glance around. A large floral couch took up most of the living space, and old photographs dotted various surfaces.

Agnes returned with a tray holding a teapot and two delicate china cups. She set it down on the coffee table and poured them each a cup before settling into her armchair. "So, Lieutenant," she began, "what can I help you with?"

Cam took a sip of the tea, savoring the warmth before responding. "I'm looking into the disappearance of Misty Collins, and I understand you lived across from them at the time."

"Sure did." She nodded and took a sip of her tea, a slight palsy to her movement. "They were a beautiful family, so happy together... Until they weren't."

"Did Dennis and Misty ever argue?"

"Oh, no." She laughed. "Those two were a perfect match. Dennis made a good choice for his second wife. The first one, not so much."

Cam tipped his head. "What happened to his first wife?"

She waved a hand in the air. "She took off when David was just a little thing. She was young, felt like she missed out on her childhood, so she ran off to some big city."

The corners of her lips turned down. "I think that's what hurt Dennis the most when Misty took off. He never expected it."

"Can you tell me what you remember about that day?"

"I saw her leave that afternoon. I was sitting in the living room watching my shows. The window looked right out over the street." She took another sip of tea. "It never made sense until I heard she was missing, but..." She trailed off with a little shake of her head. "I was never sure."

Cam tipped his head. "What's that?"

"Well..." She hesitated for a long moment. "I don't think Misty was alone when she left."

"There was another person in the car?"

Agnes nodded, looking pained. "At first I thought it was Dennis, but the build wasn't quite right. I didn't get a look at his face, mind you, but I'm positive it was a man."

"Did you tell the police?"

"Later." She nodded. "After things settled down a bit. But it made sense that she was running away, if she was having an affair and all."

"Did you ever see a man at the house?"

"Never." She shook her head. "It caught me so off guard, I didn't want to believe it at first. I thought my mind was playing tricks on me, but I know what I saw."

"You have no idea who it might have been?"

"Sorry." She shook her head again. "I didn't have my glasses on. I remember thinking it was strange at the time, but a few hours later I heard about her leaving, and... Well, you know the rest."

"Dennis was supposedly at work that day. Did he happen to come home for lunch?"

"No." She shook her head. "He always stayed at the factory during lunch. Sometimes David would come home."

"David?" Cam's brow lifted at the mention of Misty's stepson. "He came home for lunch?"

"Only once in a while, but school wasn't as strict back in those days. And it's a short walk to their house."

"What can you tell me about David?"

Agnes nodded slowly, her expression lightening a bit. "He adored her, you know. Wherever Misty was, you'd find David close by." She chuckled. "He was like a puppy, that one."

"So he and Misty got along okay?"

"Like two peas in a pod. David didn't have a maternal figure growing up, and Misty really took him under her wing. He was completely enamored of her."

Her eyes grew distant as she recalled the past. "It was a difficult time. Misty was such a kind woman. She didn't deserve what happened."

"Do you remember if David was around on the day Misty disappeared?" Cam pressed, leaning forward slightly.

Agnes frowned, her brows knitting together in concentration. "Not that I remember. I'm sure the police asked him the same thing at the time."

"I'm sure they did," Cam said placatingly. "I was just hoping if he was around, he might have seen or heard something."

"I don't remember seeing him," Agnes replied, "but I suppose anything is possible. He might have come through the backyard. He did that sometimes."

"You said you were watching your shows when Misty left—do you remember what time that was?" The report didn't state an exact time, and Cam was curious if it coincided with the school's lunch hour.

She tipped her head in thought. "Maybe one o'clock?"

"Is that what time David would come home for lunch?"

"Oh, heavens no." She let out a little laugh. "They started the day so early, they would eat around ten or eleven, if I remember correctly."

Damn. Even if David had come home for lunch, Misty had left almost a full two hours later. Still, maybe he'd noticed something about her behavior that day that could help. "Thank you, Mrs. Duncan. I really appreciate you taking the time to speak with me."

He thanked Agnes for her help and promised to keep her informed of any developments. As he left the facility, Cam couldn't shake the feeling that he was onto something. He drove back to the station, replaying Agnes's words in his mind.

Once he'd settled at his desk, Cam reached for his phone and dialed Collins's number again. One ring rolled into two, then finally sent him to the same automated voice messaging system. He hung up and tapped the phone against his lips. Had David seen something that day?

His fingers moved swiftly over the keyboard as he typed "David Collins" into the employee database. The search yielded a list of possible matches, and Cam honed in on David's most recent place of employment: a construction company named Ridgeway Builders. He picked up the phone and dialed the number listed on the screen.

"Ridgeway Builders, this is Amanda. How can I help you?" a cheerful voice answered.

"Good morning, Amanda. This is Lieutenant Cam McCoy with the Brookhaven Sheriff's Department. I'm trying to get in touch with one of your former employees, David Collins. I haven't been able to reach him, and I'm hoping you can help."

There was a brief pause before Amanda replied. "I'll transfer you to his former supervisor, Mr. Harlan. Please hold."

A minute later, a gruff voice came on the line. "This is Frank Harlan. What can I do for you, Lieutenant?"

"Mr. Harlan, I'm looking for David Collins. I understand he worked for you recently."

"That's right. David was with us until a few weeks ago."

Cam jotted down notes as he continued, "I've been trying to get in touch with him but haven't had any luck. Do you happen to know where he might be?"

Frank sighed, a sound of regret and resignation. "David quit suddenly. Said he had some personal issues to sort out. I tried to get more information out of him, but he was pretty tight-lipped. Mentioned he was planning to move, but didn't specify where."

"Did he leave any forwarding address or contact information?"

"Afraid not, Lieutenant. He cleared out his locker and left without much of a word. I wish I could be more helpful."

"Anything at all you can remember might help us. Did he seem different before he left? Any changes in behavior or anything that stood out?"

Frank hesitated before answering. "He seemed more on edge, but I just chalked it up to stress. Construction work's not for everyone."

Cam thanked Frank and ended the call, a sense of unease settling in his chest. He needed to speak with David now more than ever.

CHAPTER
THIRTY-ONE

Laden down with bags, Kinley strolled out of the office supply store armed with colorful markers, notebooks, and classroom decorations for the upcoming school year. A wave of excitement washed over her. Organizing her classroom was one of her favorite rituals, a fresh start for both her and her students.

Dusk had fallen, and lights blazed brightly overhead in the parking lot. She quickly skimmed the rows of cars, trying to remember where she'd parked. Finding her vehicle a few rows down, she stepped off the sidewalk and cut across the lot.

She felt better than she had in weeks. Everything was finally falling into place with her house, and soon she would need to find a new place to live. And that brought to mind a whole new issue—where to go next. She'd been thinking a lot about both Ainsley and Cam's offers to stay with them. Ainsley was getting married soon, but they had the extra space, and Kinley could come and go without disturbing them. And Cam...

She swallowed hard. Over the past couple of weeks since she'd been released from the hospital, she hadn't allowed herself to really examine the feelings that had swamped her when she'd been injured, but now it hit her harder than ever. Something seemed... different with Cam.

There had been a moment at the wedding when she swore he was about to say something. And what was that joke about getting marred? That was a joke... right?

Her pulse raced just thinking about it. Was he serious? He'd been more protective than ever, constantly calling or stopping by to check in. It was nothing she wasn't used to, but sometimes she caught him watching her when he thought she wasn't looking. And that look in his eyes, like he couldn't tear his gaze away from her...

So lost in her thoughts, she was completely caught off guard when a hard hand wrapped around her throat. "Scream and I'll kill you."

The shock paralyzed her for a split second. She felt the cold steel of a knife pressed against her side, and a gruff voice hissed in her ear, "Do what I say, and you won't get hurt."

She had no idea where the man had come from, but he must have been waiting for someone to come out of the store. Kinley quickly glanced around the parking lot, wondering if anyone would hear her if she tried to scream.

She tried to lift her hands in a placating gesture, but the weight of the bags pulled them down. "I'll do whatever you want."

"Give me your purse and keys."

She dropped her hands, shaking them free of the plastic bags encircling her wrists, and shrugged her purse from her shoulder. She didn't want to touch him—didn't want to even look at him. Doing as he ordered, she dropped everything to the ground where he could easily grab it.

"Good."

She bit her lip as the blade of the knife dug into her side, and the man bent to scoop up her keys that lay at their feet. Kinley risked another quick look around. People moved around inside the store behind the brightly lit windows, but she couldn't see a single person in the parking lot.

One black-gloved hand palmed the key fob and pressed a button, and a moment later, the trunk released and popped open.

Fear skittered through her. "Please, whatever you want, it's—"

Before she could finish, his hand wound tightly in her hair, jerking her head back. From this angle, face tilted toward him, she could see that he wore a ski mask that covered everything except his eyes and mouth. She searched his features, but it was almost impossible to distinguish exactly what color his eyes were as they glared into her own.

"Shut the fuck up. Say another word and I'll slit your throat right here."

She flinched at his words and nodded shakily. Tears sprang to her eyes as he tightened his grip on her hair to prove his point, then thrust her toward the car.

"Get in the trunk!" he growled, yanking her toward the open space. Kinley's heart pounded as she struggled against his iron hold. She saw the desolate lot stretching out before her, the shopping complex just a sprint away.

Her gaze darted toward the trunk, then back to him. She couldn't get inside. If she did, she was dead for sure. Her mind seemed to slow down as she fought to figure out what to do. Her thoughts scrambled, and her feet remained frozen to the asphalt.

"Get in!"

The man gestured with the knife toward the trunk, and she took advantage of the split-second distraction. She threw her weight backward, trying to push her assailant off balance. The man tightened his grip, his knife slicing into her forearm as she twisted in his grasp. The pain was sharp and immediate, but it fueled her desperation.

With a surge of adrenaline, she stomped hard on the man's foot, forcing him to loosen his grip. She spun around and struck out with her elbow, hitting him square in the jaw.

He let out a grunt of surprise and pain as he stumbled into the SUV behind him. Kinley didn't waste a second. She bolted toward the shopping complex, her injured arm throbbing with each step as she zigzagged through the parking lot, weaving between cars to put as much distance between herself and her attacker as possible.

"Help! Someone help me!" she screamed, her voice raw with terror. Her legs burned as she sprinted across the hot asphalt, each stride taking her closer to safety.

Kinley's fear propelled her forward, and she could see the figures of people pouring out of the stores, their heads turning toward her cries. She stumbled into the crowd, gasping for breath, her injured arm throbbing dully.

Pushing past a group of people, she threw the door open and dashed inside, looking around frantically. Ignoring the surprised looks the patrons inside sent her way, she launched herself toward the check-out counter. "I need help! I... I was attacked outside in the parking lot, and I dropped my purse so I don't have a phone, and I need to call for help..."

She took a moment to drag in a breath as the attendant looked on with concern. "Can I... Can I use your phone?"

He immediately maneuvered around the counter, then gestured toward the back of the store. "Come with me."

He flicked a quick look around the room like he was searching for the man who had accosted her outside.

"You'll be safe in here," he assured her as he led her

into a small break room. "Do you want me to send one of the ladies back here to sit with you?"

It took a moment for her mind to slow down and try to process the question. She appreciated the gesture, but she shook her head. "No. I just need a phone."

He seemed to understand how rattled she was, because he kept a healthy distance between them as he moved toward a cordless phone on the desk. He picked up the handset and extended it toward her, and she accepted it with shaking fingers as he moved toward the doorway once more.

Her entire body shook as she listened to one torturously slow ring, followed by another. Finally, a familiar voice filled the line.

"Campbell McCoy."

"Cam, it's... it's me."

"Kins?" His tone was drenched with a combination of worry and concern. "What's wrong?"

"I..." She swallowed hard, trying to remain calm, but she was sure that Cam would read right through it. "I'm at the office supply store. Somebody came after me in the parking lot, and I—"

"Are you safe?"

His tone was strong and clear, and it helped to ground her a bit. "Y-yes. I'm in the manager's office."

"Did you call the police yet?"

"N-no." Her teeth chattered. "Not yet."

"I'll take care of it," he promised. "Just stay where you are, and I'll be there in fifteen."

"Okay," she whispered. "See you then."

She clicked off the phone and set it on the edge of the desk, then curled up in the chair, wrapping her arms around her legs.

She was wrong. Whatever was happening at her house, it wasn't getting better. It had just gotten worse.

CHAPTER
THIRTY-TWO

Cam hit the parking lot running. A hundred different scenarios had flitted through his mind on the drive here, all of them involving some kind of bodily harm. She sounded healthy enough, but still... He wouldn't be able to relax until he saw her with his own eyes.

Inside the store, he flashed his badge to the store manager who led him to the break room, then left Cam to speak with Kinley alone. His lungs felt tight, his chest so constricted that he couldn't drag in a full breath until he saw her sitting in a chair beside the desk, looking small and vulnerable as hell.

Thank God, whatever had happened must have just scared her, because she didn't appear to be hurt in any way. Whatever it was had to be serious, though—Kinley wasn't the type to make a big deal of nothing. In fact, she tended to downplay things, so it made him even more curious to find out what the hell had happened.

He stopped a foot away, scanning every inch of her from head to toe. His chest constricted as he peered down into those big blue eyes. "Are you okay?"

She nodded but didn't say a word, and he extended a hand her way. She slipped her palm into his and stood, moving instinctively toward him. A moment later she leaned into him, giving him all of her weight, and he pulled her into his embrace. Keeping one arm locked around her lower back, he buried his free hand in her hair as she tucked her face into his chest.

He wondered if Kinley could hear his heart slamming against his ribs where she rested against him, her cheek pressed to the space over his heart.

Her body shook but she didn't cry, and neither of them said a word for what felt like forever. The silky curtain of hair tickled his skin, and he slid his hand down to cup the back of her neck. Her face lifted, and he brushed a lock of hair away from her cheek. "Don't ever scare me like that again."

She nodded again, and Cam shifted her against her side, keeping one arm wrapped protectively around her shoulders. "Can you tell me what happened?"

A shiver racked her body, and she fixed her gaze to a spot on the floor before continuing. "I was walking out to my car, and I'd just unlocked it when a man came out of nowhere. He was... He had a mask and gloves, and he pointed a knife at me and told me to get in the trunk."

His blood boiled, and a red haze bled into his vision at the thought of anyone pulling a knife on her.

His grip on her tightened. "What did you do?"

Her gaze slowly rose from the floor, over his feet and legs and finally up to his face. "I hit him."

His eyes widened with surprise, and he saw a tiny flicker of a smile dancing at the corners of her mouth. "I—I stomped on his foot and hit him as hard as I could, then ran inside."

Most people, men and women alike, would have followed the man's instructions and climbed right into the trunk, hoping that he would eventually let them go. But not Kinley.

Now that the fear had finally begun to recede, pride glowed brightly in her eyes, and she straightened away from him. He stared down at her as she slipped her palm into his. He squeezed her fingers gently before lifting both hands to cup her face.

"You gave him hell, honey." He stroked her hair, her cheeks, every inch of her pretty face, thanking every deity known to man that she was okay. "I'm proud of you."

"Thanks." A real smile finally broke through, and his heart seized in his chest.

He hated to abandon her now, but there were some loose ends that needed to be tied up before they could leave. "Will you be okay here for a few minutes? I need to speak with the manager."

Understanding lightened her eyes, and she gave a sharp nod. "I'll be fine."

He gave her hand a quick squeeze before pulling away. "I'll be right back."

Cam left the office and wound his way down the stark white hallway toward the store. He caught the manager's gaze and tipped his head, indicating for the man to join him. "I understand you have cameras covering the parking lot?"

The manager, Roy, nodded, already turning to lead the way. "Yes, yes we do. Follow me."

They retraced their steps down the hallway until they reached a small office across from the break room where Kinley currently sat waiting. Roy fumbled with a set of keys before unlocking the door.

The office was cramped, filled with stacks of papers, old receipts, and a couple of outdated computer monitors. Roy gestured to one of the screens, where a grainy black-and-white feed from the parking lot was displayed.

"Here it is," Roy said, tapping a few keys to bring up the recorded footage from earlier that day. "This should be around the time it happened."

Cam leaned in, watching intently as the footage played. The camera's angle covered a wide section of the parking lot, but the resolution was poor. He could see Kinley walking to her car, carrying a few bags. Suddenly, a figure emerged from behind another vehicle, moving swiftly toward her.

"Can you zoom in on the attacker?" Cam asked.

Roy shook his head. "This is as good as it gets, I'm afraid."

They watched as the figure approached Kinley. There were no distinguishing features, just a dark silhouette. The attacker grabbed her, and there was a brief struggle. She fought back fiercely, kicking and striking at the man. Cam's heart pounded as he saw her break free and run toward the store, her face a mask of terror.

The man didn't pursue her. Instead, he turned and fled in the opposite direction, disappearing out of the camera's range.

"Damn it," Cam muttered. "No clear image, no license plate, nothing."

Roy nodded solemnly. "I'm sorry, Lieutenant. I wish I could offer more."

Cam sighed, running a hand through his hair. "It's not your fault. We'll have to work with what we have."

He turned to the young officer. "Get a copy of this footage and distribute it to all units. Maybe someone will recognize the way he moves, or his build. It's a long shot, but it's all we've got."

As the officer set to work, Cam turned back to Roy. "Thank you for your help. We'll need to keep in touch in case anything else comes up."

Roy nodded. "Of course, anything you need."

Leaving the office, Cam couldn't shake the frustration gnawing at him. Kinley had escaped, but her attacker was still out there. The image of her terrified face replayed in his mind, fueling his determination to find the man responsible.

Striding toward the parking lot, Cam dug his phone from his pocket and dialed Dare. The sheriff answered on the fourth ring, his voice tired. "Yeah?"

"We have a small issue." Cam's gaze swept the parking lot, quickly finding Kinley's car. "Kinley was attacked this evening."

Cam relayed the story to Dare as he gathered the things Kinley had dropped in the parking lot. "We checked the cameras but didn't get shit."

"Did she see anything?"

Cam transferred the bags and her purse to the back seat of his car. "Not that she could remember, but I'll ask her again later when she's calmed down a bit."

On the other end, Dare swore softly. "Have you found anything else on Hayes?"

"Not yet."

"I'll reach out to a few local departments, see if anyone's seen him. In the meantime, keep an eye on her."

"Will do." Cam disconnected then headed back into the store. He rapped quietly on the break room door before opening it.

Kinley's wide eyes met his, and he forced a small smile. "Ready to go?"

She nodded and pushed from the chair, and he settled a hand on her lower back as he guided her from the room. Outside, she paused. "Oh! I completely forgot—"

"It's fine." He waved her off. "I already got all your stuff."

Relief flooded her expression. "Thanks."

He nodded. "Are you up for driving home? If not, I'll make arrangements to have your car brought back."

She blew out a shaky breath. "I can probably manage..."

He scrutinized her for a moment before shaking his head. "Let me drive. We'll stay at my place tonight."

"Okay."

She moved a little closer, crowding into his side, and Cam tightened his hold on her. "Don't worry. We're going to figure out what the hell is going on."

CHAPTER
THIRTY-THREE

Cam's grip tightened slightly on Kinley's elbow as he led her up the steps to his front door. He could still feel the adrenaline coursing through his veins, and his mind was a maelstrom.

He pushed open the door and gently guided her inside. The warmth of the house enveloped them, a stark contrast to the chill of the night outside. He moved to the end table and turned on the lamp before guiding her to the couch. She sat automatically when he pressed a hand to her shoulder, but her body trembled with remnants of fear.

He squatted next to her. "You holding up okay?"

"I feel so cold." She glanced up at him and briskly rubbed her upper arms. "Like I can't get warm."

Cam nodded. "Why don't you go take a hot shower? I'll make you a cup of tea while you're in there."

She nodded and swallowed hard but made no move

to get up. He lightly grasped her hands and pulled to her feet. "Come on, sweetheart. I'll get the water going for you."

He wrapped one hand around her elbow, and Kinley sucked in a sharp breath. Cam immediately froze, his hand falling away. "What's wrong?"

"It's nothing."

She shook her head, but a glance at his hands showed a crimson stain on his fingers. Shock rolled through him. "Kins, you're bleeding."

She looked down at her dark sweater and bit her lip. "I know."

He stared at her for a second. "Why didn't you tell me?"

She glanced down, avoiding his gaze. "I didn't want to go back to the hospital," she admitted, her voice barely above a whisper.

Cam understood. The hospital was the last place she wanted to be after the ordeal she'd just been through. He gave a small nod. "I get it. Let's take care of it here then."

Inside the bathroom, he guided her toward the counter.

"Sit here," he said, helping her onto the top of the vanity. She had a smear of dirt on one cheek, and he tenderly swiped it away before pulling out a bottle of antiseptic, a tube of ointment, and a roll of bandages.

Kinley hesitated for a moment, then started to pull her sweater over her head. Her movements were slow and cautious, and a wince creased her face as the fabric tugged at the cut on her forearm. Cam stepped forward to help, gently easing the sleeve down her arm, then pulling the sweater over her head.

She wore only a black satin bra beneath, and he quickly averted his gaze, swallowing hard as he dropped the garment to the floor and turned his attention to her arm.

He saw the wound clearly now—a shallow cut, already starting to clot but still angry and red. She was lucky it wasn't worse.

"This might sting a bit," he warned as he soaked a cotton pad with antiseptic. She nodded, flinching only slightly when he cleansed the wound.

"You're doing great," he murmured, pitching his voice low and soothing.

He applied a thin layer of ointment over the wound before wrapping it with a bandage. He kept his touch gentle, his motions cautious, making sure not to wrap it too tightly. "There," he said, securing the end of the bandage. "That should do it."

Kinley nodded, a small smile tugging at the corners of her lips. "You're pretty good at this," she said, her tone teasing.

Cam chuckled. "Comes with the territory," he replied as he lowered her to the ground. "Let's get you into the shower."

He reached for the shower handle and turned it on with a flick of his wrist. Kinley moved in front of him and extended one hand under the spray, testing its warmth.

He couldn't say what prompted him to do it. Maybe it was the residual fear he'd felt from the evening; maybe it was the culmination of everything that had happened over the past two years. But he surprised them both when he slid his hands onto the curve of her waist, then dipped his head and kissed the slope of her shoulder.

For the briefest moment Kinley tensed; in the next second, she turned to putty in his hands. Her head dropped back as he grew bolder, trailing kisses along the base of her neck and up the side of her throat. Kinley turned at the same time he curled his arms around her, their mouths unerringly meeting in a clash of fiery need.

She buried her hands in his hair as his mouth slanted over hers. One hand coasted downward and fisted in his shirt, and she yanked on the hem. Between kisses, he managed to pull it up and off before attacking her bra. He practically ripped the material in his haste to get it off her, and he let out a low growl as her full breasts filled his palms.

Her fingers tightened in his hair as he dipped low and took her nipple between his teeth, then sucked hard. She arched into him and he grabbed her ass, grinding into her. Kinley's eyes fluttered closed and her teeth cut into her bottom lip as myriad sensations played across her face.

Cam shoved his jeans down, then stripped her out of her shorts and scooped her into his arms. His mouth fused to hers once more as he stepped into the shower, dousing them under the warm spray. Kinley wrapped her legs around his back and shifted her hips, digging in her heels as she positioned herself over him. He slid deep, heart racing as he pinned her to the slick wall.

A thousand emotions volleyed inside him as he drove into her, lifting and lowering her until she finally broke on a ragged cry, fingernails digging into his shoulders. He kissed her hard as contentment and pleasure swept over him and everything else around him faded except the feel of the woman in his arms.

CHAPTER
THIRTY-FOUR

Cam raked one hand over his face, a combination of fury and regret welling up inside his chest. They'd interviewed Kinley this morning regarding the incident in the parking lot last night, but she wasn't able to recall anything of value.

Once they were done, Cam had requested that her sister, Ainsley, come pick her up since Kinley's car was still in the parking lot of the office supply store.

He shook his head. "Kinley told me she was having issues at the house. I just... I didn't believe her at first. I thought after the whole thing with Joel..."

Sawyer offered a sympathetic smile from where he sat behind his desk. "I understand. What did she say?"

"At first, she thought it was her head injury, that she was forgetting things." Cam shook his head. "I should have known. I downplayed it at first, because, hell... She's been through a lot, and I thought she was just stressed. But then she mentioned the handyman she'd hired—Hayes."

Sawyer's eyes flicked down to the papers strewn across the desk in front of him, and he nodded. "He would've had access to her house, could have maybe gotten a copy of her key or something. But according to Kinley, he supposedly disappeared the day after she hired him and hasn't been seen for weeks."

"Right," Cam said, brows furrowed. "But if he was in her house, he could have taken whatever he wanted and been gone before she even knew it."

Sawyer contemplated that for a moment. "What would he have to gain from scaring her?"

"I have no idea." Cam spread his hands wide. The same thought had been circulating through his brain for the past twelve hours. "Why the sudden escalation? Why go from moving things at the house to trying to abduct her?"

"You're sure it's the same person?"

Can snorted. "Of course not. She says she didn't see the man in the parking lot. But who the hell else could it be?"

"Her ex."

Sawyer lifted a brow his way, and Cam paused. Had he been thinking more clearly, he would have considered the possibility before now. Ted and Kinley had broken up a few months ago; what reason would he have to scare her like that? It didn't make sense. Besides, that wasn't Ted's style. He was a smarmy prick, but he gravitated toward emotional manipulation, not abduction.

Cam shook his head. "They didn't part on good terms, but Ted doesn't have the balls to pull off something like that."

Sawyer lifted a shoulder. "We saw what happened when Ainsley left Parsons..."

That was true. Then again, that situation was entirely different. Joel had been openly abusive and possessive; Ted was just an entitled prick who threw a tantrum when he didn't get his way. "Maybe, but it doesn't feel right. I don't see the motive."

"Is there anyone else who might hold a grudge against her?"

"Aside from Hayes—who she already told you about—and her ex, I can't think of anyone." Cam shook his head. "She's a teacher, but school is out."

"No disgruntled parents of students?"

"Not that she's ever mentioned."

Sawyer nodded. "So we're back to square one. Kinley has issues with the house, then all of a sudden she's being abducted from a parking lot. That's a huge jump."

"Someone obviously wants to scare her—but why?" Cam sank back in the chair and steepled his fingers, deep in thought.

"When did it all start?"

"As far as I know, just a couple weeks after she hired

Hayes. He's our best suspect at the moment, but I haven't been able to find the asshole."

Sawyer made a face. "You think maybe he took her money, thought he could scare her away and come back for more?"

"He could have robbed her at any time." Cam shook his head. "Why do something public like try to abduct her?"

"Hell, I don't know." Sawyer scrubbed a hand over his face. "There has to be something we're missing."

Cam threw himself back in the chair, thoroughly disgusted. "We need to find Hayes first and see what the hell he knows."

"Why don't you go by his house again, see if anyone's seen him." Sawyer pushed out of the chair and grabbed his jacket, then slipped it on. "I'll pay Ted a visit and see where he was last night."

Cam left the station and headed once more to Hayes's house. He couldn't shake the feeling of unease that lingered. The pieces of the puzzle were all there— they just didn't quite fit.

CHAPTER
THIRTY-FIVE

Cam's phone vibrated on the nightstand, yanking him from a deep, contented sleep. As soon as he blinked into the darkness, he knew something was wrong. Grabbing up his phone, he glanced through bleary eyes at Dare's name.

He swiped his thumb across the screen. "Yeah?"

"We've got a homicide."

Fuck. Dread settled in his gut, and he grimaced. "Same as the others?"

"Male this time."

He blew out a breath as something like relief washed over him. At least it wasn't another woman. "Where?"

"Cam?"

Kinsey's sleepy voice drifted toward him, and he caught her small hand as it coasted over his chest. He gave her fingers a soft squeeze. "Everything's fine, honey. Go back to bed."

On the other end, Dare snorted. "That didn't take long. Tell Kinley I said hi."

"Fuck off."

Dare chuckled. "I'll send directions to your phone."

"Thanks. Be there as soon as I can." Cam hung up and rolled to face Kinley, who was now propped on one elbow, blinking sleepily at him.

"What's wrong?"

"Nothing to worry about." He leaned in and kissed her forehead. "It's still early; go back to sleep for a while. I'll see you after work, okay?"

"Okay." She nestled back into the covers. "Be safe."

Those sweet words tugged at his heart strings, and he couldn't resist the urge to steal one more kiss. "I will. See you later, Kins."

"Okay," she murmured around a yawn, already drifting to sleep again.

A smile tugged at his mouth as he reluctantly pushed from the bed. He wanted nothing more than to climb right back in beside her, but there was a crime scene waiting—and the sooner it was sorted it out, the sooner he could get back to her.

Nearly twenty minutes later, he pulled up to the scene. A cruiser sat at the mouth of the alley, lights bouncing off the windows of the surrounding buildings. Cam recognized Forester's form nearby as he parked the car and killed the engine.

Cam nodded his way as he climbed out of the car. "I assume the medical examiner has been contacted?"

"Yep. He should be here soon. Not that we'll need any help identifying the cause of death," he said dryly. "Single gunshot wound to the head. Probably close range from the look of it."

The narrow beam of the flashlight bobbed in front of them as they made their way down the narrow alley, following the low hum of voices that floated toward them on the quiet morning air.

"I'm going to wait for the ME," Forester said, hitching a thumb over his shoulder toward the road. "I'll bring him over as soon as he gets here."

"Thanks." Cam gave him a clipped nod, then made a beeline for Dare. The officers had assembled near the entrance to an old brick building, and one of the deputies was busy marking off the crime scene as Cam approached.

Dare was speaking with another of the men from night shift, and he caught Cam's eye as he approached. Dare slapped the man on the back before breaking away and heading toward him.

"Hey." He dipped his chin at Dare as he drew even with him. "What do we know so far?"

"Not much." Dare shook his head. "A homeless man found him about an hour ago when he went into the building. As soon as he saw the body, he went to the station to report it."

"Any idea how long he's been here?"

"I'm guessing it's been a while." He grimaced. "Webb is working on getting an ID."

The arrival of another vehicle drew their attention, and Cam swiveled toward the medical examiner as the older man collected his things, then headed toward them.

"Doc," he greeted the older man. "Sorry to start your day this way."

Dr. Seidel offered a tired smile. "This is getting a little too frequent for my taste."

"Same here," Dare commiserated as he ducked beneath the crime scene tape, then led the way toward the building.

Inside, the doctor took one look at the victim, then glanced between Dare and Cam, surprise etched into his aged features. "I have to say, this is different. I was expecting another female."

"I hate to say it, but I'm relieved it's not." Cam blew out a breath. "That case is a nightmare. Hopefully this will be open and shut."

The doctor nodded as he pulled on a pair of gloves and knelt next to the man sprawled face-down on the rough concrete floor. He gestured to the bullet wound. "I would guess this is the cause of death, but I'll do a full examination to be certain."

Dare nodded. "Time of death?"

"Judging from the state of decomposition," Doc replied as he inspected the man, "I would say several days. Maybe a week or two."

Cam's lips pressed into a firm line as he glanced around, taking in the scene. The floor was dirty, covered with a thick layer of dust in places—but not here. Whoever killed the man had cleaned up after themselves, ensuring that no footprints were left behind.

Webb strode toward them, evidence bag in hand. Inside was a small rectangle, and Cam held it up to see it better. His lips pressed into a firm line as he recognized the driver's license labeled with Corey Hayes's information.

He glanced at the man's face, comparing it to the ID. "That's him."

"Sheriff?" Cam and Dare turned simultaneously toward Duke Turner who stood a dozen feet away. "We've got something over here."

Cam fell into step next to Dare as he crossed the room. In the corner, a subtle glimmer caught his attention. As Cam drew closer, the object began to take shape. With a jolt, he realized it was a small keychain—a silver charm shaped like a star. His heart skipped a beat.

"Fuck."

The epithet slipped out before he could stop it, and Dare turned a concerned glance his way. "You recognize it?"

Cam swallowed hard and nodded. "It's Kinley's."

Expression shuttered, Dare nodded slowly. "You're sure it's hers?"

"Positive." Cam slipped on a pair of gloves, then carefully picked up the keychain by the ring, his mind racing. Why was this here? It made no sense. Kinley wouldn't be involved in something like this. She was kind, responsible, and had no reason to hurt anyone. But seeing the keychain here, at the scene of a murder, was deeply unsettling.

Cam took a deep breath, trying to steady his thoughts. "It doesn't make sense. She would never do something like this. But it does mean Hayes was in her house. He must have taken it."

Dare frowned. "It does look bad, though. We need to talk to Kinley, find out what she knows."

CHAPTER
THIRTY-SIX

Kinley pulled open the door the moment she heard Cam's car pull into the driveway. But when her gaze landed on his face, she froze. The last time she'd seen him look this serious, she'd been in the hospital. She watched him warily as he slowly slid from the driver seat, then strolled up the sidewalk as if he carried the weight of the world on his shoulders.

When he finally met her eyes, worry skittered through her. "What's wrong? Did something happen?"

Panic rose within her at the thought of her sisters or parents being hurt, and she suddenly felt lightheaded. A strong hand curled around her elbow, lending silent strength. "Everyone is fine. Let's go inside."

Cam guided her to the couch and she sat automatically, her gaze fixed on his. He let out a sigh as he sank down next to her.

"I need talk to you about a case we're working on,"

Cam began slowly. "That call I got this morning—it was for a homicide."

Her eyes widened with worry. "I'm sorry. What happened?"

"The man was Corey Hayes."

The wheels in her mind turned the name over and over until it finally clicked. Kinley jerked upright. "Oh, my God. Hayes? The handyman?"

Cam nodded, his expression somber. "Yeah, that Hayes. He was found in an old abandoned building downtown."

Kinley sank back into the couch. "Who would do such a thing?"

He hesitated for a long moment before speaking. "Kins, we found something at the crime scene... Something I think belongs to you."

"Something of mine?" Shock saturated her tone. How could something of hers possibly end up at a crime scene? It didn't make sense.

Cam reached into his pocket and pulled out a small plastic baggie. Her brows drew together as her gaze landed on the silver star keychain inside. He held it out to her, and she stared at it in shock.

"What—?" She shook her head. "I thought I lost it. I..."

She abruptly trailed off as what he'd said earlier sank in. She'd first noticed the keychain was missing after the man had accosted her in the parking lot. But it had somehow ended up at the scene of a murder. How was that possible?

"It was found in the building near Hayes's body," Cam explained gently. "We need to understand how it got there."

Cold washed over her as she tore her gaze from the keychain and glanced up at Cam. "I... I don't know. I mean, I noticed it was missing, but I don't know how long it's been gone."

She hated that her voice trembled as she spoke. She passed the evidence bag back to Cam and wrapped her arms around her waist. Her breaths came too fast, like she couldn't draw in enough air.

"Hayes was working on your house, right? It's possible he took it," Cam said, trying to sound reassuring. "But we need you to come down to the station so we can take your prints."

A sharp pain ricocheted through her heart. "You think I did this? You really think I could be involved in something like this?"

"No, sweetheart, I don't think you had anything to do with it," Cam said soothingly. "It's just procedure."

She stared at him in shock. "Of course my prints are going to be on it. It's my keychain!"

He held up a hand to reassure her. "And that's exactly what we need to know. We need to collect your prints, that way we can narrow down who might be responsible."

She stood up, wrapping her arms around herself to

ward off the chill that had settled deep in her bones. Tears burned across the bridge of her nose as a hollow feeling took root in her chest. Emotion clogged her throat, and she turned away from him, desperately trying to keep him from seeing how deeply his words had affected her. "You know I wouldn't do this."

"I know that," he said, standing as well and taking a step towards her. "I'm not accusing you of anything," he said softly. "I would never do that."

His hand landed on her arm, but she pulled away. Kinley cleared her throat. "Fine. Let's get this over with."

She stalked toward the door, but Cam caught her by the waist and pulled her to a halt. She kept her gaze down as he swiveled her in his arms, unwilling to look at him. He knew her better than anyone. How could he do this to her?

Logically she knew he was just doing his job. He had to be thorough so that the killer didn't get away. But it felt like the sharpest betrayal.

His thumbs slid across her cheeks, swiping the tears away. "I'm so sorry, sweetheart. Please don't cry."

He kissed her forehead, his lips lingering against her skin. "I'm just trying to protect you. The sooner we clear this up, the sooner we can focus on finding the real killer."

"I understand."

She did. Truly. But the hurt didn't abate as she grabbed her keys and purse, then followed him to the car. Silence stretched between them, heavy with unspoken words. The drive to the station was tense, neither of them speaking.

When they arrived at the station, Cam led Kinley inside, the familiar sights and sounds of the precinct feeling suddenly foreign and uncomfortable. He guided her to his office, where Sawyer was waiting to take her prints.

"This won't take long," Cam said, trying to sound reassuring.

They worked quickly, taking her fingerprints and comparing them against the ones found on the keychain. After what felt like an eternity, he nodded to Cam. "I've isolated her prints, which leaves us an unidentified partial to work with."

"Perfect." He turned to Kinley and gave her hand a little squeeze. "That's exactly what we needed."

Kinley nodded, her shoulders sagging. "I'm glad. But this still doesn't explain how my keychain ended up there."

"Do you happen to remember when it went missing?" Sawyer asked.

Kinley shook her head. "I noticed it was gone after..." Her voice cracked, and she started over, gesturing toward Cam. "After Cam picked up my things in the parking lot, I realized it was missing. I figured it fell off or got broken when I dropped my keys."

"Don't worry." Sawyer offered her an encouraging smile. "We'll figure out what's going on. You just stay safe in the meantime, keep an eye on your surroundings and let us know if anything strange happens."

"I will."

Cam looped an arm around her shoulders. "It's been a long day. Let's head home."

God, yes. She liked the sound of that.

CHAPTER
THIRTY-SEVEN

Kinley absently traced the rim of her coffee cup as she stared blankly at the kitchen table. The buttery glow of morning sunlight spilled through the window across from her, illuminating the room with a cheerful glow. But at the moment, she felt anything but cheery.

She'd lain awake most of the night, thinking about everything that had happened over the past couple of weeks. It all seemed to point to Hayes. But if Hayes was dead, then he couldn't possibly be responsible for everything that had been happening. So who was?

Lance.

The realization hit her like a punch to the gut. Lance, the seemingly kind realtor she'd met at the coffee shop... and the hardware store. She thought back to the moment when they'd first met, and how smoothly he'd moved in to offer his assistance.

Because he'd been watching her?

Goosebumps prickled along the backs of her arms, and her stomach revolted. It could be a coincidence—Brookhaven was a small community, after all—but she seriously doubted it. Now, each encounter with him felt like calculated moves on a chessboard, each one placing him in her path.

Had he known all along? What if Lance had been following her, learning her routines, her vulnerabilities? She felt sick just thinking about it.

It made perfect sense. If Lance had been behind the strange occurrences, it would explain everything. He'd given her advice on which particular locks to use; ever since then, she hadn't had any more trouble with the doors.

How could she have been so stupid, so naïve?

The doorbell rang, splintering her attention and sending her pulse skittering in her veins. Oh, God. Was it him? Was it Lance?

The possibility rendered her motionless, frozen in place, and she jumped when the doorbell rang a second time. It felt like a vise had closed around her lungs, making it hard to breathe. She took a tiny step toward the living room, keeping close to the wall, and peeked around the corner. Through the frosted pane of glass in the front door, she spied a male figure standing on the front porch.

Wary, she kept her steps slow and light as she cut

across the room, taking care to stay out of sight. Angling to the side, she peeked out the window. The air bottled up in her lungs rushed out in a whoosh of air.

Damn it. The car sitting in the driveway was undeniably Ted's expensive BMW. Why the hell was he here?

Reluctantly, she opened the door and his familiar smile greeted her, the sight of it twisting her stomach into a knot. "Kinley."

She didn't bother with niceties. "What can I help you with?"

"Well, I..." His gaze skittered away for a second, then landed on her once more. "Can I come in?"

She shook her head. "I don't think—"

"Please." His eyes implored her to listen. "It's about Addie."

Her hatred for Ted was forgotten immediately at the mention of his little girl, and she relaxed her hold on the door. "Is she okay? What happened?"

"She's fine." He gestured toward the interior of the house. "May I?"

"Um..." She bit her lip, debating her options. Finally, curiosity getting the better of me, she stepped back. "Sure."

He stepped inside, and she closed the door behind him. Turning to face him, she watched as Ted walked casually around the living room. She crossed her arms over her midsection and ventured deeper into the room, keeping the couch between them as he examined the room.

He turned toward her, a huge smile on his face. "This place looks amazing. You've worked wonders."

She could count on one hand how many times he'd been in her home. They'd spent most of their time together at his house, because he'd said it was easier. She knew now that he was full of shit. He was ashamed of her, ashamed to be seen in this house with her, as if he were better. Her hackles rose at his backhanded compliment. "Thanks. Cam has been a huge help."

"That's... great." The confidence in his features leached away. "I... I made a mistake, Kinley."

"Oh?" That was a first. She couldn't remember ever hearing Ted admit weakness of any kind—especially where his ego came into play.

Ted turned to face her, his expression earnest. "I've missed you, Kinley. I've been doing a lot of thinking recently, and I realized how perfect we were together. I made a mistake letting you go."

Anger and frustration surged through her. "What are you talking about?"

"I never should have left you." She was so completely taken aback that she had no idea what to say. Ted rushed to fill the silence. "I miss you, sweetheart, I miss what we had together."

This time she couldn't help the mirthless laugh that fell from her lips. "What about Megan?"

"Lauren," he corrected, then waved a hand through the air as her eyebrow ratcheted toward her hairline. "Nevertheless, it's over between us."

What the hell did he expect her to do with this information? He couldn't possibly think he had a chance now, after everything that had happened.

Ted reached for her but she backpedaled, and his face fell. "Lauren and I are no longer together. It wasn't right. I was trying to move on, but I couldn't stop thinking about you."

She shook her head, struggling to keep her composure. "Trying to move on? You told me you'd been seeing her for months before we even split up."

"I would never do that to you," he said, stepping closer. "I was just trying to make you jealous. But I've changed, Kinley. I realize now that you were the best thing that ever happened to me. We were good together, and I want to make things right."

Kinley dropped back a step and shook her head. "I'm with someone else now, Ted. I'm with Cam."

Ted's expression darkened, and a flicker of irritation crossed his face. "Cam? He's your best friend, Kinley. But I love you. We belong together."

She felt a chill run down her spine at the intensity in his eyes. "Ted, please. You need to leave. Cam and I are happy together."

Ted made no move to leave. Instead, he stepped even closer, his presence suddenly feeling suffocating. "No,

Kinley. You don't understand. Cam is just your friend. He doesn't love you the way I do."

Before she could react, Ted reached out and grabbed her arms, his grip firm and unyielding. "Ted, stop it," she said, her voice shaking.

"Just listen to me," he insisted, his face inches from hers. "We can make this work. I know you still have feelings for me."

Kinley tried to pull away, but he held on tighter, his intense gaze unwavering. "Ted, let go of me," she said, panic rising in her chest.

"Come on, sweetheart. Let me show you how good it was."

He leaned in, and she turned her face away, pushing against his chest as hard as she could. "Ted, stop! I'm not—"

Her words were abruptly cut off as Ted's weight lifted away from her body and he was yanked roughly backward. She blinked in astonishment as Cam suddenly appeared and a moment later, Ted hit the ground—hard.

Suddenly, Cam was there, handcuffs snapping into place around Ted's wrists while the man on the floor writhed and pleaded. "Let me go!"

Cam ignored Ted's pleas as he read him his rights. "She told you to stop. You should've listened."

Kinley watched, wide-eyed, as Cam hauled Ted to his feet, then turned him toward the door. He paused halfway across the room and glanced over his shoulder at her. "I need to take care of this, then I'll be home."

He shot her a quick wink, then disappeared, pushing a struggling Ted toward the cruiser. Kinley moved toward the door on autopilot, still rattled from the whole ordeal. Hands shaking, she managed to close the door, then leaned against it and shook her head. What the hell had just happened?

CHAPTER
THIRTY-EIGHT

Once at the station, Cam led Ted into an interrogation room and gestured for him to sit. "The sooner you admit to everything, the sooner we can get you booked."

"I don't know what you think I've done," Ted said as he dropped into the chair, "but it certainly isn't whatever you think it is."

Cam took a seat across from him, fixing Ted with a steely glare. "You forced yourself on her. That's assault. And that's only the beginning in a long list."

Ted scoffed. "I'm not going to sit here and listen to some manufactured list of offenses. I want my lawyer."

"Sure thing." Cam nodded. "But first, tell me something. I'm sure by now you've heard about the trouble Kinley's been having."

Ted tipped his head slightly to one side, apparently unconcerned. "From what I can tell, that was her sister's doing."

Cam's hand clenched into a fist and he forced himself to relax. "Ainsley had nothing to do with it. Her ex attacked Kinley. But that's not what I meant, and we both know it."

Ted's lips lifted in a semblance of a smirk. "Do I, though?"

Rage shuddered through Cam. Next to him, Sawyer sat up straighter, prepared to take over, but Cam spoke up before he had the chance. "First there was the incident downtown. The one where she was almost hit by a car. Then the forced entry to her house."

He stretched the truth a bit on that, but he needed to see Ted's reaction to the information. "Then there was the attempted mugging two nights ago."

Ted's confident expression slipped a bit. "What?"

"Don't play stupid." Cam leaned forward in his chair, pinning the other man with a hard stare. "You really think I believe you showing up at her house today was a coincidence?"

A muscle ticked in Ted's jaw. "I don't have to explain anything to you."

"The hell you don't," Cam snapped. "From where I'm sitting, it looks like a jealous ex-lover trying to target her."

Ted looked away.

"Tell me about the night of the mugging."

Ted shrugged. "I don't know anything about it. I wasn't there."

"Do you have an alibi?" Cam asked, leaning forward.

Ted smirked. "Yeah, actually. I was at Joey's Bar with some friends. I'm sure you can check the security footage if you don't believe me."

Cam noted the confidence in Ted's voice, but he wasn't about to let him off the hook that easily. "We'll see about that."

He nodded at Sawyer, who left the room to verify the man's information.

"In the meantime, do you know anyone who might have a reason to target Kinley?"

Ted's expression shifted slightly, a hint of amusement dancing in his eyes. "You really don't know, do you?"

"Know what?" Cam snapped, his patience wearing thin.

"Hmm..." Ted leaned back in his chair with a smirk. "Interesting."

Cam ground his molars together. "What's interesting?"

Ted laced his fingers together over his stomach and regarded Cam, one insolent eyebrow cocked toward his hairline. "I thought you were besties. Thought Kinley shared everything with you."

"She does." Cam growled. What the hell was this asshole implying? "If you have something to say, say it."

Ted chuckled, a low, mocking sound. "Not sure I

want to tell you. After all, if Kinley hasn't mentioned him..."

Him? Every nerve ending went on alert, a prickling awareness spreading through his body. "What the hell are you talking about?"

"I'm talking about Kinley's new special friend." Ted arched a brow. "Lance. I'm sure you know him."

Cam's fists clenched under the table. He knew Ted was trying to get under his skin, but the fact that Kinley hadn't mentioned this Lance person was unsettling. "Who is Lance?"

Ted leaned forward, his smirk widening. "I ran into Kinley at the coffee shop a couple weeks ago. She was there with him then. They looked pretty cozy."

Cam's mind raced as he processed this new information. Why hadn't Kinley mentioned it? Was she hiding something, or was this just another one of Ted's attempts to stir up trouble?

"You think this Lance is behind the threats and the incident in the parking lot?" Cam asked, trying to keep his voice steady.

"Maybe," Ted said with a shrug. "You should probably ask Kinley about it. But you might want to find out more about Lance first. You know, just in case."

Sawyer reentered the room and dipped his chin in a brief nod, silently conveying that Ted's alibi was solid. Cam bit back a growl. Goddamn it. They were back to square one.

He didn't trust Ted, but he couldn't ignore the

possibility that Lance—whoever the hell he was—was involved. He shoved his chair back and stood, shooting a glare at Ted all the while. "Stay available. We might need to talk again."

Ted smirked as he stood. "Whatever you say, Lieutenant."

The man turned to leave, but Cam refused to let him have the last word. "And, Ted?" He waited until the man turned back to him to speak. "Stay away from Kinley."

A muscle ticked in his cheek, but Ted wasn't stupid enough to argue. With a slight dip of his head, he strode toward the door, and Cam let out a deep breath. He needed to find out who Lance was and why Kinley hadn't mentioned him.

Cam left the station at a fast clip, his mind a tumult of thoughts as he replayed the conversation he'd just had with Ted. The revelation about a man named Lance gnawed at him, leaving him both unsettled and frustrated. Why hadn't Kinley mentioned him before? What else was she hiding?

Determined to get answers, he got into his car and drove to her house, his grip on the steering wheel tightening with every passing mile. At her house, he strode to the front door and knocked hard.

Kinley opened the door just seconds later, as if she'd been watching for him. "Cam? What happened with Ted?"

"Forget about Ted for right now." Cam turned to

face her, his expression hard. "Why don't you tell me about Lance?"

Kinley's eyes widened and she opened her mouth to speak, but Cam cut her off. "Ted told me about him. Said he saw you on a date with this guy at the coffee shop."

"I was—kind of. It was just pretend." Kinley stumbled over the explanation. "I saw Ted there with his new girlfriend, and I was going to leave but then this guy—Lance—walked in and pretended to be my boyfriend, and—"

Cam held up a hand to stall the flow of words. "Who is he?"

"My realtor." Her wide blue eyes peered up at him. "I thought it was so ironic that I ran into him right after you and I talked about selling the house. I didn't think much of it at first, but—"

Cam's gaze narrowed. "What do you mean, 'at first'?"

She swallowed hard. "So, remember when I showed up at your house that night after I ran into Ted at the coffee shop?"

She shot him a guilty look. "That wasn't the whole story. It was nothing major," she continued quickly when he glared at her, "but that was the first time I met Lance."

"You ran into him at the coffee shop?"

"Yeah." She twisted her fingers together. "I walked in and saw Ted with standing there with his new girlfriend. As soon as I saw them, I started to turn around and leave. All of a sudden, this guy—Lance—was there. He pretended to be my boyfriend, and—"

"He *what*?"

"Nothing happened," she rushed to assure him. "It was all to put on a show. He suspected something was off between Ted and me, so he bought me a coffee, pretended we were on a date, then gave me his business card before he left."

Cam ground his molars together, trying not to snap. "And then what happened?"

"Nothing. At least, not right away. But... a few days later I ran into him at the hardware store."

"Jesus, Kins." Worry and anger caused Cam's voice to rise several octaves. "Why the hell didn't you tell me this sooner?"

"I didn't want to seem paranoid. And honestly, I wasn't sure if it was just a coincidence or if there was something more to it," Kinley admitted, indignation fueling her tone.

Cam blew out a hard breath and paced the room, trying desperately to rein in his temper. "So you think he could be the one responsible for the disturbances here? The missing items, the strange noises?"

Kinley nodded slowly. "It makes sense, doesn't it? I mean, he's had access to the house. He knows the layout. And if he's been following me since the very beginning..."

"Then he's had plenty of opportunities to mess with

you," Cam finished, his jaw clenched. "We need to find out more about this guy. If he's involved, we need to know why and what he's planning next."

Kinley's eyes met his, a mix of fear and determination shining through. "What do we do now?"

Cam placed a reassuring hand on her shoulder. "You stay the hell away from him. Don't speak to him, don't take his calls. I'm going to find out whatever I can about him and what his end game is."

CHAPTER
THIRTY-NINE

Cam sat in the small interview room, a cup of coffee growing cold as he studied the man across from him.

"Thanks for coming in, Lance," Cam began. "I just have a few questions for you."

Lance nodded. "Of course, Lieutenant. Anything to help."

"Good," Cam said, leaning back slightly. "Do you know a woman named Kinley Layne?"

Lance's steady gaze held Cam's. "Yes, I know Kinley. She's a client of mine."

Cam nodded. "Where did you meet her?"

"At a coffee shop," Lance replied. "We ran into each other there a few times. I also saw her at the hardware store, and I'm the realtor who listed her home for sale."

Cam somehow managed to keep his expression neutral despite the turmoil swirling in his gut. "That's quite a few places to run into someone."

Lance shrugged one shoulder. "Brookhaven's a small town, Lieutenant. It's not unusual to see the same people in different places."

Cam leaned forward. "Is that so? Did you also know that Kinley has been having some trouble lately?"

Lance's brow furrowed. "I mean... I saw the stitches and all, but I didn't want to ask, you know? She seemed pretty self-conscious about it."

"Someone tried to run her down with a car," Cam said. "And she was almost mugged just a few nights ago."

Lance's eyes widened in shock. "I had no idea. That's terrible."

Cam watched him closely, looking for any sign of deception. "You sure about that? It seems a bit coincidental that you've been around her so much, and now she's in danger."

Lance's face turned red with frustration. "I'm a realtor, Lieutenant. I meet a lot of people, and I run into them around town. Yes, I've seen Kinley at those places, but that doesn't mean I have anything to do with her being in danger."

Cam's eyes narrowed. "So you're saying it's all just a coincidence?"

"Yes," Lance said firmly. "I've got nothing to hide. I've done my job and nothing more."

"And does your job include pretending to be a woman's boyfriend?"

Red swept up the man's neck and face. "Not usually,

no. But she seemed uncomfortable, and I didn't like the look of the guy, so... I figured I would try to help any way I could."

Cam leaned back, silent for a moment, letting the tension build. "All right, Lance. Let's talk about your whereabouts on the days Kinley had her accidents." He rattled them off, one by one. "Can you account for your time?"

Lance took a deep breath. "I can. I was showing houses, meeting clients. I also have regular office hours. I keep a detailed schedule."

"Can anyone verify that?" Cam asked, raising an eyebrow.

"Yes," Lance replied. "My assistant and several clients can vouch for me. I can give you their contact information."

Cam studied him for a long moment, then nodded. "All right, give me the list."

Lance scribbled down the names and numbers on a piece of paper and handed it to Cam, who took it without breaking eye contact.

"Thanks, Lance. We'll be checking your alibi." Cam leaned forward. "One last thing—Would you be willing to submit your fingerprints for the investigation?"

Lance looked surprised but nodded. "Sure. I have nothing to hide."

Sawyer produced a fingerprinting kit and methodically took Lance's prints. "This will only take a moment," Sawyer said before leaving the room to run the prints through the system.

Cam stayed seated, his gaze fixed on Lance. "So, Lance, let's talk more about Kinley. Have you ever been to her house?"

Lance frowned. "Of course. She's a client of mine; I was there to take photos for the listing."

"That's interesting, because Kinley's also experienced trouble at her house. Someone's broken in twice now."

Lance's jaw tightened. "I'm a realtor, for God's sake, not a criminal. I have no reason to break into someone's house."

Cam leaned back, his eyes never leaving Lance's face. "Understand, we have to look at everything. If there's something you're not telling us, now's the time to come clean."

Lance drew in a breath. "I understand that, but I've told you everything. There's nothing more to say."

The door opened, and Sawyer walked back in, his expression grim. He handed Cam a piece of paper. "We got a match," Sawyer said, his voice low.

Cam scanned the report quickly before looking up at Lance. "Care to explain why your fingerprints were found at a crime scene?"

Lance's face drained of color. "What crime scene?"

"A few days ago, Corey Hayes was found murdered in a building downtown," Sawyer said, his eyes narrowing. "Your fingerprints match a partial pulled from a keychain found at a crime scene."

"No." Lance shook his head vehemently. "That's impossible. I had nothing to do with that."

"A keychain belonging to Kinley Layne was found near the victim—and your prints were on it." Cam's voice was cold. "How do you explain that?"

Lance's gaze darted frantically around the room. "I... I don't know. I've never even heard of that guy."

"Do you recognize this?" Sawyer slid a photo of the keychain across the table, and Lance shook his head emphatically.

"I've never seen that."

"Yet your prints are on it?" Sawyer scoffed. "That's a stretch, don't you think?"

"It's the truth," Lance insisted, his voice rising in desperation. "I swear—I would never hurt Kinley, and I certainly wouldn't murder someone."

Cam and Sawyer exchanged a look. He sounded awfully sincere, and he hadn't displayed an ounce of recognition when he saw the keychain.

"All right, Lance," Cam said slowly. "We'll need to take you into custody until we can sort this out."

Lance's face contorted with panic. "No! You can't do this. I didn't kill anyone!"

"We'll see about that," Sawyer said, moving to stand beside Lance. "For now, we'll have to hold you."

As they escorted Lance out of the room, Cam couldn't shake the feeling that there was more to the story. Lance's reaction seemed genuine, but the evidence was damning.

The connections between Lance, Kinley, and the recent troubles in Brookhaven were too strong to ignore. They needed to dig deeper, and fast. He couldn't afford to let anything slip through the cracks—not when lives were at stake.

CHAPTER
FORTY

Kinley couldn't relax. For the past half hour she'd paced around the house, nerves battering her insides. The ringing of her phone split the air, and she grabbed it up. Seeing Cam's name on the screen, she quickly tapped the button to answer. "Did you find anything?"

"We got a match," Cam said, a combination of relief and fatigue saturating his voice. "The partial print on your keychain belongs to Lance Barton."

For a moment, the room spun, and Kinley had to steady herself against the back of the couch. "You're sure?"

"Positive," Cam replied. "We've got him in custody right now."

Kinley nodded, though she knew Cam couldn't see her. "Okay," she managed to say. "Thanks for letting me know."

"Stay safe," he added before the call ended.

Kinley lowered the phone, her mind reeling. He really was involved. It still didn't seem quite real. He seemed so nice... How could he be involved in something so sinister?

A knock on the door startled her, making her jump. Her heart raced as she walked to the door, then peeked through the peephole. A man stood on the front porch, the familiarity of his features tugging at the periphery of her brain.

All of a sudden it clicked. She'd met him the day she'd listed her home. Pulling open the door, she pasted on a smile. "Max. What can I do for you?"

"Hey, Kinley." His easygoing smile gave away to concern. "Is everything okay?"

Kinley forced a smile, though her nerves were still on edge. He must not have heard about Lance yet. "Hey. Sorry, just got some... bad news."

He looked genuinely worried. "I'm sorry to hear that. I hate to do this to you now, but... we had a last-minute showing scheduled for this afternoon."

She blinked at him before realization hit. "Oh! Of course. I—I'll go change and get out of here for a bit."

He shot her a relieved smile. "Thanks, Kinley. And take your time. I'll wait outside until you're ready."

Kinley closed the door and leaned against it for a moment, trying to collect herself. She had trusted Lance, had let him into her home and into her life. The thought that he might have been hiding something so dark made her skin crawl.

She went upstairs and quickly pulled on a pair of jeans and shoved her feet into a pair of flats. As she pulled her hair into a messy bun, she couldn't shake the uneasy feeling that had settled in her stomach.

Something wasn't right.

David Collins stood at the basement door, a key in his hand. He glanced around to make sure no one was watching before slipping the key into the lock. The door opened silently, and he stepped inside, closing it behind him with a quiet click. The dim light from a small basement window cast long shadows, adding an eerie atmosphere to the cluttered space.

He moved quietly through the basement, memories flooding back as he navigated the familiar territory. This had once been his home, and in his mind, it still was. As he moved farther into the basement, his footsteps were light, barely making a sound on the concrete floor.

He reached the stairs and began his ascent, each step careful and measured. The house was quiet, save for the distant hum of a refrigerator and the occasional creak of settling wood. At the top of the stairs, he paused to listen. He could hear soft sounds coming from upstairs —Kinley moving about in her bedroom, likely getting ready to leave as she had mentioned.

He took a deep breath, steeling himself, and moved silently through the hallway. The familiar layout of the house came back to him effortlessly, guiding his steps as he made his way toward the stairs that led to the second floor.

Each step on the wooden staircase was a calculated risk. He placed his weight carefully to avoid the known creaky spots, his ears attuned to any sign that Kinley might hear him. The old house seemed to conspire against him, the wood groaning softly despite his efforts.

Finally, he reached the top of the stairs. Her bedroom door was slightly ajar, allowing him to peek inside. Kinley stood near her dresser, her back to the door, oblivious to his presence. For a moment, he simply watched her.

She was such a beautiful girl. It was such a shame that it had come to this. The secrets he thought he'd buried had come to light. Now it was time to lay the past to rest once and for all.

CHAPTER
FORTY-ONE

"Bad news." The door to Cam's office opened, and Deputy Duke Turner stepped in. "I just got off the phone with the lab. Lance's prints are a match for the ones on the keychain, but his alibi is airtight."

Cam bit back a curse. "That fingerprint was a match. If Lance didn't leave it behind, then how the hell did it get there?"

Hayes was dead. Ted and Lance both had alibis. The logical suspects were falling away, leaving them grasping at straws.

Turner grimaced. "I wish I knew. But there's something else. I still haven't been able to reach David Collins."

His absence was looking more and more suspicious by the minute. "Any financial activity? Credit cards, bank withdrawals?"

"Nothing. It's like he vanished into thin air," Turner replied.

Cam's mind raced. "We need to dig deeper into David's background. Friends, acquaintances, anyone who might have a clue where he could be."

Turner nodded. "I'm on it."

As Turner left the office, Cam leaned back in his chair, staring at the ceiling. Every dead end, every unanswered question, brought him closer to the edge.

He was lost in thought when a knock on the door jolted him back to the present.

"Come in," he called out, looking up to see Deputy Evan Landry stepping inside.

"Someone's here to see you, Lieutenant," Evan said. "She says she's an old friend of Misty's—Tammy Holbrook."

Cam sat up straight in the chair. "Send her in."

A moment later, a middle-aged woman stepped into the room.

"Thank you for seeing me. I heard about Misty's death and... I needed to come. I wanted to know if you have any leads."

Cam gestured for her to sit down, offering a reassuring smile. "We're doing everything we can, but I'm afraid I can't share much at this point. It's still an active investigation."

Tammy nodded. "I get it. I just... needed to know that someone is looking out for her. Misty deserves justice for what happened."

Cam leaned forward, sensing there was more she wanted to say. "If you have any information that may help us..." He trailed off, allowing Tammy to move at her own pace.

She hesitated for a long moment, then took a deep breath. "I don't know if it's relevant or not, but... Misty was pregnant when she disappeared. No one else knew; she was waiting for the right time to tell everyone. She confided in me because she was so excited and couldn't keep it to herself."

Tammy shook her head. "My kids were still young then, too, and I lent her some books on pregnancy and babies. I thought about telling the police at the time, but decided against it. Dennis was torn up enough as it was. He'd lost his wife—he didn't need to know she'd taken his child, too."

Cam absorbed this new detail, thinking about the implications. "Did you ever see those books again?"

Tammy shook her head, her expression troubled. "No. No one ever mentioned them. I figured Misty took them with her when she left. But now... now I'm not so sure."

Cam rested his elbows on the desk, watching Tammy intently. "What can you tell me about Misty's stepson, David Collins?"

Tammy shifted uncomfortably, her gaze dropping to her hands. She took a deep breath before answering, clearly wrestling with her thoughts. "David was..." She swallowed hard, her gaze darting toward the wall. "Well, everyone knew he loved Misty."

"It seems so," Cam said quietly. "Did you ever notice any discord between them?"

Tammy sighed, her fingers twisting together nervously. "No, they never fought. The opposite, in fact. He followed her everywhere. It was like he only had eyes for her. He would often come home for lunch just to spend time with her alone. It was... strange."

Cam's mind raced with possibilities. "Did Misty ever mention feeling uncomfortable about his behavior?"

"She thought he was just a lonely kid who needed attention. But I often wondered if there was something deeper there. His attachment to her..." She shook her head. "It didn't seem healthy."

"Did you ever see anything that made you think their relationship was more than it should be?" Cam asked, his voice low and careful.

Tammy hesitated again, her eyes flickering with uncertainty. "I never saw anything outright inappropriate, but sometimes... The way he looked at her... it gave me chills."

She bit her lip. "I mentioned it to Misty once, but she just laughed it off. I mean, his mother left when he was little, so... maybe she was right."

But she didn't appear convinced, and neither was Cam. "How old was David when Dennis married Misty?"

Her eyes rolled heavenward in thought. "Fourteen or fifteen, maybe?"

His stomach churned violently. "Do you think David knew about the pregnancy?"

"I don't know. As far as I know, Misty didn't tell anyone except me. But if he was as obsessed with her as it seemed..." She made a little face. "He might have figured it out."

"Did Misty ever mention anything about David's behavior getting more intense or troubling?" Cam pressed.

"No." She shook her head. "She always defended him. And I couldn't come right out and ask, you know?"

"I understand." Cam offered a small smile. "Thanks for letting me know. This was a huge help."

"I hope so." Her smile was brittle as she stood. "I hope you find who did this."

"Me, too."

Once she was gone, Cam sank back into his chair, contemplating the implications. David had been a teenager in the throes of puberty. Was it possible he felt more for his stepmother than familial love?

He pushed from his chair and the soft tread of footsteps drew his attention to Sawyer as he entered the office. The detective caught his gaze and stopped dead in his tracks. "What happened?"

"I'm not sure," Cam replied. "But I just had a very interesting visit with an old friend of Misty's."

"Yeah?" Sawyer changed direction as they headed toward Dare's office. "Hopefully we'll get a break."

"Maybe," Cam murmured as he knocked on Dare's door. The sheriff waved them in, and they dropped into the chairs across from him.

Dare turned his attention their way. "What's up?"

"A friend of Misty Collins's just came by."

Dare nodded. "What'd she have to say?"

"For starters... Misty was apparently pregnant when she died."

His eyes flew wide. "Well, that's interesting. Wonder how the stepson felt about that. A lot of kids would feel like they're being replaced with a new baby."

"That's the thing..." Cam gave a slow shake of his head. "According to Tammy, David was very close to Misty—almost obsessively so."

Sawyer frowned. "You think David's feelings for Misty went beyond a normal stepmother-stepson relationship?"

"It's possible." Cam shrugged. "If David was in love with Misty and found out she was pregnant, he might have become jealous of his father. If he felt that Dennis was a threat to his relationship with Misty, it could have led to... something drastic."

Dare arched a brow. "Are you suggesting that David might have had something to do with Misty's murder?"

"It's a theory," Cam said. "Turner and I have been trying to get ahold of him for almost two weeks now, but we can't find him. It can't be a coincidence that we find Misty's body and David just conveniently goes missing at the same time."

Dare's expression darkened. "Get a BOLO issued. I'll work on getting a warrant."

Cam felt a knot tighten in his stomach. The pieces were starting to fit together in a way that painted a disturbing picture. They needed to find David, and fast.

CHAPTER
FORTY-TWO

Just as Kinley took a step toward the doorway, a strange noise drifted toward her. She froze, her pulse sprinting in her veins. She knew that sound—the same soft groan the old wood emitted from the third step from the top of the landing.

Someone was in the house.

Was it Lance? No. She mentally shook off the thought. Cam said they had him in custody. Pulse pounding rapidly in her ears, she tentatively ventured forward just as another almost inaudible creak of wood met her ears. She peered around the doorframe and her gaze collided with Max's dark eyes.

For a moment, neither of them moved. Her mind spun with confusion. He'd said he was going to wait outside—and she'd locked the door...

Hadn't she?

She opened her mouth to speak, but the words jumbled on her tongue. Her gaze slid over his face, then lower. The sight of the key in his hand stopped her cold. Confusion gave way to deep, icy fear.

Her gaze jumped back to his, and the look in his eyes, once seemingly kind, now glinted with a dark intent that sent a chill down her spine.

Panic surged through her veins, and without another word, she slammed the door close, throwing all her weight against it. She fumbled with the lock, hands shaking, before finally managing to turn it with a satisfying click.

The tumbler of the lock slid into place not a moment too soon. Kinley suppressed a shriek as the door jumped in its frame. Heart in her throat, she slowly backed away, retreating deeper into the bedroom, mind racing. What the hell was going on?

"Open up, Kinley," he called through the door. "I just want to talk."

Every cell of her body trembled with fear, and her muscles felt jerk, uncoordinated, as she moved to put as much distance between them as possible. She couldn't wrap her mind around it. Was Max truly behind everything? As a realtor, he had access to her house... But why would he want to hurt her?

"Goddamn it, open up!" came his angry shout from the hallway.

Goosebumps sprouted over her skin, and she tossed

a desperate look over her shoulder. The only way out was the window, but it was a straight drop from the second story. While she might be able to escape him, she would more than likely be injured from the fall.

A loud bang echoed through the room as Max threw himself against the door once more, making Kinley jump. The wood shuddered but held—for now.

"Open the damn door!" he shouted, pounding maniacally on the slab of wood.

She ignored him, her breath coming in short, panicked gasps. She couldn't stay here. She had to find a way out. Her eyes fell on the window again. It was her only option.

Another bang against the door, louder this time, echoed through the room, making her hair stand on end. The frame creaked ominously, then began to give way, the wood splintering with a sharp crack.

Her thoughts now focused only on escaping, she rushed to the window, throwing it open and looking down. The ground seemed so far away. Her heart raced as she considered the jump. Could she make it without breaking something?

A third bang, and the door bowed violently, hinges screeching under the strain. She was out of time.

She swung one leg over the windowsill, gripping the frame tightly as she shifted her weight cautiously over the edge. Just as she was about to hoist herself out, the door burst open with a final, deafening crash and slammed against the wall.

Max stormed into the room, his eyes wild. She scrambled to contort herself through the small space, but he was on her in an instant. Two strong hands wrapped around her, and she thrashed against his hold. "Let me go!"

Digging his fingers into her flesh, he dragged her back inside. She hit the ground hard, and stars danced before her eyes. He grabbed at her hands, but she fought back as hard as she could, kicking and clawing at him.

She tried to crawl away, but he was too fast. He pinned her down, his weight pressing her into the carpet. She struggled, every muscle in her body fighting against him, but he was stronger. Pain sliced across her face as his palm connected with her cheek, making her teeth rattle together. Damn, that hurt!

With a sudden burst of adrenaline, she bucked and writhed against his grip. The world suddenly turned topsy turvy as they rolled, and Kinley blinked against the glare of the overhead light, momentarily disoriented.

Unable to form words, a series of low grunts left her throat as she thrashed against his hold. Suddenly, the weight pinning her arms loosened. The hope that sprang up in her chest was doused almost immediately as the man shifted his grip, his forearm moving up and constricting around her neck.

He leaned backward, forcing her back to arch, and the motion put strain on her throat. Black spots danced before her eyes as she struggled to draw in a breath. Two seconds passed, then three. Her lungs felt tight, like they were burning, and Max tightened his hold even more. The blackness around the edges of her vision slowly bled inward, and she lost the fight to stay awake as her body went limp.

CHAPTER
FORTY-THREE

David Collins was like a phantom, slipping through their fingers at every turn. No one had seen or heard from him in weeks.

The warrant had come back, and Cam and Sawyer now pored over the data from David's phone records.

"Got something," Sawyer said, his finger tracing a line on the screen. "His phone pinged off a tower about an hour away, just last week."

"So he's in the area. But there's no credit card activity, nothing under his name at all. Let's try checking under Dennis's name," Cam suggested, a hunch forming in his mind.

Sawyer tapped away at the keyboard, pulling up records linked to Dennis Collins. But there was nothing. No transactions, no new addresses, no sign of life.

"Nothing here either," Sawyer said, frustration creeping into his voice. "He's like a damn ghost."

There was no record of the man's death, but neither was there any indication of where he might be. If David had caught wind of the fact that the police had retrieved Misty's body from the lake, it was only natural that he would want to be here, to lay her to rest after nearly three decades. Unless he was responsible for her death.

But if that were the case, what would prompt him to quit his job and return to the scene of the crime, so to speak? If he was trying to hide from authorities, it would have been smarter to disappear a thousand miles away.

"We're missing something," Cam muttered as he scanned the pages for the umpteenth time. "There has to be a connection we're not seeing."

Sawyer leaned back, rubbing his eyes. "Maybe we need to take a different approach. What about David's past? Someone from his school days might remember something useful."

Cam nodded slowly and pushed from his chair. "It's worth a shot. Let's head over to the school. It's summer, so the staff will be limited, but maybe someone there can point us in the right direction."

When they arrived at the school, the parking lot was nearly empty, the building echoing with the silence of summer break. They walked inside and approached the front office, where a lone secretary sat behind the desk.

"Excuse me," Cam said, flashing his badge. "Lieutenant McCoy, this is Detective Reed. We're looking for information on a former student, David Collins."

The secretary looked up, curiosity piqued. "David Collins? That name sounds familiar. What do you need to know?"

"We're hoping to find someone who might remember him," Sawyer explained. "Anything you can tell us would be helpful."

The secretary thought for a moment, then nodded. "We keep old yearbooks in the back room. Maybe you can find something there."

She led them to a dusty storage room filled with various office supplies and paraphernalia. Several boxes had been stacked in the back corner, filled to the brim with yearbooks dating back decades. Cam and Sawyer found the correct years and began to flip through the pages, scanning for any mention of David. After several minutes, they found a picture of the school newspaper staff.

"Looks like David worked for the school newspaper," Cam said, tapping the photo. "And I believe the editor at the time was a girl named Rachel Thompson."

"Let's see if she's still local." Sawyer pulled out his phone and made a call to the station, asking one of the deputies to pull Rachel's contact information. A few moments later he hung up and turned to Cam. "She married now and lives about two hours away, but Landry is sending her number now."

As if on cue, Sawyer's phone dinged with the arrival of the contact information. He dialed the number, then hit the speakerphone function, and after a few rings, Rachel answered.

"Mrs. Wilcox, this is Detective Sawyer Reed with Brookhaven Sheriff's Office. We're investigating a case involving David Collins. We understand you were the editor of the school newspaper when he was here. We were hoping you could help us."

There was a pause on the other end before Rachel replied. "I remember David. Shame what happened to his family. What can I help with?"

"We're trying to locate him," Cam said. "Anything you can tell us about his time at school, his interests, or people he was close to could be helpful."

Rachel sighed. "David was pretty private, but he did spend a lot of time with the journalism teacher, Mr. Harris. They worked on a lot of stories together. If anyone knows more about him, it would be Alan Harris."

"Is Mr. Harris still at the school?" Sawyer asked.

"No, he retired a few years ago," Rachel replied. "But I think he still lives in town."

Cam thanked Rachel and wrote down the address. "Let's go talk to Mr. Harris."

Cam and Sawyer arrived at the small house where the retired journalism teacher greeted them with a curious glance before leading them to a cozy living room.

"Thank you for seeing us, Mr. Harris," Cam said as

they settled into armchairs. "We've reopened Misty Collins's case."

The older man frowned sympathetically. "Horrible what happened to her."

"We're trying to find the person responsible, so we're checking with everyone who may have come into contact with the Collins family that day. We've spoken with Rachel Thompson, the former editor of the school newspaper. She mentioned that you and David worked together often."

Mr. Harris nodded. "I remember David well. What specifically are you looking to know?"

Sawyer leaned forward. "Do you remember if David was acting strangely the day that Misty disappeared?"

Mr. Harris frowned. "David was always a bit... eccentric, for lack of a better word. He loved working for the paper and often got lost in whatever he was working on. But he was excited to be working on a new story, I remember that."

"Mr. Harris, can you confirm if David went home for lunch?"

Mr. Harris adjusted his glasses as he thought back. "Hmm... He often did, so I'm almost positive he left for lunch that day."

Sawyer glanced at Cam. "And when he came back, did he mention anything about what he was doing or working on?"

Mr. Harris shook his head. "No, he didn't say much. He

returned after lunch, went straight to the newsroom and used the computer, then left again rather quickly. I didn't ask, but I figured he was working on his new story. David was the type of student every teacher wants—he got his work done on time and didn't need to be micromanaged. He found a story and followed it until the end."

Cam leaned forward, considering the implication. "So, after lunch, David came back to school, used the computer, and left in a hurry. Did anything about his behavior seem out of the ordinary to you at the time?"

"Not really. David was always deeply involved in his work." Mr. Harris lifted one shoulder. "It wasn't unusual for him to dive right into whatever he was working on. He was intensely self-conscious of sharing his work with anyone until it was ready, so I left him to it."

Cam and Sawyer exchanged a look. "So, you didn't find anything about his behavior that would make you suspect he might be involved in Misty's disappearance?"

Mr. Harris's eyes widened in disbelief. "Not at all. David was always very dedicated to his journalism. I didn't connect it to anything out of the ordinary, especially not something as serious as a murder."

"Thank you for clarifying that, Mr. Harris," Cam said as he stood up. "We appreciate your assistance. If you recall any further details or if anything else comes to mind, please reach out to us."

Mr. Harris nodded, a look of concern crossing his face. "I will. I hope you find the answers you're seeking."

As they left Mr. Harris's house, Cam's mind spun with the new information. The fact that David's behavior had been so routine made it easier to overlook. But now, with David's actions under scrutiny, it raised questions about what might have been hidden behind the normal façade of his daily work.

They were getting closer; he could feel it. Each new piece of information brought them closer to uncovering the full truth behind Misty Collins's murder—and the true killer.

CHAPTER
FORTY-FOUR

Kinley's eyelids fluttered as she fought through the heavy cloak of darkness seemed to cling to her. Dim light penetrated the edges of her vision, growing stronger with each passing moment. She pushed through the fog of unconsciousness, blinked rapidly as the overhead light came into focus.

Her eyes closed once more of their own volition, wincing against the sharp burst of pain in the back of her brain. Averting her eyes, she blinked them open and focused on the wall across from her as a wave of memories washed over her.

Max—no, not Max... David—watching her intently from his place near the steps. Breaking down the door and subduing her. Her lungs tight and aching until everything went black.

Chills raced down her spine. She had to get out of here.

Kinley shifted, trying to shift to her feet, but her body remained stubbornly immobile. Panic surged through her, and she struggled harder. Rough material tugged at her flesh, and a horrifying realization dawned: her wrists and ankles were bound tight.

Oh, God. She had to get out of here... But how? And where was David? She froze where she lay on her side and listened intently. For several seconds, she heard nothing. Then, the slight creak of a board came from somewhere overhead. Her heart pounded in her chest, her thoughts a cacophony of fear as she listened to him make his way across the attic, his footsteps echoing in the silence.

How long had she been unconscious? Not very, if he'd left her and gone straight to the attic. Her throat still felt a little sore, but mostly from the pressure he'd put on her windpipe. She cleared her throat softly, checking for damage, but her voice seemed strong enough. He hadn't done any real damage, then. Maybe she could get to the phone and call for help before he got back.

Rolling to her back, Kinley scanned the room for her phone. Where the hell had she put it? *There.* She spied it sitting on the edge of the dresser.

Upstairs, she could hear David shuffling boxes and shifting things around. What was he doing up there? It didn't matter. She needed to call for help before he found whatever he was looking for and came back.

He'd tied her hands behind her, which hampered

her movements drastically. She began to wiggle frantically, trying to roll to her stomach, and finally managed to get her knees under her. Her muscles ached from the effort, but she pushed through the discomfort. Tucking her toes under her, she rocked her body backward.

With her ankles still bound, she lost her balance as she rose to her feet. Her breath caught in her throat as she stumbled, hopping awkwardly in her attempt to stay upright. She bumped into the dresser, and tears burned her eyes as the sharp corner dug into her hip.

Her movements had jolted the phone, and it skittered across the surface of the dresser. Damn it! Biting back the pain radiating from her hip, she focused on the phone. She turned her back, watching in the mirror as she grabbed for it. Just a few more inches...

The sound of David descending the stairs had her pulse quickening with renewed fear. Tossing a look in the mirror, she lifted up on her tiptoes and arched her back, stretching as far as her bound hands could reach. She made another grab for the phone and her heart leaped in her chest as her fingers brushed the black plastic.

A low chuckle came from the doorway, and Kinley whipped her head toward David. She turned her body, trying to shield the phone from his view, but he shook his head as he closed the distance between them.

"Trying to hide something from me, Kinley?"

She watched helplessly as he deftly reached around her and scooped up her phone, then pocketed it. Her heart dropped to the pit of her stomach, but the despair dissipated a moment later when a flash of silver at his side stopped her heart mid-beat. A knife dangled from the fingers of his right hand, the metal glinting ominously.

He followed the direction of her gaze and lightly tapped the blade against his thigh. "Play nice and I won't hurt you," he said softly, his tone deceptively gentle.

His words offered no comfort. Kinley's heart raced, her mind screaming at her to run, to fight, but she was completely at his mercy, a prisoner in her own home.

"Max—"

"David."

She blinked at him, caught off guard. "What?"

"My name is David Collins." He swept one arm in a wide arc. "I used to live here."

Oh, God. She'd heard Cam and Dare talking about the Collins family, and everyone in town knew about Misty Collins. "Wh-what do you want?"

David sighed, looking almost regretful as he began to speak. "It's unfortunate, really. You were just at the wrong place at the wrong time. Hayes, too—I couldn't risk either of you poking around and finding my secret."

He paced the room as he spoke, and she kept her gaze locked on the knife hanging loosely in his hand.

"You see, Kinley, there are things about my past that no one knows. Things that I've had to keep hidden." He tossed a meaningful look her way. "And when you started renovating this house, I couldn't take the chance that you might uncover something."

Kinley's mind raced, trying to piece together his words. What could possibly be so important, so dangerous, that it would drive him to such lengths?

David stopped and looked at her, his eyes dark with an intensity that sent chills down her spine. "I'm sure you've heard about Misty, haven't you?"

She hesitated, then nodded at the rhetorical question, sensing that he was searching for some sort of acknowledgement. "I—I heard she was the woman they found in the lake. The one who was m-murdered."

"Such an ugly word." His face contorted into an expression of distaste. "It's not like I wanted to hurt her. I didn't have a choice."

He dropped down on the edge of the bed, his gaze distant as he began to speak. "I loved her, you know. She was kind and beautiful, everything my real mother wasn't. I thought..."

He trailed off for a long moment. "She loved me, I know she did. But when I found out about the baby..."

Kinley listened, her heart aching as she heard the pain and anger in his voice. She wanted to scream, to beg him to let her go, but all she could do was try to reason with him. Maybe if she won his trust, he would let her go.

"I didn't know about a baby," Kinley said softly.

He glanced up at her with a cold smile. "No one did. She kept it a secret from all of us." His gaze slid away again. "I wonder how long she would have waited had I not found her."

Kinley waited a beat, but he didn't continue. She felt compelled to fill in the eerie silence. "Was it... yours?"

He let out a cruel laugh that turned her stomach. "It should have been. But no. It was my father's—the baby would have been my brother or sister."

"What happened?" she pressed gently.

He gestured with the knife. "I came in through the back door that day—caught her red handed. She was sitting right there at the kitchen table reading a book. She tried to hide it, but I already knew."

He gave a little shake of his head. "She made me promise not to tell. Said to get out, or she'd tell my father that I was harassing her."

He clenched his fists, the knife trembling in his grip. "I didn't mean to hurt her. Really. I just wanted to stop her. I couldn't let her say those things about me."

The admission hung in the air like a dark cloud, suffocating Kinley with its weight. "I'm sorry."

"I didn't realize what I was doing until I had the knife in my hand." David held up the weapon in question. "Have you ever just... lost time? Like you're so focused on something, then all of a sudden you wake up? That's what it felt like."

He abruptly stood and stepped closer to Kinley. She

fought the urge to cower away from him, fear twisting her stomach into a tight knot. His eyes bored into hers, and for a moment, she saw a flicker of the man she had thought was kind and caring. But it was quickly replaced by the cold, calculating gaze of a killer.

"It had to look like she'd left by herself, so I cleaned everything up and hid the knife, then went back to school and typed up the note. Then I put her in the car, drove her to the lake..." He shrugged one shoulder. "Then I was back at school before the final bell."

She shivered but forced herself to keep her gaze locked on his. "How could you be sure no one saw you?"

He reached out and ever so gently brushed a strand of hair from her face. His touch was gentle, but it sent a wave of revulsion through her. "You know, that's the great thing about blending in. No one notices when you're gone."

"I-I won't tell anyone," Kinley stuttered desperately. "I promise. No one knows who you are. I won't say a word."

"Of course you won't," he said softly. "I'll make sure of it."

Kinley's mind raced, desperate for a way out. She tried to jerk away from him, but her body refused to cooperate, still bound by the thick ropes. She teetered as she tried to run, then pitched forward, her chin glancing off the floor. Tears burned her eyes as David rolled her to her back.

"Silly girl. You're going to hurt yourself." David knelt beside her, then pulled a roll of duct tape from the pocket of his sweatshirt and tore off a strip. "I wish things could have been different, Kinley. But you've left me no choice."

She tossed her head, fighting against him, but she was no match for his strength. He easily overpowered her and secured the tape over her mouth. She watched helplessly as David stood up, the knife flashing in the overhead light. Panic raced along her nerve endings as he flipped the blade, then tucked the knife into his pocket. A whimper escaped as she struggled against the rough ropes binding her wrists and ankles, her heart pounding in her chest.

David stared impassively down at her. "Time to go."

Grabbing the rope lashed around her ankles, he dragged her out of the room. The carpet scratched over her skin, burning her back, and she arched violently, her muffled cries barely audible behind the duct tape. The old wood creaked as they neared the stairs, and Kinley fought against him, bucking as hard as she could to get free.

With a vicious yank he pulled her forward, and tears sprang to her eyes as her flesh scraped along the hard wood. His footsteps thudded on the stairs, and dread curled through her stomach. She felt the top step drop away into nothingness; a moment later, the breath was stolen from her lungs as the hard treads of the stairs cut into her back.

Her head snapped back, hitting the hard floor, and agony ripped through her skull. David was relentless as he dragged her downward, and pain radiated through every cell of her body. They finally reached the bottom, where she flopped helplessly as a rag doll, tears streaming from her eyes. Behind the tape, Kinley gagged but managed to battled the nausea back. That was the last thing she needed.

David paused, listening intently, giving her a moment's reprieve. It didn't last long. Satisfied that they were alone, he dragged her through the living room and kitchen, then opened the back door. Twilight had fallen, bathing the landscape in a deep lapis. The cool night air was like a balm to her burning, battered flesh, and she dragged in a lungful of the blessedly refreshing air.

A moment later she found herself dumped onto the lawn, the hard ground and cool, dewy grass forming a dichotomous sensation on her wounds. With another quick look around, David dragged her toward his car, using the key fob to unlock it. The trunk of his car stood open, a dark, yawning void waiting to swallow her whole.

With a grunt, David lifted her and unceremoniously dumped her inside the trunk. The lid slammed shut, plunging Kinley into darkness. The engine roared to life and a moment later she felt the car lurch forward as David drove away from the house.

Her teeth rattled at every bump and turn as the car sped along the road. Suddenly the car slowed, and

Kinley's heart raced even faster. She heard the sound of the driver door opening and closing, then felt the car shift slightly as he moved around it.

In the dark confines of the trunk, Kinley closed her eyes and tried to focus. She couldn't give up. There had to be a way out of this, some way to survive. But how?

CHAPTER
FORTY-FIVE

Cam drummed his fingers on the desk, eyes flicking to the clock. He'd messaged Kinley multiple times, but there had been no response. It wasn't like her to ignore his calls or texts, especially not now, after everything that had happened.

He couldn't shake the suspicion that David was behind everything. Hayes' murder, the strange occurrences at her house—it all pointed back to him. David Collins was the common denominator.

He glanced at his phone again, the screen still infuriatingly blank. Time seemed to drag, each second amplifying his anxiety. He had to do something.

Cam pushed back his chair and grabbed his jacket. He had to see Kinley, needed to make sure she was all right. He drove toward her house, his mind a whirlwind of worry. Up on the front porch he knocked hard on the door, only to be met with eerie silence. He knocked again, harder this time.

Maybe she hadn't heard him. Or maybe she was in the shower. He swallowed hard, heart in his throat. He couldn't risk it. He needed to see her—now. His pulse thrummed rapidly as he unlocked the door and stepped inside.

"Kinley?"

His voice echoed in the small space, and a shiver raced down his spine. The house was too quiet, too still. Desperately he moved through the rooms quickly, hoping he was wrong. When he reached the top of the stairs, his heart dropped to his toes. The door had been broken in, splintered wood littering the floor. The room was in chaos, personal items scattered in disarray, a clear sign of a struggle.

Oh, God. Where was she? What had David done? He pulled out his phone and dialed Sawyer's number.

"Kinley's gone," he said, cutting off Sawyer's greeting. "The house is a mess, her bedroom door's been broken in, and—" The rest of the words jammed in his throat as a million scenarios crowded his brain, all of them worse than the last.

"Damn it," Sawyer muttered. "You think it's David?"

"Who else?" he asked angrily. "He's our only lead at this point."

"All right. I'm headed your way right now."

Cam glanced around the room, desperate for any

clue that might lead him to Kinley. His eyes landed on her nightstand, where her phone charger lay empty. If he could track her phone, it might give them a lead.

"We need to find Kinley. I'm going to try to track her phone."

Hanging up, he pulled up the app that connected Kinley's phone to his. His stomach tumbled wildly as he waited for the data to load. He had to find her. She had to be okay. There was no alternative.

His heart leaped as the small pulsing dot appeared on the screen. He switched screens and dialed Sawyer. Cam sprinted out of the bedroom and was halfway down the stairs before the call connected.

"What—?"

"I've got an address," he said before the other man could finish his sentence. "The phone coordinates put her on Elm Street."

"Elm?" Dimly, Cam heard the soft squeal of rubber on pavement as Sawyer presumably whipped the cruiser around to head in that direction. "I'll call it in and meet you there."

Cam's mind whirled as he launched himself out the front door, barely remembering to close it in his haste to find Kinley. Elm Street was in a commercial area—a few fast food joints, a grocery store, and gas station. Why the hell would he take her there?

Cam's heart beat double time as he raced toward the opposite side of town. He pressed down on the accelerator, one eye on the pulsing blue dot as it moved steadily, turning onto the road that led to the highway.

Far up ahead, the red glow of taillights cut through the black night. Cam's pulse sped up, and he watched on the screen as the distance between his vehicle and the blue dot slowly closed. Switching screens, he called Sawyer. "There's a vehicle ahead, getting ready to enter the highway. We need to check it out."

"Be there in two," came his reply.

Cam ended the call, then hit his lights as he approached the truck. The driver slowed and steered to the side of the road. Cam's pulse raced as he waited for backup, and a moment later the sound of sirens cut through the air. Sawyer arrived next, followed by another cruiser.

They circled the truck, their flashlights cutting through the shadows. A middle-aged man emerged from the truck's cab. "Can I help you officers?"

Cam flashed his badge. "We're with the sheriff's department. We need to search your truck."

The driver looked taken aback. "Search my truck? What's going on?"

"We're tracking a phone signal linked to a missing person," Sawyer explained. "It pinged from this location."

The driver lifted his hands placatingly and stepped aside. "Go ahead, officers. I've got nothing to hide."

Cam nodded toward the deputies who began their

search, checking every nook and cranny. It didn't take long for Turner to spot something shiny on the bumper.

"Over here," he called out, carefully holding up Kinley's phone between gloved fingers. "He must've put it here to throw us off."

"Goddamn it!" Cam slammed his fist against the hood of the car, frustration and helplessness washing over him. Where the hell could she be? His chest felt tight, like a vise was slowly closing around his lungs, cutting off his air supply. The thought of her alone with Collins... God, he couldn't bear it.

"We'll find her."

Sawyer placed a hand on his shoulder, but Cam shrugged it off with a scowl. "How? We've been two steps behind this whole time!"

Sawyer eyed him grimly and propped his hands on his hips. "David is leading us on a chase. We need to think. Where would he go?"

Cam took a deep breath, trying to calm his racing thoughts. "He's not at Kinley's house. We don't know where the hell he's been staying. We don't have a goddamn thing to go on."

Forester spoke up, his voice calm and analytical. "We need to consider his motives. Why take her? What does he want?"

"Fuck if I know," Cam seethed. "Everything started when Kinley said she'd been having trouble at her house."

"*His* house," Sawyer said slowly. "They moved soon after Misty disappeared. Remember what Yvonne said? David came home from school one day and everything was all packed up."

Forester stared at him, but Sawyer nodded emphatically, looking more certain of himself with each passing second. "There's something in the house."

At Cam's glare, Sawyer elaborated. "Think about it—he's been trying to get Kinley away from the house. He tried scaring her out first. When she hired the handyman, David had to get him out of the way so he didn't find whatever was inside. It's not Kinley he's after—it's been the house this whole time."

"That's great and all, but that doesn't tell us where the hell she is," Cam snapped.

"Let's think about this logically," Sawyer said evenly. "He needs a place that's isolated, somewhere he can control the environment."

"That makes sense." Forester glanced at Cam. "But where would he take her?"

"I don't know!" Cam yelled, shoving his hands through his hair.

Sawyer turned to Cam. "Listen, I know you're—"

"You have no fucking idea how I'm feeling right now." Cam whirled on Sawyer, rage thrumming through his body. "We need to find her!"

"I understand that, but you're not thinking clearly," Sawyer said, a hard edge to his voice. "If you can't control your emotions, maybe you should head back to the office and let us handle it."

"Fuck you!" Cam shoved at Sawyer's chest. "You can—"

Forester threw himself between them. "Enough! Take a deep breath."

Cam glared at Sawyer but stepped away. "This is bullshit."

"Maybe Sawyer's right," Forester said, lifting a hand Cam's way when he scowled. "Maybe you should go back to Kinley's house and see if you can find anything that might tell us where they went."

Bitter helplessness weighed on Cam's shoulders. "I love her." His voice cracked on the words. "I can't let anything happen to her."

"You won't," Sawyer replied quietly as he stepped forward. "I won't let that happen."

"What if...?"

"No what ifs," Sawyer cut over him. "Let's start from the beginning. You said Kinley was having issues with the house, which is the same house David grew up in. We know he came home at least twice the day Misty disappeared."

"And now that we know she was murdered..." Cam ventured.

Sawyer nodded. "The stab wounds say it was a crime of passion, not premeditated. He was only seventeen at the time, so he likely would have tried to cover it up as quickly as possible."

"So he made it look like she'd run away." Cam nodded, catching on and running with the theory. "Packed up her things, took the body and the car, dumped them in the lake."

"But we never found the murder weapon," Turner chimed in.

Cam glanced his way. "That's probably what was in the house. He would have hidden it where he thought it would never be found. Even if his prints washed away, it would still have Misty's blood and DNA on it."

"Until now." Forrester's mouth turned down in a grimace. "When we found Misty, he knew he had to tie up the loose ends."

"So that brings us back to Kinley." Sawyer glanced at Cam. "Where could he go that he wouldn't be noticed?"

Cam's mind spun with possibilities. There were a thousand ways to dispose of a body, but the easiest was to use an existing location that wouldn't be disturbed later. There was a landfill outside of town, though that was risky. There were also several active construction sights on the outskirts of town. "There's that new housing allotment going in—Briar Cove. Turner, Forrester, check it out. Sawyer, head over to the landfill. I'll check the lake, just in case he went back there."

"Copy." Forester called it in on the radio as he slipped into the car and he and Turner took off.

Sawyer tossed a look at Cam. "You sure you're good?"

He nodded. "I have to be. Let's find her."

Cam sprinted back to his car and threw it in gear, his mind fixed on Kinley. Come hell or high water, he was going to find her—even if he had to tear this whole damn town apart.

CHAPTER
FORTY-SIX

A tear leaked from her eye, then slid down her cheek. Everything hurt. Her wrists and ankles ached from where the rough rope abraded her skin, and her back and head ached from David dragging her down the stairs.

The car hit a bump, jostling her slightly, and she let out a muffled cry as a fresh wave of pain speared through her. Her breaths came in shallow gasps, the effort of moving exhausting her. But she couldn't give up. Not now.

Kinley's thoughts drifted to Cam, her heart aching with the need to get back to him. He would be looking for her, she knew that. But how long until he realized something had happened? How would he figure out David's identity? She couldn't wait to be found—she had to find a way to escape.

Her mind raced as she tried to formulate a plan. If

she could just get the trunk open, she could roll out. Her movement was limited because of the rope around her feet, so she couldn't run. Maybe there was something in the trunk she could use to cut through them.

Lying on her side in the dark trunk, she felt around with her hands. Her fingers brushed over the rough carpet that lined the space, and she wiggled backward. Her hands brushed the vinyl lining of the car, and she felt along the edge, searching for any sharp object.

She hadn't been paying enough attention to the vehicle's model before he'd dumped her inside, but some had hooks or latches inside the trunk area for storage. Bolstered by the possibility, she wriggled around blindly, feeling her way over the surface. Hope sprang up as her fingers encountered what felt like a hard plastic hook.

She angled her arms, trying to loop the rope over the hook. It took several tries but finally caught, and her heart leaped. Ignoring the pain that rippled along her back, she shifted side to side, rubbing the rope over the hook to create friction.

Was it just her imagination, or could she feel the ropes getting just a little looser?

Suddenly the car slowed, and she heard the familiar crunch of gravel beneath the tires. Kinley froze, listening intently as the gravel disappeared, giving way to something far more forgiving. It lacked the hard sound of asphalt, and she strained to hear anything else around her that might indicate their location. If she could get the duct tape off and call for help...

She rubbed her chin against her shoulder, desperately trying to work a corner of the tape free. One corner gradually rolled inward, closer to her mouth. She stuck her tongue out, wetting it from the inside, loosening it even more.

The car jerked slightly as it came to an abrupt stop. Kinley lay still, her heart pounding so hard she could hear the blood rushing in her ears. She could hear David moving, felt the shift of the car, then the sound of his door opening and closing.

Her pulse quickened, fear nearly overwhelming her. But she couldn't afford to panic. She needed to focus, needed to keep her wits about her and wait for the right moment to escape.

With a soft click, the lid of the trunk sprang open, and a rush of cool night air washed over her. David's shadow loomed above her, his face a dark silhouette against the night sky.

"We're here," he said softly, his voice sending chills down her spine.

He reached in, his hands sliding under her back and knees to lift her out. Fresh pain rolled over her as he grabbed her injured back, and she cried out.

"Now, now," he murmured softly. "Best to stay quiet so no one hears you."

His shoulder dug into her stomach as he flung her over his back, and she felt bile rise up in her throat with every jolting step. Kinley closed her eyes and forced it down, dragging calming breaths through her nose.

Suddenly, his words penetrated the haze of pain that clouded her mind. He said someone might overhear—that meant there were people around.

Blinking away the sweat and tears obscuring her vision, she tried to place their surroundings. The moon peeked out from behind a cloud, and the mirrored surface of the lake rose up in front of them as he cut across the dewy grass.

David's heavy tread clomped against the wooden planks of a dock, and panic seized her chest. Oh, God. He was going to throw her into the lake—just like Misty.

Before she'd worked out a plan in her head, they'd reached the end of the dock. David dropped her unceremoniously on her back, and the breath rushed from her lungs. She stared up at him, every cell of her body aching, tears streaming down her cheeks.

Not sparing her a glance David retreated, moving back toward shore, but was back less than a minute later. In his hands, he held a large rock.

Fear ricocheted through her, and she resumed her efforts to struggle, yelling as loudly as she could behind the tape. The cold night air stung Kinley's skin and she struggled weakly, the pain making her movements sluggish and uncoordinated. She refused to go down like this.

"Shut your mouth!" David whisper-yelled.

He dug a knee into the soft cavity of her stomach, driving the air from her lungs. Tears scalded her eyes and slipped down her temples as she stared at the moon high overhead.

David deftly looped a coil of rope around the rock, then wove it through the bonds that secured her ankles. She felt the coarse fibers dig into her skin, filling her with a paralyzing dread.

A soft grunt escaped her lips as David picked up the rock and settled it on her torso. Satisfied with his work, he scooped her into his arms and stepped up to the edge of the dock.

He stared out at the lake for a moment, myriad emotions playing over his face. Was he thinking of letting her go? Hope swelled in her chest as he remained frozen, just staring out at the water.

Finally, his gaze dropped to hers. Then... he let go.

Her scream came out muted as she hurtled backward through the air. It felt like she was falling forever before her body hit the water and terror sliced through her.

The icy water swallowed her whole, and the shock of it stole her breath away. The coldness of the water was like a thousand needles pricking her skin. It was all around her, pulling her under, wrapping her in cold, inky darkness. Her chest tightened as the frigid liquid seeped into her clothes and hair, making her movements slow and heavy.

She bucked frantically, trying to reach the surface, but the rock tied to her feet was relentless, dragging her deeper into the dark abyss. Kinley thrashed against the restraints, the weight of the rock pulling her down faster than she could fight against it.

The tape on her mouth curled up, then lifted away completely and drifted toward the surface. Kinley blinked against the hazy, swirling water as the weight of the rock dragged her downward. The ropes around her hands felt looser, and she yanked on them as hard as she could.

She kicked wildly with both feet, trying to propel herself toward the surface. She hadn't had a chance to drag in a breath before she'd gone under; her chest felt tight, and her throat began to burn with the desperate need for oxygen.

Then the fear set in.

The world above became a distorted blur of moonlight and ripples as she sank deeper into the dark, frigid depths. Her descent slowed as she neared the bottom of the lake, and she felt herself come to rest on the soft silt of the lakebed.

Disoriented, she tried to make sense of her surroundings. The underwater darkness was oppressive, and she had to squint to see anything at all. Her heart pounded in her chest, each beat echoing in her ears. Kinley's lungs screamed for oxygen, the tightness in her chest becoming unbearable.

Suddenly, the ropes binding her wrists came free, sliding down and over her hands like a water snake. Determination surged within her. She grabbed hold of the rope and the rock with one hand, then levered to her feet and pushed as hard as she could, using every ounce of strength to propel herself upward.

Her movements were slow, the weight of the rock dragging her down as she fought against the relentless pull. She paddled furiously with her free arm, her muscles burning with effort.

Seconds ticked by in agonizing slowness as she felt herself rising, inch by inch. The surface seemed impossibly far away, a distant, shimmering hope. Her vision blurred and her lungs ached, desperate for air. She kicked harder, pulling with her arm, fighting against the weight. Her body screamed in protest, but she ignored the pain, focusing only on the need to survive.

The moonlight grew brighter and brighter, illuminating her path to survival. Suddenly, with one last stretch, she burst free of the surface.

CHAPTER
FORTY-SEVEN

The hairs on the back of Dare's neck stood on end. Something wasn't right.

On the counter his phone vibrated an alert, compounding his worry. The dread in his stomach solidified when he saw Sawyer's name scroll across the screen.

Just a few feet away, Ainsley stood next to the oven, and she tossed a glance over her shoulder at him. Her brows dipped when her gaze landed on him. "Everything okay?"

No. He had a horrible feeling everything was not okay.

Swallowing down the age-old instinct, he forced a smile to his lips. "Just work, honey. I'll be right back."

He slipped from the room and lifted the phone to his ear. "Yeah?"

"We have a situation." Sawyer didn't beat around the bush. "Kinley is missing."

Goddamn it. He pitched his voice low. "What do you mean she's missing?"

"Cam stopped by her house after work, found signs of a struggle." He gave Dare a quick rundown of everything that had happened. "We've got deputies canvassing the town, but we need all hands on deck for this one."

"Any leads?"

"Nothing concrete, but we're still trying to track down David Collins."

Dare's mind raced. "I'll be there in ten."

He hung up and headed back into the kitchen. The moment she heard his footsteps, Ainsley whipped toward him, eyes wide with fear. "What is it? What's wrong?"

He took her shoulders in hand and gently squeezed. "Kinley's not at home." He searched her questioning eyes as he delivered the news. "We're having trouble locating her."

The blood drained from Ainsley's face, and she swayed on her feet. Dare caught her to his chest. "It's okay, sweetheart."

"No." She shook her head as she pushed against his hold. "Not my sister."

Dare pulled her back to him and locked one arm around her back. "Take a deep breath, honey. The guys are already out looking for her. We're going to do everything we can to find her."

She peered up at him, agony carved deep in her expression. "We have to find her. We have to do something!"

"I know." He ran one hand soothingly over her back as he settled her in a stool at the island. "I need you to focus, sweetheart. Look at me."

Her big blue eyes met his, heartbreakingly vulnerable, and his chest tightened. She'd been through too much lately—they both had. He couldn't let anything happen to Kinley.

"I'm going to go help look for her. I need you to call your family and friends—anyone who can help look for her—and have them assemble at the station. Call Marley and Troy, too. Can you do that?"

Her hands shook as he pressed her phone into her palm. "It's going to be okay, sweetheart. I promise."

Ainsley swallowed hard. "Please bring her back."

He gave her a quick, hard kiss. "I will."

One way or another, he would find her sister and bring her home. Dare whistled for Sarge, then grabbed his keys and headed for the door. "Call me if you need anything. I'm taking Sarge with me."

"I'll organize everyone I can," Ainsley said, her voice firm despite her fear. "We'll search all night if we have to."

Dare nodded, appreciating her strength. "We need to move fast."

Ainsley nodded, already dialing numbers on her phone as Dare strode out of the house and headed for his cruiser. Sarge trotted beside him, his keen eyes scanning the dark surroundings.

As Dare opened the back door of the cruiser, Sarge suddenly tensed, his ears pricking up. A low growl rumbled in his throat, and without warning, he took off like a shot into the night.

"Sarge! Halt!" Dare yelled, but the dog didn't slow. What the hell? He'd never done anything like this before.

Dare took off after the dog, following the dark blur of his body as he bolted across the black landscape. Dare ran as fast as he could, watching his footing carefully in the moonlight.

From one of the houses along the shore, the sound of an engine roared to life. A moment later, headlights swept over the terrain as the car sped away, its tires kicking up gravel. Dare's heart raced as he sprinted after Sarge, the dark shapes of trees and bushes blurring past him.

He reached the edge of the lake just in time to see Sarge bolting down the dock, then leap into the lake. Dare followed the path of the dog's body, and his eyes locked on a figure bobbing in the water. His heart clenched with fear and hope.

Above the splashing he could hear the person gasping for air, struggling to stay afloat. Without hesitation, Dare tossed his phone to the ground, then waded into the water after the dog. The icy chill of the lake bit into his skin, but he pushed through, diving under and swimming as fast as he could.

Breaking the surface, Dare gulped in air and swam harder, his eyes never leaving the struggling person. As he got closer, he could see Sarge had reached her, the dog's powerful jaws gently grabbing onto the fabric of her shirt to keep her above water.

Dare reached out, his fingers brushing against the person's arm. "I've got you!"

The moonlight broke through the clouds once more, illuminating the face of the person Dare was holding.

"Kinley!"

Thank God. Relief coursed through him even as Kinley gagged and sputtered, coughing up water.

"Hang on, I've got you," Dare reassured her.

He wrapped one arm around her ribs, then began to tow her back toward the shore. Sarge swam along beside them, keeping them in his sights at all times.

Dare's feet finally found purchase on the sandy bottom, and he lifted Kinley into his arms. Something heavy bumped into his leg, but he paid it no heed as he pushed forward. Water saturated their clothes, streaming from the fabric in waves, slowing their movements to a crawl.

Sarge reached the shore first and shook off, water flying in every direction. He stood there patiently, waiting for Dare and Kinley, his dark eyes assessing.

"Good boy," he encouraged the dog.

Lifting Kinley higher, Dare carried her out of the water and onto the sandy shore. The heavy weight bounced off his leg again, and Dare paused. What the hell?

In the dim light, he could barely make out a large object swinging from a rope... attached to Kinley's legs.

Jesus Christ. Dare clenched his molars together as he strode inland, far from the gently lapping waves, then settled her on the ground. He ran his gaze over her from head to toe, checking her over for any injuries. Her feet were bound with rope, and the weight of the rock had caused it to cut deeply into her skin. Blood trickled from the wounds, mixing with water and dripping from her skin in rivulets.

She had similar abrasions on her wrists, but she must have managed to get the rope off because it was nowhere in sight.

He turned her on her side and she coughed violently, spitting water onto the beach. "Get it out," he murmured softly.

He gently rubbed her back, and she sucked in a sharp breath. Dare's stomach twisted as he inched up the fabric of her shirt. Even in the dim light he could see the dark bruises already forming, harsh abrasions covering her flesh from her hip bones all the way up to her neck.

He bit back a curse and carefully lowered the soaked fabric back into place. "Kinley, can you hear me?"

She nodded weakly but didn't say a word. Goosebumps broke out over her flesh, and her body trembled from the cold. "It's going to be okay," Dare promised, brushing a strand of wet hair from her face. "You're safe now."

He pressed his fingers to the base of her throat, taking in the thin, thready pulse. Her eyes fluttered open, her face pale and her breathing shallow. Her eyes focused on him for a moment, then closed again.

"Dare." The single word was barely audible.

"Hey, you." He couldn't help but smile. "Gave us a scare."

"You found me," she whispered, her voice weak.

"Sarge found you." Dare scooped up the phone from where he'd dropped it earlier and dialed as he spoke. "Everything's going to be fine, Kins. You're okay now."

His heart rate finally began to slow, and the call connected a moment later. "Yvonne, I found her—I found Kinley. Send an ambulance to my place."

He hung up and pocketed his phone, then turned his attention back to Kinley. "I know your back probably hurts, but I'm going to pick you up, okay?"

She nodded a little and grimaced as he slid his hands under her, then carefully lifted her once more.

Dare turned and strode back toward his house, keeping his gait slow and steady so he wouldn't jostle her too much. "I'd let the ambulance come here, but your sister will give me hell if she doesn't see you first."

"Damn right." Her lips curled up slightly at the corners, and Dare grinned.

"I might be the luckiest son of a bitch in the world," he said as he carefully skirted a fallen tree branch. "We've got everyone out looking for you, and you fall into my lake? What are the odds of that?"

Her smile slipped away, her brows furrowing. "Did..." Her breathing was shallow and labored. "Did you... find him?"

"Find who, Kinley?"

"Max." Her eyes closed again and a violent shiver racked her body.

Who was she talking about? "Don't worry about it right now," he soothed. "Just relax. Everything's going to be fine."

CHAPTER
FORTY-EIGHT

Cam's phone rang, cutting through the agonizing silence. Dare's name flashed on the screen, and he snatched up his phone. "Dare? Did—?"

"We found her. She's alive, but she was in the lake. You need to get to my house—now."

"Thank God." Cam's voice cracked with relief and fear. "I'm on my way."

His heart pounded as he pressed down on the accelerator. The dark road blurred as he raced around the lake, every second feeling like an eternity.

Minutes later, he skidded to a stop in front of Dare's house. Lights glowed brightly within, and Cam jumped out of the car, his pulse racing as he sprinted to the front door. He burst inside at a near run. "Dare!"

"In here!" came a familiar feminine voice.

He bolted down the hallway toward the living room, his gaze zeroing in on Kinley before he'd even crossed the threshold. She sat in the corner of the couch, wrapped in blankets, damp tendrils of hair clinging to her face. Ainsley sat beside her, one arm around Kinley's shoulders, her expression a mix of relief and worry.

"Be careful with her," Dare warned from his right, his voice pitched low. "She's hurt."

Cam nodded, his throat tight with emotion. "How bad?"

"Abrasions on her wrists and ankles... And on her back."

He swallowed hard. "He didn't..."

Dare gave a sharp shake of his head. "Otherwise she seems to be okay."

Cam managed to tear his gaze from Kinley and glanced at Dare. "Was it David?"

"I don't know." The corners of his mouth turned down. "She mentioned the name Max. Does that mean anything to you?"

Cam turned the name over in his mind but came up blank. "I don't think she's ever mentioned him before. Did Ainsley know?"

"I haven't had a chance to ask. We just got her settled when you showed up."

"Thanks." Cam dipped his chin. "I'll see if I can get some more information from her."

Ainsley met Cam's gaze as he stepped forward, and she offered him a small smile. Dipping her head, she whispered something in Kinley's ear, then gave her one last squeeze and stood, allowing Cam to take her place.

He nodded his thanks, then moved next to Kinley, his heart breaking at the sight of her shivering form. Gently, he touched her face, the coldness of her skin seeping into his fingers.

"Hey, beautiful," he said softly.

Her eyes fluttered open, her gaze meeting his. "You're here," she whispered, her voice weak and strained.

Cam leaned closer, resting his forehead against hers. "I'm here," he repeated. "Of course I'm here."

The sound of sirens pierced the air, signaling the arrival of the ambulance. Dare stood up, then moved to the front door to let them in.

"Paramedics are here," he said to Kinley, whose eyes had closed again. Another shudder worked its way through her body, and he gently chafed her arms to stimulate her muscles.

A moment later, the paramedics strode into the room with a stretcher, and Cam reluctantly stepped back, giving them room to work. Dare stood beside him, one arm wrapped around Ainsley's waist as they watched the proceedings warily.

They worked quickly, assessing Kinley's condition and preparing her for transport.

"We'll get her to the hospital," one of the paramedics said, carefully lifting Kinley onto the stretcher. "She needs to be checked for hypothermia and any other injuries."

As they loaded Kinley into the ambulance, Dare

placed a reassuring hand on Cam's shoulder. "She's tough. She'll pull through."

Cam nodded. "I'm going with her to the hospital. Keep me updated."

"Of course," Dare said. "We've got every deputy in the county looking for David. We'll find him. And if you can get Kinley to talk, let me know what you find out about this Max person."

The ambulance doors closed, and Cam climbed into his car, heart racing as they sped toward the hospital.

CHAPTER
FORTY-NINE

Kinley awoke to the sterile smell of disinfectant and the soft beeping of medical equipment. Her eyelids felt heavy, and she blinked against the harsh fluorescent lights overhead.

God, she hated hospitals. She hated the noises, the smells... If she never saw the inside of a hospital again, it would be too soon.

Drawing in a deep breath, she glanced to the side and saw Cam slumped in a chair beside her bed. He looked exhausted, his eyes closed and his head resting against the back of the chair. The sight of him brought a wave of relief, a sense of safety that she desperately needed.

As if feeling her gaze on him, Cam stirred and sat up, his eyes meeting hers. A smile spread across his face, filled with so much love and relief that it made her heart ache. It was like déjà vu, a painful reminder of when she'd been attacked a few weeks ago and had woken up to find him by her side.

"Hey, sweetheart," he said softly, pushing out of the chair and moving to sit on the edge of her bed. "How are you feeling?"

"Like I've been run over by a truck," she whispered, her voice hoarse. "But it could be worse. I'm still here."

"Thank God," Cam breathed, leaning down to kiss her forehead. He slid onto the bed next to her, careful not to jostle her too much, and gently wrapped his arms around her. His warmth enveloped her, chasing away the chill that had settled deep in her bones.

"I was so worried about you," he murmured, his lips brushing against her hair. "When Dare called and said they'd found you in the lake... God."

Kinley nestled closer to him, feeling the steady beat of his heart against her cheek. "I'm sorry. I didn't mean to scare you."

"It wasn't your fault," Cam said, his voice thick with emotion. He squeezed her a little tighter. "I don't know what I'd do if I lost you."

"You didn't." She rested her head on his shoulder. "I'm fine."

"I know." He drew in a deep breath. "I love you, Kinley. More than anything."

Tears welled in her eyes as she looked up at him. "I love you too, Cam," she whispered, reaching up to touch his face. "I'm so glad you're here."

"I'm not going anywhere," he promised, kissing her softly. "You're stuck with me."

They sat in silence for a moment, the weight of the recent events hanging heavily in the air. "I still can't believe it," she said quietly. "One second, I swore I was going to drown, and the next..." She gave a little shake of her head. "Sarge was there, then Dare was pulling me out."

His hold tightened. "We were looking everywhere—we had no idea where you were. I was headed that direction, but..." He trailed off for a second. "It was a stroke of luck that you were on the side of the lake near his house."

"I wasn't even certain where I was until Dare took me back to the house."

She shivered at the memory, and Cam kissed her temple. "Can you tell me what happened?"

She took a deep breath, then launched into her explanation. "After you called to let me know about Lance, Max showed up at the house."

"Max?"

She turned slightly to face him. "He's a realtor who works with Lance."

Understanding lit his eyes. "Do you know his last name?"

She let out a bitter laugh. "I know his real name—David Collins."

Cam blinked, and Kinley sighed. "I met Max at the

brokerage when I hired Lance to list my house. I didn't think anything of it at the time. But he admitted yesterday that his real name is David Collins. He's the one who used to live in my house—the one who killed Misty."

"You're sure?"

His brows drew together, and she nodded. "He admitted everything."

"Hold on one second." He dug his phone from his pocket and tapped a button to call Dare. Switching it to speakerphone, he held the phone between them.

When Dare answered, voice groggy and thick with sleep, Cam directed his words to Kinley. "Tell him what you just told me."

Kinley relayed the story from the beginning, telling him where she'd met Max, and how he'd shown up at her house.

"He must have known we had Lance in custody," Cam said. "He figured he would be long gone by the time we realized we had the wrong guy."

Dare made a disgruntled sound on the other end. "I'll get everyone on it, see what we can find out about Max."

"Call if you need me," Cam replied. "I'm going to stay here with Kinley."

He hung up, and Kinley tipped her head up to him. "You can go if you need to."

He shook his head. "Hell, no. Not yet, anyway."

Kinley understood. She leaned into him, exhaustion washing over her. "I hope this brings some closure. For Misty's family, and for everyone."

Cam kissed the top of her head. "It will. And we'll make sure David faces justice for all of it."

CHAPTER
FIFTY

Cam's phone rang, and he awkwardly juggled the cup of coffee as he dug it out of his back pocket. Dare's name popped up on the screen, and Cam lifted the phone to his ear. "You find something?"

"We've reached out to the realty office," Dare began. "Got Max's name and information. Local police checked his home this morning."

"And?" Cam left the hospital cafeteria and strode toward the elevators that would take him back to Kinley's room.

Her family had shown up late last night after Ainsley rallied everyone, but she was still exhausted from the ordeal and wasn't feeling up to having visitors. They'd made plans to come back first thing this morning, and Cam decided to give them some time alone with her.

On the other end, Dare sighed, his frustration evident. "They found Max Everett dead. Looks like he was killed a few weeks ago. We're assuming David killed him and used his identity to get a job at the realty office."

Cam shook his head, disbelief and anger coursing through him. "So David's been hiding in plain sight all this time, using Max's name. And no one suspected a thing."

"We just put in a request to search Max Everett's bank statements and credit card information, so as soon as we get the warrant, hopefully we'll have an idea where he's gone."

"I'm coming in, too." Cam stepped into the elevator and punched the button for Kinley's floor.

"We can take care of it. Kinley needs you there."

"Kinley needs me to find the asshole who tried to kill her," he snapped. Finding David Collins and bringing him to justice had become a personal mission for him.

Dare hesitated, and Cam continued, "Her family is here anyway, I'll just be in the way. I need to do something useful."

"I understand. See you soon."

Cam disconnected, then strode from the elevator, making his way toward Kinley's room. Inside, the Layne family took up most of the free space, and their eyes turned his way as he entered the room.

The moment Kinley laid eyes on him, something shifted in her expression. He walked straight to her side and picked up her hand. "I have to go to work for a bit. I'll be back as soon as I can."

She studied him for another long moment, then nodded. "Be safe."

"I will." He dropped a quick kiss on her lips, then turned to face her family. "If you need anything, call me."

Ainsley and Brynlee both shot him a smile and a little wave. Charlene stood and pulled him into a hug. "We'll be right here 'til you get back."

He squeezed Mrs. Layne tight, then nodded toward her husband, Garrett, who clapped a hand on his shoulder. "We'll take care of her while you're gone."

"Thank you."

Cam tossed one last look at Kinley before he left the room and headed toward the station. Inside, it was controlled chaos. Cam moved into his office and glanced at Sawyer. "Have you found something?"

Reed glanced up at him. "Good timing. We just got the warrant, so we're checking the records now."

Dare moved into the room behind Cam. "How's she holding up?"

"Good so far, thanks."

The men huddled around the computer, combing through Max Everett's bank statements and credit card transactions.

"Got something," Sawyer said, stopping at a recent transaction. "Here's a charge last night from a motel."

He pulled up the browser and typed in the motel's

information. It's about fifty miles away. David must have checked in right after he attacked Kinley."

Dare nodded. "Let's go. The sooner we get there, the better."

The drive to the motel was tense, the silence in the car charged with a sense of urgency. They arrived at the small establishment just after 10AM. The neon vacancy sign flickered in the morning light, and a few cars were scattered around the parking area.

Sawyer nodded to a small sedan in the corner of the lot, partially concealed by a rusty fence. "Looks like Max Everett's car."

They shared a quick look before sliding from the vehicle and crossing the small gravel lot in search of the office. Inside the lobby, a young woman stood behind the counter, idly flipping through a magazine. She looked up as they entered, her eyes widening slightly at the sight of their badges.

"What can I do for you?" she asked.

Dare stepped forward and introduced himself. "We're with the Brookhaven Sheriff's Department. We need to ask you about a guest who checked in last night."

Cam held up a photo of David Collins. "Have you seen this man? We believe he checked in under the name Max Everett."

The clerk took the photo and examined it. After a moment, she nodded. "I wasn't here last night, but I can check the logs." She turned her attention to the computer and tapped away for a moment before nodding. "Checked in late last night, used a credit card. He's in Room 14."

"We need to apprehend him immediately. Stay here, and lock the doors after we leave."

The clerk nodded nervously, eyes wide as she watched them file out of the office.

Outside Room 14, Dare positioned himself to the side of the door while Cam and Sawyer flanked the other side. Dare knocked firmly.

"David Collins, this is the Brookhaven Sheriff's Department. Open the door."

There was a moment of silence, then the sound of movement inside. Dare knocked again, louder this time. "David, we know you're in there. Open the door."

The door remained closed.

Dare took a step back, then tipped his head toward the door. He kicked the door open, and they burst into the room, weapons drawn. David Collins stood in the middle of the room, eyes wild with shock and fear. He lunged for something on the nightstand, but Cam was faster, and he tackled him to the ground.

Sawyer moved swiftly, securing David's arms behind his back with handcuffs. "David Collins, you're under arrest for the attempted murder of Kinley Layne, as well as the murder of Max Everett."

Dare began to read the man his Miranda rights. With a shake of his head, Cam took in the pistol lying on the bedside table.

David struggled briefly, then went limp, realizing the futility of resistance. His mouth settled into a petulant moue. "I didn't do anything. You're making a mistake!"

"I seriously doubt that," Dare said coldly. "Right now, you're coming with us."

CHAPTER
FIFTY-ONE

The case had taken several twists, but they finally had solid evidence tying David to the recent list of crimes.

"The gun we found in his motel room is registered to Max Everett," Sawyer said, handing Dare the ballistics report. "His prints are all over it."

Dare skimmed the report. "And the ballistics?"

Cam nodded. "Confirmed. The bullet that killed Max matches the gun we found in David's possession. But that's not all—the ballistics also match the bullet used to kill Corey Hayes."

Dare took a deep breath, absorbing the information. "All right. Let's see what he has to say."

David Collins looked up, his eyes flickering with a mix of fear and defiance, as Dare pushed open the door to the interview room. Dare dropped into a chair behind the stainless steel table and stared at David for a long moment before speaking.

"Why don't you tell me what happened?"

David lifted his chin defiantly. "I want a lawyer."

"Sure, you can have a lawyer. But I should tell you first..." The sheriff leaned forward, resting his elbows on the table as he stared intently at the man before him. "The gun we found in your motel room has now been linked to two murders—Corey Hayes and Max Everett. Recognize those names?"

David's face paled, and he swallowed hard.

Dare leaned forward, his gaze intense. "Tell me—did you kill Max Everett to steal his identity?"

The man refused to respond, and Dare pressed on. "When we found Misty's body, you knew you were caught, didn't you?"

David's eyes flashed with anger, and a muscle ticked in his jaw. "I don't know what you're talking about."

Dare hummed a noncommittal sound. "Kinley told us all about how you killed your stepmother and stashed the weapon, disposed of her—"

"She's lying," David retorted angrily.

Cam bristled as he watched the interview on the screen. "Motherfucker."

"Don't worry," Sawyer said quietly. "We've got enough to put him away."

True, he would face charges for killing two men, but they still didn't have the murder weapon from Misty's murder. And if they didn't find it soon, Collins would get away with it.

On the screen, Cam watched as Dare tipped his head toward David. "Let's talk about Max. Why him?"

David expelled a deep breath before speaking. "I was at a bar one night when he sat down beside me. He starting making small talk, telling me how he'd just finished his certification to become a realtor." He shrugged. "I figured it was a good cover."

Dare nodded slowly. "So, you killed him, took his identity, and got a job at the realty office."

David's confidence began to leach away by degrees. "Working as a realtor would allow me the freedom to come and go. I knew Kinley was working on her house. I was going to approach her, but then Lance signed her as a client instead."

"You planned to make him take the fall for Hayes's murder. How did you manage to get Lance's fingerprint and plant it on Kinley's keychain?"

David glanced to the side. "Lance left his coffee cup in the office one day. I lifted the print and waited for the right moment. I needed a way out, and framing Lance seemed perfect."

Dare leaned back, arms crossed. "Why kill Hayes?"

David's shoulders snapped straight and he shook his head. "I want my lawyer."

Dare studied him for another long moment before nodding. "Fine."

He pushed from his chair, then signaled to two deputies waiting outside. They entered the room to escort David back to his cell.

Though they didn't fully understand the man's motives, they had enough to convict David for the murders of both Corey Hayes and Max Everett. His dark secrets had been exposed, and the town of Brookhaven could now move forward, one step closer to healing the wounds of the past.

CHAPTER
FIFTY-TWO

The sun had just begun its ascent, casting long shadows over the fields as Harry Crawford worked on repairing the fence line that bordered his property. He skillfully maneuvered the wire, securing it to the wooden posts. He enjoyed these quiet moments, just him and the land. It put things in perspective for a man.

He straightened up to stretch his back, allowing his gaze to wander across the field. His gaze slid over the gently waving fronds of hay, then snapped back as a glint of something shiny in the grass a few yards away caught his attention. Curious, Harry wiped his hands on his overalls and walked over to investigate.

As he drew closer, the object became clearer. A knife, its blade dull with age, lay half-buried in the tall grass.

Harry frowned as he glanced toward the road that ran about ten yards from where he stood. There was no hunting allowed on his property, and he hadn't seen any strangers around recently. Had someone tossed it out of a passing car? And if so, why?

He bent down to inspect it more closely. The blade was clean, but the knife itself was of a kind not typically used around these parts—definitely not a hunting knife. More like the kind that came out of a kitchen set.

A sense of unease crept into his bones. Deciding it was better to be safe than sorry, Harry pulled out his cell phone and dialed the number for the sheriff's office.

Cam's ass had just hit the chair in his office when his phone rang. He picked it up on the second ring. "McCoy."

"Lieutenant, I've got Harry Crawford on the line. Think it might be related to the Collins murder."

His pulse leaped with anticipation. "Patch him through."

A moment later the call connected, and Cam introduced himself. "Yvonne said you found something?"

"That's right. I was out workin' the field this morning and found a knife pretty close to the road. Looked a little out of place, so I figured I should report it."

"Have you touched anything?" Cam asked as he

pushed to his feet and met Sawyer's gaze across the room.

"No, sir. Left it right where I found it."

"Perfect. We'll be there in twenty."

Sawyer followed suit and stood as Cam hung up, then pulled on his jacket. "Someone found a knife in a field off the old highway."

Sawyer's brows shot up, a dubious expression etched on his face. "You think it could be that easy?"

"I can only hope so," Cam muttered. The case had been a clusterfuck; they needed an easy break.

Less than a half hour later, Cam and Sawyer parked along the side of the road and cut through the tall grass to where Harry stood next to a barbed wire fence line.

"Morning, Lieutenant. Detective." Henry tipped his head their way. "It's right here. Haven't moved it."

"I appreciate that." Cam knelt down to examine the knife, careful not to touch it. "You've done the right thing calling us, Mr. Crawford. We'll take it from here."

Harry nodded. "Hope it's nothing serious, but you never know these days."

Cam took out an evidence bag and carefully placed the knife inside, sealing it tightly. "We'll find out soon enough. Thanks for bringing it to our attention."

They thanked Harry one last time, then headed back to the cruiser. Cam dug his phone from his pocket on the way and called the Medical Examiner's office to speak with Dr. Seidel.

"Doc, we have a weapon here that we need to test ASAP. Mind if we stop by?"

"I'll be here," the doctor promised.

Cam cranked the engine and headed toward the ME's office. From the passenger seat, Sawyer tossed him a look. "We still need to test the DNA to link David to Misty's murder—if this is the knife."

Cam nodded. "But if we can find any blood on here and match it to Misty..." He shrugged. "Maybe he'll give us the answers we need."

A few hours later, Cam walked into Dare's office, a preliminary report in one hand, the evidence bag in the other. "Dr. Seidel found traces of blood on the knife we collected from Crawford's farm. Type matches Misty Collins."

"And..." Sawyer dragged out the word. "From what Seidel can tell, the blade matches the wounds inflicted on Misty's ribs."

A smile curled Dare's lips. "Just what I wanted to hear."

Extracting the bag from Cam's outstretched hand, Dare weaved through the station toward the interview room and gave a quick knock.

Dare pushed open the door and glanced at David's lawyer. The sharp-eyed woman sat beside her client, her expression unreadable, and he tipped his head her way. "Glad I caught you before you left."

The woman arched a perfectly manicured brow, and Dare dropped into the seat across from her. Gaze fixed on David, he reached out and set the evidence bag in the middle of the table.

The moment David laid eyes on the knife, his entire body went rigid. A dozen emotions played over his face, but he didn't say a word.

He knew he was caught.

Dare leaned forward. "David, this knife was found near the road by Harry Crawford's farm. Have you ever been out that way?"

David's lawyer placed a firm hand on his arm. "Don't say anything. We can discuss this later."

She started to stand, but Dare continued. "We found traces of blood on the blade." He tipped his head to one side. "Want to guess whose blood we found on there?"

"Sheriff, you can't—"

"It's okay." David's eyes remained fixed on the knife, his face a mask of defeat. He shook his head slowly, his voice trembling. "There's no point in lying anymore."

The lawyer tightened her grip, her voice low and urgent. "David, don't say another word."

Ignoring her, David looked up at Dare, his eyes filled with a haunted regret. "It was an accident—I swear. Just a stupid, terrible accident."

Dare had suspected as much, but hearing the confession was crucial.

David's lawyer sighed, releasing her grip. "David, this is not the time or place—"

The whole story poured out then—how David had killed his stepmother and hidden the weapon, then disposed of her body. How, when he'd heard that the police had found her body in the lake, he'd immediately returned to Brookhaven.

He'd killed Max, then stolen his identity so he could move around undetected. He'd had eyes on his old house—Kinley's house—and had learned that she'd hired Hayes to do some work.

"He did steal her money and probably had no intention of going back." David shrugged. "But I couldn't risk it. If he found the weapon and made the connection..."

The lawyer's face was a mix of frustration and resignation. She knew there was no stopping this confession. "David, you've just admitted to multiple crimes. This will go on record."

David slumped in his chair, the weight of his actions pressing down on him. "I know."

As the officers moved in to transport David to the county jail, the lawyer threw a disgruntled look Dare's way. "Better hope that holds up in court."

With that she was gone, and Dare barely repressed the urge to roll his eyes. Fucking lawyers.

Back in his office, Dare sat with Cam and Sawyer, going over the details of David's confession.

Cam shook his head. "It's hard to believe he admitted everything just like that."

Sawyer leaned back in his chair. "Sometimes, the guilt becomes too much to bear. He knew he was caught the second he saw that knife."

Dare nodded. "We've got him for all three murders now. This is the closure we needed for Max, Hayes, and Misty."

Cam made a face. "Like she said—we need to go through the evidence, make sure everything will hold up in court. But with his confession, it should be straightforward."

Dare nodded his way. "We need DNA to confirm the knife was used in Misty's murder, so put a priority on that. But regardless, he's going away."

Sawyer agreed. "And Lance will be cleared. We need to make sure he knows that."

Dare smiled slightly. "He'll be relieved to hear it."

The dark secrets were finally coming to light, and justice would be served. It was a small victory in the grand scheme of things, but for the victims and their families, it meant everything. The people of Brookhaven could move forward, free from the shadows of the past.

CHAPTER
FIFTY-THREE

The hospital corridors were bustling with activity, but Cam's focus was solely on Kinley as he wheeled her out the front door and into the bright sunlight. Her release from the hospital was a welcome relief after everything she'd been through.

When they reached his car, he helped her into the passenger seat with a gentle smile. "Ready to go home?"

She nodded but didn't say a word, and silence stretched between them as he climbed into the car and headed toward her house. He snuck looks at her from time to time, tempted to ask what was going through her mind. He bit his tongue, determined to let her come to him in her own time.

All too soon they pulled up in front of her house and parked. Cam moved around to the passenger side and helped her out. He trailed just behind her as she made her way up the front stairs toward the door, her steps slow and tentative.

Her hands shook as she juggled the keys, and he gently extracted them from her fingers. "Let me."

He unlocked the door, then pushed it open. She hesitated on the threshold for a moment before stepping inside, and he watched her intently as she moved into the living room, her gaze sweeping the small space.

A shudder racked her body, and he settled a hand low on her back. "Kins?" His brows pulled together as he waited for her to turn and meet his gaze. "You okay?"

She offered a small smile, but it didn't reach her eyes. "Yeah, I..." She blew out a breath. "I'll be fine."

"My offer stands," he said quietly. "If you're not ready to be here..."

He trailed off, letting his words hang in the air between them. She studied him for several seconds, then glanced around the room again. "It's weird. I already knew I wanted to sell the house, but now... knowing what happened..." She shook her head. "I can't be here. It feels too... dirty."

"I can understand that." His hand slid to her waist. "Come home with me."

"Are you sure?" Kinley took a deep breath. "I just don't want you to regret it and—"

"Never," he replied without hesitation. "I wanted you with me before all this even started."

He turned her in his arms and pulled her close.

"Move in with me because you want to—not because you need to. We'll start fresh, be a real couple."

A small smile curved her lips. "A real couple?"

He peered down at her. "I love you, Kins, and I want to be with you. We'll take things as slow as you want, and I'll give you whatever time and space you need."

Tears glazed her eyes and her smile wobbled tremulously. "I don't need time. When I woke up in the hospital with you next to me..." She shook her head. "It felt different between us. I didn't want to admit how much I'd fallen for you, but... I did."

He curled a hand around the back of her neck and lightly stroked the tendons with his thumb. "Good. Because I've wanted you for as long as I can remember."

He dipped his head and kissed her, the gesture full of emotion. After a moment Kinley pulled back and looked up at him. "Thank you for everything," she said quietly. "I don't think I could have gotten through this without you."

"You're stronger than you think, Kins. You can do anything." He smiled and gave her one last little squeeze. "Come on, let's get you packed."

They moved through the house, gathering her essentials and stuffing them into duffel bags and suitcases. The rest could wait until later. Once they finished packing, Cam loaded her belongings into the car, then helped her into the passenger seat and headed to his place.

Hours later they were settled on the couch, the TV

playing softly in the background, when Kinley finally broached the subject. "What happened?"

Aside from taking her statement, they hadn't spoken of the recent events. Cam drew in a deep breath. "We found David Collins in a hotel about an hour away. He admitted to everything—the murders of Misty, Hayes, and Max Everett. He's in custody now."

Kinley's eyes widened and she swiveled his way. "He confessed?"

Cam nodded. "It almost feels too good to be true. Everyone thought she disappeared for decades."

"Too bad Dennis didn't live to see justice served," she murmured quietly.

He nodded in commiseration. "Her funeral is scheduled for tomorrow. Justice is being served, and she can finally be at peace."

Tears welled in Kinley's eyes, and she swiped the moisture away. "I can't believe it's finally over."

"It's over." Cam pulled her closer and dropped a kiss on the top of her head. "It's finally over."

The day dawned bright and sunny, a stark contrast to the somber pall that hung over the small cemetery where Misty Collins was finally being laid to rest. The morning light filtered through the trees, casting dappled shadows on the freshly turned earth.

The small town gathered at the cemetery, a sea of

black-clad mourners standing in silence around Misty's grave. A gentle breeze rustled the leaves of the nearby trees, the only sound breaking the heavy silence.

Kinley felt the weight of the community's grief pressing down on her, mingling with her own guilt and sorrow. She had survived, but Misty had not. The thought gnawed at her, a constant reminder of the fragility of life.

The pastor stepped forward, his voice steady and calm as he offered words of comfort and hope. "We gather here today to honor the memory of Misty Collins. A beloved wife, a cherished friend, and a kind soul who touched the lives of many. Though her time with us was tragically cut short, her spirit remains in our hearts."

Kinley glanced around at the small group gathered around the gravesite. There were no family members left to mourn Misty; her only family had long since scattered or passed away. Only her friend Tammy stood beside the casket, her face etched with grief and relief.

As soon as the service wrapped up, Kinley made her way over to the other woman. "I'm so sorry, Tammy," Kinley said softly. "I can't imagine what you're going through."

Tammy nodded and swiped at a rogue tear that trailed down her cheek. "Thank you. I'm just glad you're safe. Misty would have wanted that."

Kinley placed a comforting arm around Tammy's shoulders. "She can finally rest now," Kinley said softly.

"No more suffering, no more unanswered questions. She's at peace."

With a nod Tammy stepped forward, placing a single white lily on the casket. "Rest in peace, Misty," she whispered, her voice breaking. "You deserved so much better."

The discovery of Misty's body had reopened old wounds, but it had also brought a sense of closure. David Collins, the man responsible for Misty's death, as well as several others, was behind bars, and justice had finally been served.

Cam moved next to Kinley and wrapped an arm around her waist. "I'm glad we could bring her justice," he said quietly.

She nodded and leaned into him."Me, too."

From his other side, Dare nodded. "It's what she deserved. After all these years, she can finally rest."

CHAPTER
FIFTY-FOUR

Sam Morley tied the trash bag tightly, moving on autopilot as he got ready to close up for the night. It had been a long day at the restaurant, and all he wanted now was to get home and collapse into bed. He sighed as he grabbed his keys, then pushed open the heavy side door that led into the alley.

The night air was thick with the stench of garbage and decay as he stepped outside. The door creaked slightly as it swung shut behind him, leaving him alone in the dimly lit passage, the light from the alley's single flickering bulb casting eerie shadows over the brick walls.

Sam quickened his pace toward the dumpster, eager to finish his task and head home. As he moved, his foot caught on something, and he stumbled, the trash bag slipping from his grip and landing with a thud.

"Fuck!"

Annoyed, he glanced down to see what had tripped him. His heart skipped a beat as his gaze slid over something pale and motionless at his feet. A chill ran down his spine, and a wave of fear curled through his gut.

Fumbling, he dug out his phone and turned on the flashlight. The beam of light cut through the darkness, illuminating a ghastly sight: a young woman's body, brutally mutilated and discarded next to the dumpster.

With trembling hands, Sam dialed the Brookhaven Sheriff's Department. The phone rang once, twice, and then a dispatcher answered.

"Brookhaven Sheriff's Department, what's your emergency?"

Sam's voice was shaky, barely above a whisper. "I... I think I found Lindsey Gill."

Don't miss the final book in the Secrets of Brookhaven series. Turn the page for a first look at Out of Time.

OUT OF TIME

CHAPTER ONE

Fallon Ray turned into her driveway, her home a welcome sight after a long day of being on her feet. She pressed the button on the remote, watching as the garage door lifted smoothly, the motor's hum blending with the muted buzz of insects outside.

She pulled into the garage and cut the engine, the gentle purr fading into silence. Wearily, she climbed from the driver seat, then moved to the trunk of the car and gathered a handful of grocery bags. Balancing the bags in one hand, she moved toward the entry door to the house and used her elbow to hit the switch to lower the garage door. The mechanism groaned as the door began its descent, the sound echoing in the confined space.

Fallon headed inside, kicking the door closed

behind her before striding into the kitchen. As she began to put the groceries away, she mentally checked her list, ensuring she hadn't forgotten anything essential—milk, bread, a bottle of her favorite red wine. Satisfied she hadn't missed anything, she headed back out to retrieve her purse and cell phone from the car.

As she stepped into the garage a cool draft washed over her, sending goosebumps sprouting over the backs of her arms. She frowned, her attention drawn to the large bay door. It stood wide open, the cool night air drifting through the space.

She swore she'd closed it. Fallon shook her head. She must be more exhausted than she thought.

Shrugging off the unsettling feeling, she tapped the button again and remained frozen in place, watching as the door descended fully this time, sealing her safely inside. A sense of relief rushed through her at the sight, and she let out a soft, self-deprecating laugh as she hopped off the step and crossed the narrow space.

Just as her fingers landed on the door handle, a faint whisper of movement reached her ears. Her heart skipped a beat, her senses suddenly on high alert. Before she could react, a large hand clamped over her mouth and nose, and a damp cloth covered her face.

Instinctively she sucked in a breath, and she drew in a lungful of the noxious fume that emanated from the fabric. The acrid smell was sharp and overpowering, and it caused her eyes to water. Her throat felt as if it were on fire, and she choked reflexively, trying to expel it from her system.

Panic surged through her, and she thrashed wildly, fighting against the attacker. The arm banded around her waist held firm, the hand holding the cloth immovable. Her vision blurred, the edges going dark as the drug sank into her system and took root. She struggled to stay conscious, her thoughts becoming a jumbled mess of fear and confusion, even as her limbs grew heavy and unresponsive.

Her breaths came in ragged, desperate gasps, each one drawing more of the chemical into her system. The world tilted, and her balance slipped away as everything faded to black.

Fallon's eyes fluttered open, slowly adjusting to the dim light that cast eerie shadows across the room. Her head pounded, a dull, relentless ache that matched the cold, damp chill seeping from the concrete walls. Her body felt heavy, sluggish, and she licked her cracked, dry lips.

She blinked hard, taking in the dingy basement, the block walls stained with age and moisture. Confusion settled over her. Where was she?

With startling clarity the events of the evening came back to her, and a wave of panic surged through her.

Oh, God.

Fallon's pulse kicked up, her heart thudding

painfully in her chest. Her breaths came in rapid pants, throat aching, mind still reeling from the effects of the drug. Shoving through the foggy delirium that clung to her, she forced her muscles to move. Her hands refused to cooperate, and something cut into the flesh of her wrists.

A sickening sense of dread descended as she realized they were bound with coarse rope and suspended high over her head.

No. No, no, no.

She yanked on them to no avail, her heart slamming against her ribs, lungs hyperventilating with fear. She had to get out of here. But how?

She glanced frantically around the small room once more, and every cell of her body froze.

A man hovered on the periphery of the shadows, only his silhouette visible in the faint glow of the single, naked bulb that hung from the ceiling.

"Please." Her throat, cracked and dry, struggled to form words. "Let... let me go."

The man shifted, moving more fully into the circle of light, and she studied his features. Something about him was familiar... Did she know him?

He smiled, a gesture that should have been reassuring but only served to amplify her fear. She recoiled as he moved closer.

"Don't worry," he said with a small shake of his head. "Everything is just fine."

Fallon trembled violently as he leaned over her, his

hands moving with practiced precision as he checked the restraints. She winced, expecting pain, but his touch was gentle, almost tender. He adjusted the bindings, ensuring they were secure but not tight enough to cut into her skin.

"There now," he murmured. "We don't want you hurting yourself."

Her eyes darted around the room, searching for any avenue of escape. As she turned her head, her chin grazed something on her left bicep, and her attention was drawn downward to a thick, white bandage that stood out in stark relief against her pale skin. Fear mingled with confusion.

"What happened?" She hated that her voice shook.

The man's expression softened as he stroked his hand over her hair. The gesture felt disturbingly intimate, and her stomach revolted.

"You don't need to worry about anything now. We're going to be happy..." His eyes lit up with a strange, fervent excitement as his gaze dropped to her midsection. "The three of us."

Fallon's breath caught in her throat as he placed a hand on her belly. Her stomach swooped violently, and her blood turned to ice as her gaze moved once more to her upper arm. Horror dawned as the cold realization of truth washed over her.

"You... you took out my implant?" she whispered, her voice barely audible over the rush of her own frenzied heartbeat.

The man nodded, his smile widening. "Yes," he said, his voice filled with twisted pride. "Now we can be a real family."

Tears welled up in Fallon's eyes as she struggled against the restraints, the reality of her situation crashing down on her. She was trapped, helpless, at the mercy of a man who had taken everything from her. Desperation clawed at her throat, but she forced herself to stay calm, to think.

"Please," she said again, her voice breaking. "You don't have to do this. Just let me go."

But the man shook his head, his expression firm. "We're meant to be together. You'll see."

As he turned away, the dim light casting his shadow across the room, Fallon's mind raced. She had to find a way out, a way to survive. She had to fight, not just for herself, but for the life she had never imagined carrying within her. Determination hardened her resolve. She would find a way to escape. She had to.

Keep reading Out of Time now!

ALSO BY MORGAN JAMES

Thrillers and Mysteries

SECRETS OF BROOKHAVEN

Out of Sight

Out of Breath

Out of Time

STANDALONES

Dead of Winter

Romantic Suspense

QUENTIN SECURITY SERIES

Twisted Devil – Jason and Chloe

The Devil You Know – Blake and Victoria

Devil in the Details – Xander and Lydia

Devil in Disguise – Gavin and Kate

Heart of a Devil – Vince and Jana

Tempting the Devil – Clay and Abby

Devilish Intent – Con and Grace

Quentin Security Box Set One (Books 1-3)

Quentin Security Box Set Two (Books 4-6)

*Each book is a standalone within the series

RESCUE & REDEMPTION SERIES

Friendly Fire – Grayson and Claire

Cruel Vendetta – Drew and Emery

Silent Treatment – Finn and Harper

Reckless Pursuit – Aiden and Izzy

Dangerous Desires – Vaughn and Sienna

Cold Justice – Nick and Eden

Rescue & Redemption Box Set One (books 1-3)

RETRIBUTION SERIES

Unrequited Love – Jack and Mia, Book One

Unbreakable Love – Jack and Mia, Book Two

Pretty Little Lies – Eric and Jules, Book One

Beautiful Deception – Eric and Jules, Book Two

Hidden Truth – John and Josi

Sinful Illusions – Fox and Eva, Book One

Sinful Sacrament – Fox and Eva, Book Two

Retribution Series Box Set 1

Retribution Series Box Set 2

Retribution Series Box Set 3

The Complete Retribution Series

ABOUT THE AUTHOR

Morgan James is a USA Today bestselling author of thrillers and romantic suspense novels. She spent most of her childhood with her nose buried in a book, though she now loves to weave stories of her own. When she's not writing, Morgan can be typically be found experimenting in the kitchen (making a mess more often than not). She currently resides in Ohio and is living happily ever after with her husband and their two kids.

Keep up with Morgan and stay up to date on sales, giveaways, and new releases at www.AuthorMorganJames.com

Shop her books at MorganJamesBookShop.com